HEIGHTEN MY DESIRES
SEBASTIAN & LOLA PART II

STEELE INTERNATIONAL, INC. A BILLIONAIRES
ROMANCE SERIES BOOK 2

CHARMAINE LOUISE SHELTON

ISBN: 978-1-7352917-3-4 (Paperback)
ISBN: 978-1-7352917-2-7 (eBook)
Published by CharmaineLouise New York, Inc.
Sexy Fantasies Fulfill Your Desires Publications

ABOUT HEIGHTEN MY DESIRES SEBASTIAN & LOLA PART II

Sebastian proved a playboy billionaire never changes, or did he? Lola gave up on love and her desire for dominance thanks to his love for another. But what you see is not what you always get...

Will their love bond them, or will outside forces keep them apart forever?

Travel with this highly explosive match around the globe as they chase each other and their business dreams. New York City, Los Angeles, Paris, London, Dubai, Abu Dhabi await in this scintillating romantic suspense Sexy Fantasy.

Sebastian and Lola's love story is a standalone trilogy in the series. Get a glimpse of their dynamism in other books.

Anthem: "BedTime Story" Madonna

https://www.youtube.com/watch?v=CSaFgAwnRSc

Playlist:
https://www.youtube.com/playlist?list=
PLXwYvn0e218BG3nYwPgZE6voUwr2QbU1F

Visit CharmaineLouiseBooks.com

LOLA

"*O*h... Oh... Oh... Fuck... Yeesss... Sssir!"

The sounds coming from my mouth reverberate around the Cellar as my Master rains an onslaught of ruthless blows to my bare ass and thighs. I lie naked, face down, cuffed to the red leather spanking bench atop the main stage in the middle of the room. My poor bottom and puckered hole are on full display for all the members—the crème de la crème of society—at LEVELS New York to witness. His chosen punishment for me since I had the absolute audacity to scene with another Dom. Yes, it was revenge for my Master denying me pleasure when I wanted it and needed it the most. Do I regret it? Absolutely not, I affirm as I relish the pleasure in the pain.

"Tell me, Naughty Girl. Why did you choose to disobey me and scene with another Dom although you belong to me only and I expressly told you your climax will wait until you earned it?"

He demands in a clear voice that resonates throughout the Cellar for everyone to hear my greedy sins.

Thankful for the break in my spanking, I try to draw out the much-needed reprieve. With a voice hoarse from my cries, I tearfully reply to my Master.

"Ppp... Please—Hiccup—Please... Sir, I do not know what came over me—"

WHAP... WHAP... WHAP

I yowl from the punishing blows. Then attempt to twist my bruised bottom from his hard hand. The pain more intense since I'm mortified by the already large crowd gathered and growing quickly upon hearing my pitiful cries.

"Wrong answer, Naughty Girl. Let us try it again, shall we?"

He continues with a snarl, "Tell me, Naughty Girl. Why did you disobey me and scene with that Dom despite being told that you will have to wait until you earned your climax?"

WHAP... WHAP... WHAP... WHAP

I take a moment to clear my throat enough to squeak out my response, now chastened by his reprimand.

"Sssir... I was a naughty girl... And I was desperate for relief after you took me to the edge for over two hours this morning... I couldn't concentrate at work... Sssoo... I sought a Dom who would scene with me just until I reached my release nothing further... And... And... I did not expect you would ever find out..."

I end on a pitiful whisper, praying that my Master

doesn't punish me further for admitting the full truth. I purposefully came to LEVELS tonight seeking my unsanctioned pleasure behind his back.

WHAP... WHAP... WHAP... WHAP... WHAP

"Is this where you sought your pleasure with a Dom behind my back, Naughty Girl? On this soaking wet pussy that is dripping your juices down your thighs in a puddle on the floor?"

I cringe and scream as my Master repeatedly spanks my swollen, throbbing pussy with his unforgiving fingers. My arousal almost peaks and I pant to catch my breath so I can answer him.

"Yeesss... Ssir!"

I keep my answer brief as my Master has taught me and because I hope to assuage him quickly so that this embarrassing punishment will end.

"Well, Naughty Girl, I can tell by the sweet smell of your arousal and by your engorged clit that you are enjoying this spanking. Which leads me to believe that you need another form of correction to ensure that you understand your mistakes and will avoid such erroneous behavior."

With that, my Master squats behind me to remove the red, suede-lined cuffs that anchor my ankles to the spanking bench. I watch him from over my shoulder admiring his devilishly handsome face scowling, his eyebrows scrunched above his piercing gray eyes that lift to meet mine. I nearly swoon at the sight of him and feel my pussy clench in need of his ten-inch, thick member.

"Do you like what you see, Naughty Girl?"

He asks as he gently ghosts his fingertips along my calf, up my thigh, and up to my—

"Ooowwweeee!" I screech when his large palm slaps my sore butt cheek. Fuck, that was unexpected. Smiling faces tell lies is the truth.

My Master chuckles darkly as he strides to the front of the spanking bench where his bulging cock strains against his trousers on a level with my hooded eyes. I lick my glossy lips and seductively look up at him through my eyelashes.

"Ah, ah, ah Naughty Girl, I know how much you enjoy sucking me off, but no pleasure for you tonight. You will only have my ten inches in your tight little ass," he admonishes me. "Come."

My heart sinks.

He finishes unbuckling the cuffs at my wrists and helps me from the bench. Then takes my small hand in his large one as he leads me to the wicked St. Andrew's Cross. A cane leans against the well-worn wood, polished from so many uses by Doms and their subs. Tonight, it's my turn. I shudder at the thought, not sure if it's in fear or desire.

Without words, my Master cuffs me once again, this time spread-eagle to the cross, my back to the awe-struck audience. I close my eyes when I realize more members have gathered on the other side. High-profile faces peer at me with rapt attention. They can fully see my naked body, my heavy, D-cup breasts with pebbled nipples, and swollen

pussy lips fully exposed. My face is as red as I imagine my burning ass must be.

"Now, Naughty Girl, you will count out loud the ten lashes of the cane. If you miscount, we will start from the beginning. Do you understand?" He asks loudly, playing to the infatuated crowd who oh and ah in response.

I take a deep breath and open my eyes to look at him before I reply in a resigned sigh, "Yes, Sir, as you wish."

The whistling sound of the cane zipping through the air is my only warning. At first impact, I feel no pain. Then the sensation hits me like a shot and I scream out the first stroke.

"Ooowwww... One..."

My Master unrelentingly canes my ass and thighs, already reddened and marked with his large palm prints from the spanking that he gave me only moments before. I wantonly writhe against the St. Andrew's Cross, counting each of the savage hits until I can no longer think coherently and the sounds of the Cellar fade away.

My last image before I enter subspace is that of my climax galloping towards me. It's so intense I won't be able to rein it in. My only prayer is that my Master doesn't stop my punishment and allows me to cum. If he brings me back from the edge, that would be pure torture. Fortunately, all thought ends as the welcoming darkness of floating freely consumes me.

"No... other... Dom... is... to... ever... touch... you... Pet!"

I wake to my Master growling in my ear as he savagely emphasizes each word with a harsh thrust of his massive dick in my tight ass. Just the sound of his voice sends me spiraling towards another climax. His authoritative power makes my pussy walls clench down hard on nothing in my empty channel and takes my breath away. I pant and push back meeting every thrust with one of my own—my sore, bruised ass slapping against his groin sending shock waves through my body. Damn, he feels so, so good! This is what I needed, I resolve, secretly pleased with my punishment.

Now, as the muscles of my pussy and ass tighten from my impending orgasm, I keen and ball up my hands. My fists pound the cross I'm now braced against with my feet on the floor, my Master having removed the four cuffs. He holds me with one arm hooked around my waist and the other hand clasping my throat to keep me in a submissive position. I feel his cock swell and he speeds up his movements. My Master becomes frantic, chasing his orgasm before he throws his head back and bellows my name with his release. His dick spews copious amounts of cum, some sliding down to coat my pussy and thighs. With a final upward thrust that lifts me onto the tips of my toes, he pumps the last of his jizz deep inside of me. I scream his name as I cum with him.

"Sebaaasstiaan!"

The sound of my hoarse voice screaming aloud rips me from my dream. I bolt upright in the bed sweating, breathing heavily, wildly looking around for the LEVELS members, the Cellar, and my Dom... Sebastian.

I flop back down against the pillows, noticing that the sheets are in disarray tangled around my body. Not the arms of my former lover holding me in his warm embrace as I hoped. The realization sinks in my brain past the haze of my sexy fantasy that I'm not in New York at all. Rather, I'm at the resort in Fiji for the eight-day fitness retreat as my birthday gift to myself.

A much-deserved getaway after the last four months of expanding my luxury lingerie company, Lola's Coterie to New York City and Las Vegas. Plus the short-lived, sizzling relationship that I had with Sebastian Steele, the Alpha billionaire whose company STEELE International, Inc. owns the retail spaces that my new boutiques are in. The third and fourth after my flagship in Paris and second location in London.

I made a vow to myself I won't go into my birthday dependent on any man. So I chose to end things with Sebastian upon returning home from Vegas early to find him with Lydie Jackson in the penthouse duplex that we shared on the fifty-fifth and fifty-fourth floors. Conveniently in The STEELE Tower above my boutique. The Tower is a modern, gray-tinted glass fifty-seven story mixed-use skyscraper on Fifty-Seventh Street and Fifth Avenue on Billionaires' Row in New York City.

Better to be alone than with someone who tells me one thing but does another. For the third and final time, I will not allow Sebastian Steele to dupe me into believing Lydie is only an old family friend and confidante. Especially when I saw them with my own eyes on the bed in one of

the guest suites at the penthouse. Sebastian in only sweatpants, soothing Lydie who was in one of his T-shirts with mussed hair, smiling lovingly at him. No, my thirtieth birthday marks a whole new decade for me and the continuation of my plan to expand Lola's Coterie globally. That's my sole focus once again.

I roll over with a groan and leave the stifling confines of the empty bed. I rip the damp, silk, babydoll nightie off of my hot, drenched body that's still reeling from a sleep-induced orgasm. Then head to the en suite bathroom of my cliffside villa on the private Fijian Laucala Island to shower before my first session begins. The retreat's host is Starr Knight, the owner of the Beverly Hills-based fitness studio and wellness center Starr Light Fitness & Wellness. I pray that she can help me get my head back in the game with her mediation, yoga, Pilates, and whatever else she recommends for an aching heart. I'll need the works, I reflect with a resigned sigh.

LOLA

*L*ast night was wild. I cannot believe that I dreamed of Sebastian. Ugh!

I should have known it wasn't real. I've never and would never ever call him Master and definitely would never choose punishment butt-ass naked in front of anyone. Well, maybe with a mask on like I did that time he flogged me on a mini-demonstration stage in the Cellar during Masquerade Night at LEVELS New York.

Seriously, I wonder if my subconscious wants me to be so submissive. Or is my Independent Woman stepping up again to remind me not to be in a D/s relationship. For her, that includes the sub-during-sex-only version like I had with Sebastian. After four months of that experience—granted it was fantastic and I miss it/him—I'm still torn between letting go and just feeling as he always told me. Even more so since Sebastian has betrayed my trust. That precondition is the foundation for any D/s intimacy. I can

finally admit that I love him, but I have to love myself more. I really need—

"Lola... Hello there... Lola?"

The gentle voice seeps through my introspection and shifts my focus from the painful inner turmoil to the present.

Damn. Here I sit on my yoga mat in the middle of mediation class meant to clear my thoughts. Yet my mind is running in a million directions—and some circles—thinking about that man. Get it together, Lola!

I open my eyes to see the angelic face of Starr, her deep brown eyes filled with concern as she peers at me. She's a beautiful woman in her late twenties or early thirties. Her chestnut-colored skin dewy in the humidity. Her long, curly, dark brown hair pulled up in a topknot. Starr has a sexy body to die for—five feet, six inches, fit, yet still curvy. I smile and laugh softly, embarrassed that I didn't really meditate as that was the purpose of this session. Starr's dimples highlight her sculpted cheekbones when she returns my smile.

"Come on, girl, the session ended. Do you want to tell me all about it over breakfast?" Starr asks as she gives me a hand up from my mat. "Everyone has a story to tell. I could see by how much you were frowning while moving your lips as you talked to yourself with shut eyes. Your mind definitely has something to work out. Yoga simply won't do!"

With a loud snort of laughter at just how on point she is with her assessment, I agree and accept her invitation.

CONTENTS

Series Playlist

Discover My Desires Sebastian & Lola Prequel
(Available Exclusively to Subscribers)

Fulfill My Desires Sebastian & Lola Part I

Heighten My Desires Sebastian & Lola Part II

Ignite My Desires Roger & Leonie Part I

Stoke My Desires Roger & Leonie Part II

Justify My Desires Roger & Leonie Part III

Deepen My Desires Sebastian & Lola Part III

Capture My Desires Malcolm & Starr Part I

Embrace My Desires Malcolm & Starr Part II

Cherish My Desires Malcolm & Starr Part III

A Trilogy of Desires Sebastian & Lola Parts I-III

A Trilogy of Desires Roger & Leonie Parts I-III

A Trilogy of Desires Malcolm & Starr Parts I-III

Series Extras

ABOUT STEELE INTERNATIONAL, INC. A BILLIONAIRES ROMANCE SERIES

Welcome to the titillating world of the multibillion-dollar global company and the love affairs of the family that controls it.

STEELE International, Inc. is a series of interconnecting Billionaire romance. Follow the Steele family as they fly around the world chasing the women they love and their happily ever afters. Get ready for glitz, glamour, and steamy romance books. What's better than that? The Jet-set Lifestyle has never been hotter...

The Desires Series is not for the tea set; it's for the top-shelf vodka straight up in a pretty crystal glass coterie!

Don't miss any of the sizzling romance books in the STEELE International, Inc. A Billionaires Romance Series:

A Trilogy of Desires Roger & Leonie Parts I-III

A Trilogy of Desires Malcolm & Starr Parts I-III

Series Extras

Series Playlist

STEELE INTERNATIONAL, INC. - JACKSON CORPORATION
A BILLIONAIRES ROMANCE SERIES CROSSOVER

Tempt My Desires Lachlan & Haley Part I

Tease My Desires Lachlan & Haley Part II

Grant My Desires Lachlan & Haley Part III

Intrigue My Desires Harris & Kat Part I

Decode My Desires Harris & Kat Part II

Honor My Desires Harris & Kat Patt III

A Trilogy of Desires Lachlan & Haley Parts I-III

A Trilogy of Desires Harris & Kat Parts I-III

Series Extras

Series Playlist

ALSO BY CHARMAINE LOUISE SHELTON

STEELE INTERNATIONAL, INC.
A BILLIONAIRES ROMANCE SERIES

Discover My Desires Sebastian & Lola Prequel
(Available Exclusively to Subscribers)

Fulfill My Desires Sebastian & Lola Part I

Heighten My Desires Sebastian & Lola Part II

Ignite My Desires Roger & Leonie Part I

Stoke My Desires Roger & Leonie Part II

Justify My Desires Roger & Leonie Part III

Deepen My Desires Sebastian & Lola Part III

Capture My Desires Malcolm & Starr Part I

Embrace My Desires Malcolm & Starr Part II

Cherish My Desires Malcolm & Starr Part III

A Trilogy of Desires Sebastian & Lola Parts I-III

FREE BOOK

Get the start of the STEELE International, Inc. A Billionaires Romance Series with *Discover My Desires Sebastian & Lola Prequel* **FREE!**

Click Cover Below or visit **bit.ly/CLBooksNewsletter** to subscribe to my newsletter for latest news and launches, books from my author friends, and sizzling reads in book promotions. Plus, start reading the steamy billionaire romance *Series Prequel* of Sebastian Steele and Lola Lewis.

Their stories. Their discovery of unknown desires...

Starr loops her arm through mine as we head out of the thatched-roof, wooden pavilion overlooking the sparkling, cyan-colored South Pacific Ocean. The hues of which range from the darkest to the lightest blues and greens so varied in depth, like the emotions swirling through me.

"Okay, start from the top. No judgement and totally confidential!"

Starr says enthusiastically as she laughs and crosses her heart once we sit at a table on the veranda of the beachfront restaurant at the luxury private island.

I let my hazel gaze travel out across the vast, jewel-toned ocean. I take a contemplative moment to gather my thoughts in a coherent description of the last four months. Then I turn back to face an attentive Starr. From the moment that I met her at the welcome dinner last night, I innately knew that she'd be a caring and trustworthy person who would keep confidences. It's a combination of her hippie vibe, openness, and bubbly personality that makes me relax and fill her in on the details, not leaving one chapter out of my story.

Instantly, the soul-crushing weight of despair from the unexpected loss of another loved one lifts off of my chest by the end of my tale. Just as importantly, I'm relieved to see that Starr is true to her word and doesn't judge my chosen submissive behavior. Nor does she think me crazy to miss a man who cheated on me the entire time that we were together.

"Yeah, I guessed right, didn't I? You have some story! Whew!" Starr laughs as she jokingly fans herself from the all-encompassing heat of the intense relationship that Sebastian and I shared.

"Pretty much," I reply, joining in her infectious laughter.

It seems like such a relief to talk about it out loud to someone else—not talking to myself like Starr spied during class. I haven't even told my best friend and closest confidante Leonie *The Lion* Beaulieu, the world-renowned supermodel who's not only my BFF, but the muse for Lola's Coterie.

The stunning Parisian-born, feline beauty's name means brave as a lion. Her long, mahogany hair looks like a mane, prompting the accolade. She's the perfect spokesmodel for my lingerie company since her sensuous, statuesque figure reminds me of the bombshells of yesteryear and the '90s supermodels—full bust, small waist, shapely body. Her golden, caramel skin that looks great with any color or material reflects her biracial heritage— her mother is Tunisian and her father is French.

In fact, I haven't seen Leonie since the Las Vegas store opening nearly two weeks ago. I've been dodging her questions regarding Sebastian and our breakup because I needed time to digest it all and wasn't ready to talk about it. Now I can.

"Well, I'm glad that you joined the fitness retreat. Set on an idyllic tropical island with only yourself to focus on gives you the chance to gather yourself and to explore your fresh path," Starr says sincerely.

Holding both of my hands in hers and gazing in my eyes, she continues to drop more sage advice.

"Don't let anyone make you feel any kind of way about your past choices nor the future ones that you make. It is your life to live as you see fit. Your mistakes or successes sculpt you into who you really are destined to be. A yogic piece of advice is to be equally thankful for what you perceive to be good and for what you perceive as bad. It all happens for a reason. Either way, you don't let it disturb your inner peace. Strive for tranquility no matter the outer circumstances."

I nod with tears glistening in my eyes at her kind and impactful words. I needed to hear them and they make me realize that everything will work out fine. We sit in silence for a while, watching the waves lap lazily onto the sandy shore and allow the sounds of nature to soothe our souls.

Once the tears wash away my sadness, I turn to Starr and offer her an appreciative smile.

"Enough about me!" I start. "Tell me about you. A friend of mine who's a wellness editor told me she loves taking your classes when she's in LA. It bummed her out when she couldn't come to your first international retreat. I'm glad that I could take her spot. Lucky me!"

Starr claps her hands in delight, her chocolate brown eyes twinkling as she leans forward, eager to share her tale.

"I've always loved being active and caring for my body in a natural and healthy way. Of course I learned it having hippie parents and growing up in LA! My mother's name is Sun Knight and my dad's name is Peace Knight for goodness' sake!" She laughs and throws her hands up, shrugging her shoulders resignedly.

"No way! Are those their actual names?" I ask, giggling.

Starr shakes her head and laughs, "Absolutely not! Belinda and Jordan Knight. They met at a festival and the rest is history as they say. Anyway, I wanted to combine my love of wellness with helping others. So I completed my fitness certifications and studied at Stanford for undegrad with a BA in economics, then stayed to get my MBA. I opened my center six years ago at 25. It was my initial goal. Now, I want to expand into international fitness retreats at luxury resorts and add a second center location in the Caribbean. This retreat is a test run."

As Starr shares more of her story, I find the parallels of our lives another good sign: only children; 31 and 30; smart; independent, founders of thriving businesses with plans for growth. I definitely found a kindred spirit in Starry Knight as I nicknamed her since her eyes twinkle like stars in a clear night sky. We promise to stay in touch after the retreat ends. Especially since my LA boutique is opening in about eight months and I plan to spend a lot of time there in the coming weeks.

I also pay it forward, as Pierre Delcour did when he told Luc Montaigne about the opportunity to meet with STEELE for my expansion plan. They were looking to make up for a terrible deal and needed to move fast with one that would offset the loss. Luc along with being the billionaire CEO of Banque Montaigne and the Vice Chair of Lola's Coterie is my advisor, benefactor, and father-figure. Despite what overly possessive Sebastian believes.

Monsieur Delcour's thoughtful act led to my multiyear, multimillion-dollar partnership.

I promise Starr I'll tell Malcolm Steele who's one of Sebastian's four younger siblings and the president of their Entertainment Properties Division about her fitness center expanding into luxury resorts. We finish up our lengthy tête-à-tête, trading stories about the men in our lives. Then head to the next session where Starr will teach the attendees how to strengthen our cores with Pilates.

After a delicious dinner of native fish prepared with savory Fijian flavors, I retreat from the retreat. I stretch out in the sunken tub on my villa's veranda to soak my sore muscles from the exercises Starr and her instructors put me and the group through. For the first time in months, the aches are not from the rigors of having sex with Sebastian for hours.

It feels fantastic to lean back against the porcelain and let the fragrant essential oils—amplified by the warmth of the water—lull me into a peaceful state of bliss. The sounds of the ocean waves lapping against the rocky cliff are hypnotic. Finally, I let my mind drift into a meditative trance.

BY THE END of the soul-cleansing, mind-centering retreat, I'm back on track. I've stuck with my original plan to stay in New York as my base and will visit my Paris flagship and London boutique every few weeks or as needed. Once the LA construction starts, I'll go to the West Coast as often as necessary—the retail space is still undecided at this point.

The most important decision is that I will not let the situation with Sebastian change my mind about returning to my childhood home. I left it once before when I graduated from the Fashion Institute of Technology and moved to Paris. Since my parents died in a tragic car crash, New York was no longer home for me. My goal with the initial expansion was to buy an apartment in New York to split my time between there and the other cities. I will not allow the Sebastian fiasco to deter me.

Therefore, I took time before leaving to make some very necessary arrangements to prepare for my return. The realtor, Robin Sanchez-Waghorn—who helped me to find the Sutton Place penthouse of my dreams that unfortunately fell through—has arranged a rental apartment. Hopefully, I'll stay for only two months until she can help me find a permanent place. Blair Thomas, my New York assistant, has already moved our offices from The STEELE Tower's executive floor to the third floor of our New York boutique. After we signed the deal, Sebastian had arranged for me to be close, but not distractingly so as he stated. Thankfully, Blair also moved my things out of Sebastian's penthouse and into the rental, leaving the keys with the building's concierge. Now, I'm all set for my new decade of Independent Woman.

RAWR!

SEBASTIAN

wo Weeks Prior
Damn, I miss Lola. These past few weeks leading up to the openings of her New York and Las Vegas boutiques have been hectic for her. Suddenly having to stay an extra week in Vegas to wrap up some issues added to her schedule. I understand and respect her determination to grow her company. Hell, I'm no different with my focus on replacing my father as the CEO of STEELE International next year. But I still miss my Petite Seductress.

Who would have thought the self-proclaimed playboy would end up in an instant, living-together relationship with a woman whom he can see spending the rest of his life?

I preferred one night only. Perhaps two if the woman wasn't clingy or a gold digger. But only two fucks, enough time to satisfy my Dom needs and physical release for the moment. Only a short-term encounter to balance out my business-focused life. If someone would have told me that four months ago, I would have told them they have the wrong guy. No. Way. No. How. Not. This. Guy.

Well... I'm lying in bed missing my baby and wanting to wrap myself around her curvy, sexy as fuck body. My dick is hard thinking about Lola. Rolling over, I let out an agonized groan when I see the time is only 11:30 p.m. and I've been in our big, empty bed for only half an hour. Fuck! I need to take a long, cold shower and jerk off my aching, weeping cock before it explodes from the pressure of being engorged. Maybe I should call Lola for some FaceTime sex. That would—

The ringing of the penthouse intercom interrupts my pathetic pity party. Who the hell would visit me at this hour, I wonder. I tick off in my head where my family could be other than in their penthouses on the fiftieth through fifty-seventh floors above and below mine. My parents are on holiday at their Italian Rivera villa in Positano; Malcolm is at STEELE St. Barth's to review logistics for the second Jackson Hole at STEELE Resorts beach club project; Roger isn't in the city, rather at his flat in Paris where he spends around eighty percent of his time; the twins Harris and Haley are downstairs in their respective penthouses. Besides, to reach me all they'd have to do is take our private elevator and not go through the lobby. So, I pray that it's merely a late-night visitor and not some unwanted news.

"Steele," I answer as I slip into a pair of sweatpants so as not to greet them naked.

"Mr. Steele, this is Blake the concierge. I apologize for the late call, but there's a woman here demanding access to your penthouse."

In the background, I hear a woman yelling, sounding belligerent towards a security staff member before the concierge moves away from the disruptive scene. He continues in a lowered voice.

"Excuse me, Mr. Steele. The woman appears highly intoxicated and her behavior is erratic. Would you like us to call the police or escort her off of the property?"

I have to think who the hell it could be since Lola is in Vegas and The Tower's residential and commercial staff know her. Suddenly, I hear the woman screech her name. Fuck me, it's Lydie Jackson.

My mind goes into overdrive. Despite assuring me she understood we could never have an intimate rapport and Lola is my girlfriend, Lydie's gone on an obvious bender. Drunk off her ass if the commotion is any sign of her state.

We're only family friends and I'm her confidante. Damn, her younger brother Lachlan is my best friend. Now Lydie is in the lobby at this late hour to speak with me. Knowing I can't let her carry on nor do I trust her to go home and stay if my driver took her, I have to let her come up. I'll put her in a guest suite and deal with her in the morning once she's sobered up. Thank God Lola isn't home, or she'd have my balls and I'd have two emotional women on my hands. Damn.

"Thank you, Blake. I will handle the situation. Please escort Ms. Jackson to the family's private elevator and enter the code for my first floor," I tell him.

"Yes, sir, right away. Good night, Mr. Steele," Blake responds.

I take the stairs down and turn on the lights for that floor and start the coffee machine in the kitchen. The voice-controlled virtual assistant that Haley designed—the little techie nerd—handles the tasks. Then, I head to the front door to await the screaming banshee.

As soon as the elevator doors open onto the foyer outside of my duplex, I can smell the liquor rolling off of Lydie in waves. She's in a complete state of dishevelment. Her mussed hair tangled with knots as though she had been running her fingers through it or pulling it out. Makeup smeared around her eyes gives her the look of a raccoon. Black streaks of mascara from crying coupled with her puffy and red face attest to her despair. What appears to be an entire bottle of Scotch stains her light green dress. I notice the broken high heel of her shoe as she limps unevenly, staggering towards me.

"Sssebbieee."

She sing-songs, her arms reaching out to me as she stumbles across the tile floor. I cannot believe this is the polished, well-kept, in control woman who is the overall vice president of Jackson Corporation and who garners the utmost respect from hard-as-nails titans. Lydie is a total mess.

I'm shocked speechless and surprised as she jumps and

wraps her legs around my torso. I have no choice but to catch her and hold her under her ass as I stagger backwards from the unexpected collision.

"Arrre youu feeeelinggg meee up, Sssebbieee?" Lydie cackles before leaning down to bring her lips to mine as she humps her pussy against my stomach.

I nearly drop her on her ass—feeling her up. Fuck no!

Without answering her, I put her back on her feet. As she slides to the ground, I grip her elbow. I really don't need this shit, but I have a responsibility to take care of her in this inebriated state. I lead her to the kitchen and settle her at the banquette—she'd fall on her face if I put her on the stool at the breakfast bar. After, I walk to the coffee machine to reverse the drunkenness with two cups of strong espresso or more. On my way back to her, I grab some crackers from the pantry. All the while, I ignore her singing at the top of her voice about her love for me à la Beyoncé.

Yeah, I think to myself, Lydie is crazy right now and Lola would definitely lose her shit. With a sigh, I unwind Lydie's fingers from my wrist as I set the cups and the box of crackers on the table in front of her. I have to get her to consume this stuff and get sober really quickly.

"Lydie"—I start, suddenly pulling away as she grapples with the drawstring of my sweats—"You need to drink this and here, have a cracker. Cut it out right now!"

"BUT I LOOOVE YOUUUU, SSSEBBIEEE!" She wails loud enough to hurt my ears.

This situation has to get under control now. So, I switch to Dom and not a friend.

"Listen, Lydie, right now you will drink this espresso, both cups and if necessary more, and eat some crackers. After you finish, we are going upstairs to get you cleaned up and in bed—"

"Ooohhh, Sssebbieee, let's go to bed, right now!" Lydie makes a grab for my hand, but I move away in time.

I press the espresso cup to her lips and command her to drink. After what has to be an eternity, but the kitchen clock only shows half past midnight, Lydie is functional and we go upstairs. I leave her in a suite and rush to my bedroom to get a T-shirt for her to wear. Fortunately, she's in the shower when I return, so I leave the t-shirt on the bed and wait in the separate lounge. Shortly, Lydie appears looking chastened, but teary, and I motion for her to sit on the sofa while I stay in the chair opposite. With a nod of her head, she humbly agrees. We have to clear this shit up once and for all.

"Lydie—" I start, but she lifts her palm up to interrupt me.

"Sebastian, I have to apologize for my behavior. I… I had a rough day with my dad. You know the usual, proving myself to him and dodging merger marriage demands. I… I needed to take the edge off, but had too much to drink instead."

She looks down at her hands she's wringing in her lap. With a deep breath, she continues, "I'll rest until the morning and go home. That is, if you don't mind."

I will not force the issue since she looks remorseful, and it's late. So I stand and walk with her to the bedroom. Once she's settled against the pillows, I sit beside her on the rumpled bed. I stroke her face to wipe the tears from her eyes—I can't stand to see a woman cry or show such hurt, especially Lydie. I feel bad because I wonder if I led her on over the years since we've been close. I have to reassure her and let her know that I care and understand about her deal with getting her father's approval despite her happiness. It's important to me she knows that and I will support her in any way other than as the business-merger marriage that her father is insisting of her.

"Lydie, again, I want to be clear I apologize if I ever led you to believe that we could be more than friends. We cannot. Lola and I are a couple. Understand those two things. However, your happiness is a top priority for me and I will do anything to make it happen—"

A noise from outside of the room stops me and I walk over to the door, not sure whether I misheard. I hear Lydie scamper out of the bed and follow me into the hall since I see nothing in the lounge. Funny, it smells like Lola's perfume. I sniff deeper and shake my head, realizing that I miss her so much that I'm imagining her here now. I turn back to Lydie who I didn't realize was directly behind me and I bump into her. I reach out to steady her by holding her waist as I lead her to the bedroom.

"I see nothing. We must have misheard a noise... Let's get back to the bedroom."

Still a bit unbalanced, Lydie leans heavily into my side

and I guide her back to bed where she slips in and I turn off the light.

As I walk back to my bedroom in the opposite wing, I swear I can still smell Lola's alluring perfume in the hall-way. My ache for her increases tenfold, as though her perfume is a trigger for my arousal. Fortunately, she'll be home the day after tomorrow. So I'll get my fix of her body and the light she brings into my life that changed me from a playboy to a one-woman, or rather one-Lola man.

WHO WOULD HAVE GUESSED two weeks later after returning from Las Vegas, Lola would move out of our penthouse into a rental way across town somewhere and move her office from the suite on the executive floor of STEELE's headquarters to the third floor of her New York boutique?

Fuck, not me.

Well, she did and I can't even believe this shit. I should have known something was up when I called her the day after Lydie left my duplex and Lola didn't answer my calls or my text messages. It got to where I contacted Luc—I was desperate—and he told me he and Lola were in back-to-back meetings all day. Even though that niggled at the back of my mind since Lola always texted me back, I let it go. The day turned to night. Still no response. I told my flight crew to set a plan to fly out there so I could see for myself what the hell was going on. I stepped into the lobby to get into the car for the airport and stopped in my tracks.

Lola sent a text she was busy all day and going to bed. I found it odd that she texted and not called. On top of that, her text was bland with none of her usual smiley faces or xoxo. Now, I know.

She broke up with me out of the blue. Un-fucking-believable!

There I was pining away for Lola like a wuss and she dumps me with no hint of an issue. After the Vegas opening, I surprised her with a trip to Cabo San Lucas. A treat to unwind by the beach, drink Honey Bees, and get lost in each other with no distractions for a week. Unfortunately, she told me she had to stay in Vegas to wrap up some loose ends and that she was sorry she forgot to tell me.

So being the understanding boyfriend, I stayed two extra days to offer her my support. Yeah, she made up for botching my plans by treating me to a spa day with a mind-blowing happy ending. Lola played my masseuse, and I was her client with a stiff dick in need of her special rubbing.

After those two days, I fly home. Three days of missing my girl later, Lola texted me: she needs time on her own since she's been with me immediately upon arriving in New York; she feels she's losing herself jumping into a relationship with me so quickly; we should take a break and not be exclusive.

Not. Be. Exclusive. What the fuck does that mean?

Now, I'm sitting in Aquavit waiting for Lola to get here. She has to explain what changed her mind in three days from her kissing me and telling me she'll hurry home as soon as she can to bye-bye sucker.

At first I didn't know her location: Vegas or New York or on the moon. I finally persuaded her to tell me, and when she said that she'd been here for two days, I lost it.

We argued. She hung. I called back. I left voicemails. I sent text messages. Finally, she responded that we could meet today. But she refused to come to the penthouse, nor did she want to meet for dinner. Instead, it's lunch and now she's late.

It reminds me of our first night together at LEVELS. When we knew who we were as opposed to our initial first-time meeting as strangers doing a D/s scene together the night before her meeting with me for Lola's Coterie. I sat at the bar in the Cellar waiting as anxiously for her arrival, hoping that she showed up as I am now. And there she is, walking in the restaurant. Finally.

Lola is gorgeous and I feel my chest constrict when I think of us being apart after being together almost every day for four months. I was getting settled into our routine and WHAM. I watch as she makes her way to me. I can't take my eyes off of her. I want to pull her into my arms and never let her go. With a sigh, I stand when she's closer to the table to greet her.

"Hi," I start, surprised at the hitch in my usually dominant voice. "How are you?" I ask as I bend down to kiss her lips, aching to connect with her skin to skin.

She turns her head slightly so that my lips brush her cheek, then responds, "I'm good. How are you?"

So it's like that.

"I will not lie and say that I'm good—"

"Are you calling me a liar?" Lola demands, scowling up at me as she stops sitting in the chair I pulled out for her.

"Whoa, babe"—I raise my hands palms forward in defense—"I would never call you a liar. I am not good. I miss you and want to make things right between us, again. I'm confused. What happened in the three days that we were apart?" I continue as I take my seat opposite her.

Lola takes her time placing the linen napkin on her lap before looking at me. I can see her hazel eyes are shiny from unshed tears. But she blinks them away and lifts her chin, a determined expression replacing the moment of sadness.

"Like I said in my text and on the phone, I let myself get swept up and need time to refocus on me. I'll be thirty in two weeks and I promised myself that I would not depend on a man—"

I cut her off to ask if this is about her being a sub to my Dom and her struggle with letting go. She admits that's part of the problem. I remind her it's her choice and that she's the one with the power in our D/s relationship. I also tell her we can step back from it if that would make her feel more comfortable about our relationship. I will do whatever it takes to make us work. We go back and forth some more, not bothering to eat the food that we ordered —it's all tasteless to me and she struggles to eat hers, too.

After too short a period, I sit back in my chair as I watch the woman of my dreams walk out of my life.

SEBASTIAN

"*O*h, so are we back to this again so soon, Steele?"

Whack!

"What the fuck is in your *bashka, kiska?*"

Bam bam!

"Do you need me to beat it out of your *zhopa?*"

Whack! Bam bam bam!

Thunders my personal trainer and former MMA champion Borya *The War Defender* Alexeyev as he knocks my distracted ass around the mat. We're sparring in the full gym on the first floor of my penthouse duplex.

Yeah, that pretty much sums it up. We're back to working out at five in the morning before I head to the office a few floors below. Eleven is over since I no longer have Lola to roll around in our bed each morning. Either to satisfy my morning wood in her always-wet-for-me sweet pussy or waking her up with a toe-curling climax from eating her honey like a starving bear. Hopefully sparring with the giant Russian will knock some sense into me after almost two weeks of moping around or snapping at everyone. My concentration has gone to shit.

I zap back to attention when one of Borya's massive fists connects with my right flank, sending me reeling in the opposite direction, nearly off of the mat. Fuck! That hurt. I give my head a firm shake as I rub my side with my wrapped hand; I turn back to face the giant.

"Fuck you, Alexeyev! Is that the best you have for me, *kiska*?" I challenge, then go at him with a series of well-placed punches followed by a quick roundhouse kick.

"*Da*, much better, Steele. Guess you aren't getting any more of that *sladkaya kiska*! What have I told you before? Be here or go jerk off. No room on this mat for *zhopas*! Meow. Meow."

That gets my head on straight. I see red pissed he's right about me not getting any more of Lola's sweet pussy and her dumping me fucking with my capacity to function for work and life. Like hell if I'll let her craziness distract me from my duties and responsibilities to STEELE's growth and derailing me from my CEO path. If Lola wants to stay apart and deny what we had was good, then fuck it. I have to move on, too. With that in mind, Borya and I finish the rest of the session like two bulls facing off during rutting season. Game on!

"HEY, man. What's been eating your ass these last couple of weeks?"

My youngest brother Harris asks me as we're sitting in my office with Haley going over a new security protocol that they want to implement across all the STEELE divisions.

"Oh, leave him alone, nosy! If he wanted to tell you, he would," Haley admonishes with a scowl as she pushes her glasses back onto the bridge of her nose.

The twins are the youngest of the Steele clan and a double surprise for our parents, who had not planned on having more children. Then a twofer to boot. Roger is three years older and had been the baby of the family until Harris and Haley popped up—Harris older by mere minutes.

Although fraternal, they share a similar love of technology with Haley being a hacker and Harris a coder. We tease them for being nerds, but they're wizzes at what they do, which led to the approval for them to create a new subsidiary STEELE Technology and Cyber Security. As co-heads, they're responsible for all of STEELE and external clients from around the globe, including Jackson Corporation. They're smart as fuck and we've grown to depend upon them, even if they're now the babies.

Haley is a shy beauty who I can remember used to follow Lachlan and me around like a little stray puppy until she was in her gawky teens. Her looks—like Harris'—match the rest of us with jet black hair. Hers hangs midback in a silky curtain. Our signature gray eyes in her are soulful, set in her heart-shaped face with cheeks that display dimples when she smiles or laughs. Unlike now, since she's frowning in consternation at her twin.

Harris who couldn't care less that Haley does not approve of his questioning behavior rises from the conference table to stretch his much taller frame. At six feet, one inch, he's got five inches on his twin. He runs his hand through his short hair, then strides to the mini refrigerator below the drinks cabinet on the opposite wall.

"Anyone wants a bottle of water or something stronger, eh Baz?" He teases squatting down to pull one out for himself.

"Yeah, I'll only have a water, thank you very much," I respond.

I ignore the rib, grateful for the slight change in subject as I'm not eager to discuss my love life with my younger siblings.

The thought of calling the relationship that I had with Lola my love life gives me pause, and I wonder whether I love her. The more that I think about it, I'm certain that I care for her deeply and could see it growing into love easily. But... Oh well, she's squashed that with the heel of one of fuck-me sandals.

"Seriously, Baz, either you're looking like a lost puppy or you're biting everybody's heads off. I mean it, you're a mess." Harris continues ignoring Haley's loud sigh as he passes both of us a bottle.

I take my time to unscrew the cap, then swallow before I respond. We're a tight-knit family, so I'm not ashamed to admit what happened to him.

"Lola ended things almost two weeks ago out of the blue and it sent me for a loop," I confess.

Then take another sip of water and stare out of the floor-to-ceiling windows. The city stretches before me with unobstructed views of the Hudson River to the west, the East River opposite, and Manhattan to the south from Midtown to Battery Park. It's a sunny, cloudless day, so the vista is breathtaking from the forty-ninth floor of The STEELE Tower.

I get lost in thought for a moment until I hear Haley cough softly to get my attention. I return my gaze to the Dynamic Duo as we nicknamed them and smile brightly. I'm the eldest, so I want to project positivity and the ability to move past problems to my siblings. I feel responsible for them as their leader, both as big brother and as future CEO.

"So, after Borya knocked some sense into my wussy ass during our training session this morning, I'm back on track!" I tell them, slapping my palms on the table in front of me and leaning forward to look them directly in their eyes. "Now, tell me more about your latest brilliant scheme to save the corporate world from black hats."

LATER THAT NIGHT while I sit alone at the breakfast bar in my large, family style kitchen eating Indian food that I had delivered, I let my mind roam. Pre-Lola I went to LEVELS to satisfy my need to eat dinner at Level 4 Restaurant, fuck away the stress of the day, and to flex my Dom proclivities.

Now, I can acknowledge my relationship with Lola opened my eyes to me not wanting to return to my previous playboy ways of fuck 'em and leave 'em. As crude as that may appear, I was always respectful to the women, and the encounters were always consensual. I always made certain to fulfill their needs before my release—a part of my fetish.

Being in an exclusive—albeit short-lived—relationship made me realize that I'm at a point in my life where I can successfully dedicate my time to work and a woman. Neither has to suffer from lack of my attention. I'm reminded of the conversation that I had with my college roommate from Harvard right before his wedding.

"I get it Baz, and you can tease me for turning from a playboy to a soon-to-be married man. But I'll tell you now that when the right woman comes along, the one who's worth it, she'll change your mind like Lauren changed mine."

I laugh and finish putting my platinum cuff links on while I walk over to the valet for the jacket of my morning suit.

"Scott, man, you are nuts! Whatever you say, that won't be me anytime soon. I have an empire to grow and to lead—sort of what you're supposed to do with your family's business. Remember, hint, hint. No time for a relationship that will detract me from my goals."

Fast forward seven months and here I sit admitting that I want more and that Lola is the woman for me, just like Scott predicted. Sure, I'll give her some time. But I'm not giving up on us or our future together. I snagged her the first time with an offer that she couldn't refuse, and I'll reel her in again.

LOLA

"*L*ola, you have a delivery."

I look up from my computer monitor to see Blair standing in the doorway to my office on the third floor of Lola's Coterie New York. In the arms of the deliveryman is the largest bouquet of roses I've ever seen in my life. Not just your typical red roses, rather stunning lavender with silver highlights. The incredible scent of a sweet and citrusy fragrance wafts into the room.

Caught by surprise, I'm slow to ask him to place the laden vase on the conference table. So, of his own volition, he moves to it and places them in the center with a grateful sigh. Shaking his arms out as he walks to me, he withdraws a white envelope of fine linen stationary from his messenger bag. He puts the note in my hand as I sit awestruck in my chair.

"Thank you," I tell him and reach into my drawer for my wallet to give him a sizable tip.

"No, ma'am," he says shaking his head and walking backwards. "The sender already provided the tip. Enjoy your flowers!"

He turns on his heels and walks out of the door. Blair slowly leaves my office, gazing lovingly at the exceptional display of rare roses. I get up from my desk to stand beside their beauty as I open the envelope.

My Dearest Lola,

You enchant me. It was love at first sight where you enraptured me with feelings of love and adoration. I will give you time to yourself, only because you requested it. But know that you are mine and I am yours forever.

These fifty Sterling Silver Roses symbolize my love for you knows no bounds. I will never let you go. We belong together. I intend to make you face the truth and punish you soundly for your transgressions.

Your love forever,
Baz

I crumble to my knees and bow my head, overwhelmed by my former lover's declaration. It's unexpected and I have no defense against it. I love him, too. If he were here at this moment, I could not protect my heart from Baz—damn Lydie.

I love this man, so it seems as much as he loves me. As

Leonie says it's a *coup de foudre*—a stroke of lightning love at first sight. I stand and bend over the gorgeous bouquet to take a whiff of the fragrant flowers. I grip the edge of the table to maintain my balance. My eyes close as I remember our intense love affair as if it were yesterday, and we never parted.

The sound of my mobile ringing pulls me from my memories. With a sad exhalation, I head to my desk to answer the call.

"Hey, what's going on with you? You have answered none of my calls and texts!"

Speak of Leonie and she appears. I take a seat back behind my desk and gaze longingly at the roses before I answer her questions.

"Sebastian just sent the most extraordinary bouquet of silvery lavender roses with a note of his love for me," I answer.

I finger the card with his bold monogram in gray displayed on it. Then, bring it to my nose when I detect a trace of his sexy cologne, Creed Aventus. The iconic name derived from ventus the wind. Illustrating the Aventus man as destined to live a driven life. Ever galloping with the wind at his back toward success. The scent of bergamot, patchouli, musk, and vanilla tantalizes my nostrils and makes my pussy contract. I miss my lover.

"Oh, la la! What a fancy one!" Leonie laughs. "Will you give him another chance?"

I detect the note of sadness in her voice. Undoubtedly, she's thinking about her ill-fated romance with Sebastian's younger brother Roger. They, too, were a *coup de foudre*. Or so Leonie thought until Roger's demanding ways made her break free of him before it entangled them for too long. At least theirs was a fast break. Yet just as painful as I sense from the tone of her voice.

"No, I need to make my way and cannot afford to let him distract me, again. Besides, he has Lydie to make him feel better," I finish as I toss the note into the bottom drawer of my desk. I shut it with a decisive bang and return my attention to my best friend.

"Tell me what you've been up to these days. What's going on with you and Giovanni?" I ask to distract her from my melancholy love life. I think she and Roger make a better couple. But judging from the state of my relationship, I'm not the best judge of romance.

"Bof," Leonie scoffs. "He's in Paris and I'm in Milan for the shows. After Las Vegas, he told me he had to get back to his gallery to handle some business. Only, I see him on social media, all over the Internet hugging another woman. Men!" She huffs and continues on a stream of why she will never date again.

I can relate to her sentiment, as I also vowed to avoid those complications. But, as my gaze wanders to the lavish crystal vase, I can't deny the flutter in my heart that still happens when I think of Baz and what we shared. It may have been brief, but it was soul changing. As Leonie continues, I let myself drift to what should have happened upon my return to New York City from Las Vegas.

. . .

WITHOUT TURNING THE LIGHTS ON, *I strip and crawl onto the mattress to straddle Baz as he sleeps contentedly on my side of the big bed hugging my pillow close. His beautiful face is lit by the moonlight as I gaze lovingly at him.*

Gently placing my palm on his face covered in stubble, he sighs and rubs his cheek against my hand, the murmur of my name falling from his parted lips. My heart skips a beat. He's gorgeous and all mine.

"Baz, baby, I missed you so much," I whisper huskily in his ear.

The tips of my peaked nipples brush against his bare chest and cause me to shiver in anticipation of this man deep inside of me, our bodies bonding into one. Beneath me, I feel his thick shaft come to life as it grows in response to the heat of my hot, wet core eager to encase him. With a groan, Baz reaches for me, his large hands grip my hips to hold me steady. He raises his pelvis to grind his burgeoning shaft against my dripping pussy lips. I cry out and press back against him, the thin cotton of his sleep shorts not much of a barrier for our combined heat.

"Lola," he groans, thrusting up and holding me tight.

"Baz," I respond in a passionate whimper, grinding against his lengthening ten-inch dick. "I missed you so much, baby. It's so good to be home with you."

Sebastian's gray eyes fly open as he realizes this encounter is not a dream, but the real deal. Without hesitation, he easily flips us, putting his muscular body on top of my curvy one, his hips already beginning to piston against my fiery core. His Dom coming to the forefront to take control of our lovemaking.

I open my thighs wider to give him better access and lock my ankles together against his tight ass, encouraging him to drive into me. One of his hands slides between our fevered bodies to tease my engorged clit. Baz uses the other to yank his shorts past his hips, then grips his massive cock in preparation to impale me with it.

With a satisfied mewl, I throw my head back and close my eyes when his tip breeches my pussy lips. He pumps unabashedly into me, skin-on-skin. Our cries of mutual satisfaction fill our bedroom as we chase our climaxes.

Fuck, I missed my man so much. He feels so good inside of me. His guttural growls of pleasure turn me into one of Pavlov's dogs as my body responds to his—

"ARE YOU EVEN LISTENING TO ME?" Leonie's roar breaks through my reverie.

Shit, I got so caught up that I missed most of her conversation. With a contrite tone, I apologize to her and ask that she repeats herself as I promise to pay careful attention.

For the next ten minutes, I listen to Leonie and her concerns with Giovanni and Roger. Of the two, I prefer Roger, not because he's Sebastian's brother, but because Giovanni is not dependable and reappears in Leonie's life when he's in between women. Although I'm shocked to hear that he asked her to be exclusive and wants to make a go at a genuine relationship with her. Her hesitancy is because of her attraction to Roger.

He's an ass because he taunted her in Monte Carlo at

the Grand Prixe after party chatting up another well-known supermodel. I promised Leonie that I wouldn't talk to Sebastian about it. But that didn't keep me from giving Roger my death glare. What's up with the Steele men? Assholes.

Since Leonie is heading to Hong Kong next, we plan to catch up on her way back to Paris with a stopover in New York for a few days. I'm psyched to see my best friend and vow to make our time together fun and free of the Steele brothers. We'll go clubbing at the new spot Butterfly that caters to the glitterati. Giovani will think twice about his frolicking when he spies Leonie dancing the night away with hunky celebrities. We won't go to LEVELS New York like we did the last time we were together in the city. After we chat some more about fashion gossip, we end our call and I return to work.

IT'S BEEN a week and aside from the roses, I haven't seen nor heard from Sebastian. I guess he meant what he wrote in his note, that he would give me some time to myself. Just as well. Since at that moment, I was so weak I would have run right back to him and moved into his penthouse again. Not going to happen. Especially since I have a dinner meeting with Patrick Rockett. The Dom that I met at LEVELS the night Sebastian and I were hooking up for the second time and whose company Rockett Construction is the competitor to STEELE International.

Part of me accepted his offer because I knew that it would piss Sebastian off and partly because I swore to live my life. Pat is an attractive Alpha male, so it's no hardship to spend the evening with him. With that in mind, I freshen up my makeup and tidy my form-fitting, red Roland Mouret stretch-crepe dress that features a gold zipper along the entire back. It hugs my curves and with my stilettos make me feel sexy.

Blair gives me a wolf whistle as I pass her desk on my way to the elevator.

"Go home! We've reviewed the upcoming projects each night. Enough! Have some fun. I know I will," I add with a wink.

"Will do! I'll head out in a moment," Blair replies.

I wonder if she and Luc are still going strong. It's been a while since I spoke with my mentor. I make a mental note to call him tomorrow. Tactfully, I'll ask about his status with Blair. Luc is such a gentleman, that I doubt he'll reveal much of his personal life to me. Sebastian always argued that Luc wanted more from his relationship with me than just being my benefactor turned second father figure. Inwardly, I roll my eyes as I slip inside of the Bentley Bentayga.

I smile at Stan, my New York driver. Then, chuckle to myself as I think of the many nights he drove me to my trysts with Sebastian at LEVELS. Now, he's taking me to dinner with Pat at L'Atelier de Joël Robuchon, the two Michelin star restaurant at the Four Seasons Hotel New York. Oh my.

The bar area is lively as I make my way to Pat, who doesn't see me yet. His distraction with his mobile gives me the chance to observe him. He's a handsome man with a ruddy complexion, short red hair, and green eyes around six feet, three inches tall. Most intriguing about him is his sexy Scottish accent. If I hadn't met Sebastian first, Pat's charms could easily sway me.

The women near him try to catch his eye, but I don't feel a sense of jealousy as I would if he were Sebastian with hawks circling. With a devious glint in my eyes, I walk up to him and place my tiny palm on his massive chest—a reminder of his university rugby days. Damn, but he is fit. I give his pecs a squeeze and laugh softly when he jumps to his feet in surprise.

"Hey—" He starts before realizing it's me.

Pat's startled look fuels my mischief as I rub his chest more before tilting my cheek up for his kiss. Promptly, he responds as he wraps his brawny arms around my waist, lifting me to my toes to pull me close.

"Good evening, Mr. Rockett. Nice to see you," I murmur in his ear.

The women, who were only moments before ogling him, glare at me with their nostrils flared. I snicker to myself and move away from his tempting embrace. Again, he's not Baz, but I had to make myself feel better and ward off the wannabes angling for the Scottish billionaire.

"Aren't you a pretty sight, lass," Pat drawls, his accent thickened with his desire for me, his gaze caressing my body from head to toe.

With a coy smile, I respond, "Thank you. Shall we go to our table?"

"Och aye, briagha" Pat answers. The roles are reversed as his Dom replaces the startled gent, his green eyes sparkle impishly.

My pussy clenches and I lower my gaze submissively. To which a rumble in his chest emerges as a low growl. I lick my lips and press my thighs together, aching for relief I haven't had in weeks.

Pat grips my elbow and guides me to the maître d' another female who gawks at him before collecting herself. Her plump lips curve into a flirtatious smile as she leads us to our table in the center of the dining room. With his impressive physique and commanding presence, eyes follow us. I hold my head up high and gracefully sit in the chair that Pat pulls out for me.

Once we're settled and placed our order, I ask what business he wants to discuss with me.

"Ah, *leannan,* I want to finish what we started twice already, at the Cellar and the charity gala. Each time Steele rudely interrupted our dalliance. Now that you're a free woman, it's my chance to woo ye, lass."

I take a sip of my wine as I hedge for time. My mind going wild as I wonder what makes him think Sebastian and I aren't together anymore. I have told no one but Starr and Leonie. Visions of Sebastian doing a scene with another woman at LEVELS, on a date with some man-eater, or worse yet with Lydie makes my stomach flip. Could Pat have witnessed Sebastian's assignations?

Before I retch all over the pristine linen tablecloth, I excuse myself for a trip to the bathroom. In its relative safety, I can use the breathing techniques that Starr taught me. I need all the self-control that I can muster.

"WHAT... THE... FUCK... LOLA!"

I turn quickly, startled by the voice. A red-faced Sebastian stands in the doorway to the ladies' room. His fists clenched at his sides and his gray eyes shooting lethal daggers at me.

"What is it with you and bathrooms, Sebastian!" I say through clenched teeth.

I reference his invasion of the bathroom at my celebratory dinner at Per Se after we signed the expansion deal. This time, I won't let him have me. I will stand strong and not give in to his dominance. As much as I want him, I'm determined to safeguard my happiness more.

"What are you doing in a hotel with Rockett!" Sebastian yells back at me.

Da fuck!

How dare he insinuate that I'm meeting Pat for sex This man towering over me thinks so little of me and has no respect for me! He's the one running around with different women every night or his supposed family friend. Blatantly flaunting the fact that we're no longer together. I snap.

"How dare you!" I hiss, unable to contain my fury at his audacity.

Sebastian moves closer into my personal space. He

45

boxes me in and lowers his head to glare into my eyes. I refuse to move back. Instead I stand my ground lifting my chin to return his steely glare. I won't be the first to speak.

"One more time… What… are… you… doing… in… a… hotel… with… Rocket?" Sebastian grits through his teeth, his breath hot on my face.

For a moment, I'm hypnotized by his dominance. I close my eyes to gather my strength to ward off his magnetism. Although my body aches to lean into him, I straighten my spine. Opening my eyes to once again meet his gaze.

"Whatever I'm doing is of no concern of yours"—I raise my hand to stop him from interrupting me—"You and I are not exclusive. Hell, we're not even a couple. So excuse me. I have a date waiting for me."

I push a gobsmacked Sebastian out of my way, but pause at the door.

"I could very well ask you the same question, Mr. Steele," I scoff with my perfectly arched eyebrow lifted accusingly.

The parting shot ricochets off the walls as we glower at one another in a heated silence. The air is thick with tension—whether lustful or loathsome is hard to decipher. My body is afire with anger and need for this man. We're on the edge, but not pleasurably.

When Sebastian opens his mouth to respond, I remain firm. I dismissively toss my hair over my shoulder. Without a backward glance, I open the door and leave him standing with his mouth agape. I will not give him the opportunity for a comeback.

My inner cheerleader is remorseful while my Independent Woman salutes. Me... My world rocked. Sadly, not enjoyably.

LOLA

*S*weat drips down my spine, sending a shiver across my body as my feet relentlessly pound the treadmill at the swank fitness club near my apartment rental. The front and back of my Sweaty Betty Ultra Run sports bra drenched from my exertion lives up to its name. Fortunately, the black leggings camouflage and wick away the perspiration.

Every few minutes I alternate the pace or incline to maintain the burn in my muscles. Ten more minutes left in my grueling workout—my alternative form of release.

It's not quite subspace, but the rhythmic pulsations lull my mind into an active meditation. The drift happens, just not as sexually satisfying. The runner's high definitely doesn't compare to orgasmic euphoria.

I realize it wasn't the pain from the actual spanking that had thrilled me. Rather Sebastian's display of dominance that formed my need for him to possess me sexually. His power and control over me made my blood race directly to my core, engorging my clit and activating the muscles of my inner walls. The freedom from thinking for myself that allowed him to take over relaxed me.

The nerd in me researched why spanking enthralls me. According to the *Kama Sutra*'s "Blows and Sighs" chapter, spanking activates the lower chakras where sexual energy rests. The sensation moves through the entire spine like the flash of a lightning bolt. It's a way to release or awaken one's kundalini—sexual energy or chi. A spank or smack sends that chi up the spine from the root chakra, eliciting the chain reaction for a full-body orgasm.

After binge-reading the complete book—in between moments of self-induced release—I no longer feel guilty about my need for punishment and embrace my submissive desires. Even my Independent Woman approves. I won't go so far as a full-time D/s relationship, only during sex. Exactly what Sebastian and I had established and enjoyed.

Despite my revelation, I cannot go back to Sebastian. His cheating with Lydie is a nonstarter. He ruined any chance of us reigniting our passionate love affair. Yes, it is love for me. From the way he tenderly held me or the smoldering look in his gray eyes caressing my body. I sense he was on the cusp of loving me, too.

The cool-down ding from the treadmill ends my musings. My head is clear, ready for the day ahead.

* * *

"BLAIR, hey, you just poured a ton of sugar in your tea!" Billie exclaims, snagging the crystal bowl from her.

Blair mutters a curse as she moves the cup aside and rests her fingertips against her forehead. Silently, she shakes her head with her eyes closed.

"What's going on with you? I noticed you haven't been yourself since I arrived yesterday. Do you want to talk about it?" A concerned Billie asks softly.

We're at Norma's in the Parker Meridien Hotel on Fifty-seventh Street, one block west of the boutique. I figured a change of scenery for a breakfast meeting would be nice since Billie is in town. Really, I wanted to avoid bumping into Sebastian. Three times since his latest bathroom invasion is more than enough. I'm way too weak now that I've admitted my sexual preference. But smart enough to not put myself in that devil's path.

"Billie is right. You've been distracted for a few days now," I chime in.

Blair peeks at us through her fingertips before she lifts her head with a sigh.

"I'm so sorry, Lola, for letting my personal life interfere with my work—"

I raise my hand to stop Blair as I shake my head to assure her she has nothing to be sorry about. Everyone has their moments and my company is not strict where staff can't be human. Hell, my head has been in the clouds for a while. Hypercritical much?

"I'm not sure if I should discuss it with you... It's about Luc... and me," Blair pauses, raising a cautious gaze to me.

Not surprised in the least. The pair have spent a lot of time together outside of the office since we arrived in New York. Their outings to the ballet, dinners with Luc's New York associates confirmed my suspicions months ago. Luc is too much of a gentleman to discuss his private affairs, so I've only hinted at him and Blair as a couple. Each time, he changed the subject. Until now, Blair hadn't mentioned it other than to ask to leave the office early occasionally.

I place a reassuring hand on her forearm and squeeze.

"Luc is like a father to me. His well-being is of the utmost importance. However, I am a woman and know what it's like to need to talk to a friend about my love life," I smile, pleased when her eyes shine in relief.

The three of us exchange stories as we enjoy fluffy omelets and scrumptious pancakes—at least I went for a run this morning.

Luc and Blair are not officially a couple, but they've made out a few times. He's hesitant since she's seventeen years younger than him. Plus, she's the daughter of his friend who asked Luc to help her find a job.

He recommended Blair as an assistant three years ago. She was interested in fashion and not her family's manufacturing business. I was trying to handle all aspects of my company despite Luc's advice to focus on the creative design side and let an assistant handle the day-to-day tasks. After a one-month trial period, Blair proved herself to be efficient, dependable, and clever when balancing the activities that didn't need my constant or immediate attention. Blair is a valued member of my team, so I advise her to give him time.

Billie laments being single and wants a man who's a powerful match to her feisty, independent self. Someone as she says who has cojones—she's a Southern belle, not a wilting flower. Her last boyfriend only wanted the petite, brown-skinned beauty as a trophy on his arm she shares. Her big green eyes darkens with disgust.

I'm tempted to tell Billie to come with me as my guest to LEVELS New York so she can experience a Dom. Despite the concrete nondisclosure agreements they signed, I'm not revealing that part of my private life to my employees. Instead, I assure her that the man of her dreams is out there waiting for her.

My mobile chirps with a text message from Leonie. She's landed and headed to my apartment rental. I remind her the concierge has the spare key for her. As I hit send, a marvelous idea pops into my head: Girls' Night Out!

"THIS MUSIC IS PUMPING! I'm hitting the dance floor to shake my thing," a tipsy Billie announces after she applies gloss to her pouty lips.

She along with Leonie, Blair, and I sip Whiskey Sours and Manhattans gathered around our VIP booth at the opening night for the exclusive club Butterfly. I promised my girls a fun night to boot our not so titillating love lives squarely in the rear.

My gaze roams around the opulent club full of the glitterati. Celebrities, socialites, fashionistas, and billionaire tycoons wear their sexiest, most revealing outfits. Bottles of top-shelf liquor and magnums of champagne sit atop the tables in booths like ours.

Partiers pack the dance floor with their booty shaking as they grind and gyrate to the DJ's booming tunes. Those not fortunate to have a booth stand two deep at the three bars or perch on stools at high-top tables surrounding the dance floor.

"Hold on," I shout over the music to Billie. "I'm coming with you!"

We weave through the crowd as the heady scent of various perfumes and colognes mixed with sweat assails our nostrils the closer we get to the dancers. I love it! The sensuous, undulating sea of bodies calls me to revel with them.

Billie and I make quite the sight as we dance in the middle of the crowd. Billie in a glittering sea-green sequin tank dress that skims the tops of her thighs. Her ample bust nearly spilling over the top as she raises her arms overhead. She draws appreciative stares from the drop-dead gorgeous guys closing in on us as she seductively shimmies to the beat.

I match her moves with some of my own as I drop it low. The silver spangles of my fitted, strapless mini dress catch the LEDs like a spotlight. My shoulders shake as I rock back up to stand tall in my strappy sandals. Lost in the beat, I jump when brawny hands grip my hips to pull me against a massive chest. Trapped in the man's hands, I can only peer over my shoulder to see his face. Patrick Rockett. Damn.

"Aye, *leannan*, damn is correct," he rumbles in my ear. "You are a siren in your itty-bitty dress."

His warm breath sends goosebumps to the surface of my feverish skin. The sensation of his thick dick grinding into my ass as his grip tightens on my hips nearly causes me to swoon. Whether it's the cocktails or the heat, I have the sudden desire for the man in whose embrace I shiver to be—Sebastian. I shake my head at Patrick as I pull away from him. He's a Dom, but a well-bred man first. Patrick lets me go without argument.

"Hey, handsome! Who are you?" Billie's accent is as thick as Patrick's accent.

Her eyes sparkle in delight as her gaze slides over the burly billionaire. My surprised gaze lifts to Patrick, who towers over Billie and me. I notice his nostrils flare and his emerald eyes darken in lust for the petite vamp. Obviously, her siren's song is more appealing than mine, I laugh. Patrick slips his muscular arms around her tiny waist, lifting her from the floor as their hips slowly move despite the music's upbeat tempo. I won't need to invite Billie to LEVELS. She's found her Dom with very enormous cojones. To that, I can attest.

Leonie and Blair drag me back to the dance floor just as

I step off. Our shenanigans and laughter save me from asking Stan to drive me to Sebastian's penthouse pronto. Those thoughts fade away as more attractive albeit drooling guys pivot towards us. *The Lion* is on the loose and I will have fun!

LOLA

"*I* can't believe it's almost three months since I broke up with Roger," Leonie sighs as we stare at photos of him looking extraordinarily suave in a bespoke tuxedo.

Last night while we lived it up at Butterfly, he attended a charity gala with a stunning raven-haired heiress clinging to his biceps. His intense gray eyes captivate you, drawing you in even though it's only his two-dimensional image.

In another shot, despite her gaze of adoration as she presses her palm against his broad chest, Roger remains coolly aloof. His icy stare unchanged by her intimate touch.

I recall his stoic demeanor during my initial meeting with STEELE. His expression revealed no emotion, even when Leonie and the other models sashayed around the conference room in skimpy lingerie. His intense gaze redoubled.

However, that standoffish persona vanished proven when Sebastian and I witnessed Roger and Leonie at The STEELE Tower. The morning after dinner at Per Se, he carried her onto the family's residential elevator. Their long limbs tangled as their lips locked in an amorous kiss. Only Sebastian's discreet cough stopped Roger from hiking Leonie's leg around his hip as he thrust his pelvis into hers.

When he's with Leonie, the distant man changes into a fiery lover whose electricity sends shock waves through the enamored bombshell. A smoking hot couple whose flame burned out too quickly for either to come to terms. Which explains Leonie's sullen mood shift as she continues to scroll through the gossip website.

"She's the woman he wants," Leonie frowns disapprovingly as she mimics Roger's baritone voice. "A 'serious-minded partner' and not a 'wayward woman who cannot stay focused for over five minutes!'"

I hold my breath, not sure if the giggle I'm suppressing is inappropriate until Leonie bursts out in raucous guffaws. Gleeful tears trickle from the corners of her glowing amber eyes.

We cut our laughter short when the next photo pops up. Lydie stands beside the heiress; Sebastian and Roger flank them. The caption informs the viewer Sebastian and Roger are two of the world's eligible billionaires. Along with their brothers Malcolm and Harris, they're pronounced The STEELE Quaternity.

The amused tears turn tragic as Leonie and I wail over our former lovers. The fun lasted less than twelve hours.

"See I told you Sebastian lied to me the entire time we were together!" I screech in frustration. "Family friend, my ass! That bastard was fucking her for sure! That asshole jerk—"

I stalk around the living room, anger escalating. Last night I was so close to giving in to his charms. The "we belong together," his possessive Captain Caveman antics at the Four Seasons, memories of his enormous cock pounding into me had me ready to give in... again.

"No!" I slap my palm on the table so hard Leonie's iPad lifts and she jumps. "The STEELE Quaternity my ass! The Controlling Cads is more like it."

Leonie gives me a high five. "Giovanni the scoundrel, too. None of them are good enough for us, *Chérie. Tous les mecs sont des cons!*"

True, they're all assholes. We deserve better than what they offer.

The ring of my mobile interrupts our man-bashing tirade. I'm surprised to read Robin Sanchez-Waghorn's name on the display. I answer, curious what the realtor has to tell me so early on a Saturday morning. My curiosity turns to elation when she delivers monumental news. The Sutton Place penthouse is back on the market. The owner asked if I'm still interested, they re-accept my original offer plus an immediate close. Without hesitation I tell Robin to get the paperwork ready, I want to take ownership by end of day on Monday. We end the call with plans to meet at the penthouse to show Leonie this afternoon.

"Congratulations, *Chérie!*" Leonie exclaims as we jubilantly dance around the soon-to-be-empty rental.

"THE VIEW IS SPECTACULAR, Lola! You can sit on the terrace and sip tea as the sun rises or end the day with a glass of Chardonnay."

I agree with Leonie. The view of the East River sealed the deal since it reminds me of the one I had from my family's apartment further north of Fifty-seventh Street. The familiarity comforts me. It lessens the pain of the unexpected loss of my parents when they died two months shy of my eighteenth birthday. I envision myself just as Leonie described. The first night, I'll toast my parents and my return home.

The sunny, spacious penthouse in a magnificent, Rosario Candela designed building is by far my favorite of all the others Robin selected to meet my needs. It's exactly what I'm looking for in my new home. The proximity to the boutique is a bonus. A seven-block drive across Fifty-seventh Street from Sutton Place to Fifth Avenue and I'll be at the office. Sure, the crosstown traffic is daunting, but it's still a quick commute.

"You know, since you have your final project for your interior design degree, I want you to do my apartment!"

After more than sixteen years as a successful supermodel, Leonie is in her last semester at the Paris American

Academy. The years of staying in remarkable homes and hotels sparked her interest in residential design. With her desire to look beyond the catwalk, Leonie chose a path that remains a part of the creative end of business. Her taste and style are perfect for her new career.

"Oh, Chérie! Merci beaucoup pour votre gentillesse..."

Overwhelmed, Leonie's eyes fill with tears. As we embrace, I join her knowing we cry not just for happiness. But in addition to the emotions roiling in our minds about the men we love.

FORGET CLOUD NINE. My excitement breaks through the stratosphere. Robin and I finished the closing on my penthouse an hour ago. The contract included an addendum for certain light fixtures to remain. Something about the co-op board and maintenance of the property's historical value.

The process ended quickly since the seller's broker handled the signing with a general power of attorney. A niggle in my mind made me wonder why the owner was absent unlike the last time and pointed to the name appeared differently from the previous paperwork. However, Robin assured me all was in order.

What I care about are the keys in my hand—the penthouse is mine. Robin gave them to me on a sterling silver Tiffany key chain with a star charm. I plan to spend the night. So, Blair arranged a cleaning crew and a bed with linens. I'll bring my favorite Dom Pérignon Rosé Vintage 2005 Champagne and pick up dinner from Mr. Chow. Until Leonie transforms it into my home, I'll stay at the rental. But tonight, I'll celebrate.

"Lola, Luc is on the line for you," Blair's voice rings out from the intercom on my desk.

Funny, Luc usually calls my mobile. He called through the office line as an excuse to get Blair on the phone. The distance she placed between him and herself has drawn him out of his reluctance. Soon he'll give in to admitting she means more to him than he's let on. Smart move by Blair.

"*Bonjour, Renard Argenté. Comment allez-vous aujourd'hui?*" I ask, a sly smile on my face.

"*Bonjour, petite chérie. Je vais bien, merci,*" he responds distractedly.

Yup, Blair's put it on him, I giggle to myself. Go, girl!

Luc and I discuss business, including my upcoming trip to Paris and London. The past few months spent in New York and Las Vegas with only one visit to Paris and Luc handling in-person work is not enough. Meetings scheduled with suppliers and distributors among other activities require my presence. We arrange logistics and plan to meet in Paris in two weeks. With my base in New York settled, I'm ready to split my time between the States and Europe regularly.

Now is an agreeable time for the trip since my attention will focus on the LA, Dubai, and Abu Dhabi boutique openings. The LA property is perfectly situated as an anchor store amongst other high-end retailers in STEELE's outdoor mall on Rodeo Drive. Tomorrow, I meet with the Retail Properties Division team. The agenda includes the final paperwork on the LA location and discussion on two spots in Dubai and three in Abu Dhabi.

No matter how Sebastian irks me, he is extremely organized with a knowledgeable staff. The ease of our business relationship is opposite of our combustible love affair.

Once I catch Luc up on my end, I poke the bear.

"Why didn't you call me on my mobile?" I innocently ask.

A brief silence followed by a throat-clearing cough shows my theory is correct. Luc used the call as an excuse to interact with Blair. Before he can answer my question, I continue.

"Did you need to speak with Blair about something? I mean, normally—"

"Lola…" He interrupts.

Two clues he's agitated are his use of my name as opposed to *petite chérie,* and his French accent is thicker. Good, gotcha on the ropes, Silver Fox! I sit forward, ready to spar. These men will learn today, I nod decisively.

"I do not always call you on your mobile. Particularly during business hours I avoid an interruption of your creative flow or perhaps a meeting. Why are you asking me such nonsense?"

Luc's flustered. His tone is never harsh with me. Still, I won't back down. Now for the TKO.

"Hhhmmm… I'm surprised Blair answered. I thought

she'd already left for lunch with Antonio. Oh, silly me, it's not 12:30, yet."

This time, the silence is deafening. The jealousy is thick. Well… get 'em while he's down.

"Oh Luc, I need to catch her before she leaves. He's taking her to that cozy restaurant near—"

"Lola, I have another call. Adieu!"

Abruptly, Luc ends our call and I race to Blair to tell her what happened. As I reach her desk, her mobile rings and I snatch it from her hands.

"It's Luc! Let it go to voicemail!" I huff. Damn, isn't running supposed to condition me?

I relay the conversation with Blair. At first, she hides her annoyance. But by the third call in a row from Luc, she's slapping high fives with me. We listen to the messages and read several texts. We decide to not respond until tomorrow afternoon. He can roast for a little while. Maybe that will help him put on his big boy underwear.

Since neither of us has lunch dates, Blair and I order salads. We video conference Billie in from Las Vegas to give her the latest update on Luc. She gets a laugh out of it and tallies score one for Blair, zero for Luc.

Then, I get a shock when Billie tells us Patrick visited her only days after she left New York. Apparently, the bonnie Scotsman is more than entranced by Billie's siren song. He calls her each night and invited her to Hawaii for the weekend. The smart lass declined and hasn't done more than kiss Patrick. Her adage: why pay for the cow if you can get the milk for free? Billie's hard-to-get tactic works. I'll definitely keep it in mind for future use. Billie has a meeting, so we end the video call with promises of regular Girls' Chats with Leonie included in the next session.

The rest of the day goes smoothly, allowing us to leave shortly after four. At the top of the stairs on the second level of the boutique, I observe it's bustling with shoppers and attentive staff. They're not trained as salespeople, rather consultants who advise shoppers on their purchases of ready-to-wear pieces and bespoke designs. A thrill runs through me as I sense how proud my parents would be of me. With that thought in mind, I stride through the customers introducing myself and offering suggestions. So involved in helping my customers, I don't realize over an hour passed until Stan calls my mobile. I ask him to give me ten minutes to finish with a client.

My passion to give women an air of sultriness in sexy lingerie continues beyond my initial realization as a thirteen-year-old. I knew I'd found my destiny when I watched Elizabeth Taylor wearing a silk lace-trimmed slip in the classic movie *Butterfield 8*. The bombshell leaning against the wall in nothing but her slip and high-heel shoes sipping liquor from a crystal glass remains forever etched in my brain. Lola's Coterie was born.

As ALWAYS, Mr. Chow is delicious. With my hunger beyond satisfied, I make my way to the terrace where the stars glow. I envision my parents gazing down from

Heaven and raise my champagne flute in salute: Thank you, Daddy and Mommy, for loving and believing in me. I'm home, again!

Sitting cross-legged on the terrace floor, I stare at the night sky and finish nearly all the bottle of Dom Pérignon. The bubbles tickle my nose. The carefree feel the delicious vintage fills me with loosens my inhibitions. I rise from the terrace floor to make my way to the bedroom where the temporary bed awaits me.

The white fluffy pillows, downy comforter encased in silk, and matching silk sheets encase me in a cocoon of sensuality. I feel like a bride on her wedding night. With thoughts of being ravaged, I rip the tank and joggers from my body, eager to lie naked in the middle of the bed to await the command of my lover. My fingertips trail fire over my fevered body as my thoughts drift to my Dom Sebastian Steele. My nipples pebble and my pussy weeps. I miss him and want him beyond all measure of sanity. Yes, he cheated on me. But his dominance, ability to elicit multiple pleasurable orgasms from my body, and most of all his love make me burn for him despite Lydie Fucking Jackson.

I close my eyes and fantasize about my lost Baz.

"ON YOUR KNEES, LITTLE PET," his mesmerizing voice makes me drop gracefully to the floor at his feet.

My pussy quivers and my nipples peak in response to his command. I lick my lips and eye the bulge straining against the crotch of his leather pants. My Dom has a ginormous dick. I shiver in anticipation.

"Eager tonight, are you, Little One?" He asks seductively as his thumb circles my full lips. "You enjoy sucking me off, do you not?"

The rough growl causes goosebumps to break out across my heated skin. My mouth moistens at the thought of his colossal dick driving savagely down my throat as he relentlessly fucks my face, chasing his climax. I close my eyes and sigh. I love the sensation of my Dom's pulsating dick deep down my throat, twitching before it spews forth a torrent of his seed. I silently vow to swallow every bit, not allowing a drop to spill from my swollen lips.

"Yes, Sir," I moan as I squeeze my thighs together to ease some pressure built from my desire for his cock to take me.

"Have at me, Little Pet. Show your Dom how much you love to please me."

Without hesitation, my fingers pull the leather cord on my Dom's pants to loosen the lacing that separates my mouth from his thick length. As I pull the pants past his narrow hips, his bare crotch appears. So, I'm not the only naughty one tonight. I lick my lips, eager to have him in my mouth. His clipped pubic hair surrounds the beauty of his massive cock—all ten inches of it in all of its glory engorged before my hooded gaze. The pants fall to the floor and I wrap my small hand around his massive length. With a tug, I pull his bulbous tip into my mouth. My tongue circles around his massive head and pokes the slit, lapping the pre-cum from the seam. Yum.

My other hand toys with his sac, shifting the weight of his

balls in my palm. He's a virile male with loads of jizz to fulfill all of my desires. I take a deep breath to slide his thickness to the back of my throat. I moan as he throws his head back in bliss. The Dom is under my control.

I continue my ministrations easing his massive girth from my mouth then back to my throat deepening the reach on each stroke. His muscular thighs shake as he nears his peak. I slow the onslaught to make him beg me, turning the tables for only a moment. The sub becomes the Master.

"Fuuuck... Little Pet! You feel so good.... Aaaahhhhh!" He groans as his jizz gushes down my throat.

My fingers fly to my core to satisfy my pleasure. The eager digits dive between my wet, swollen folds, stroking my inner walls and G-spot in a frenzy. As I near the edge, I pinch my pleasure nub and scream my release around his turgid staff. Shock waves rip through my core. Our mutual climaxes convulse our bodies.

BAAAAAZZZZZZ!!

My sole scream reverberates around the empty bedroom—a reminder I am alone and not with my lover. I roll over onto my side to curl into a ball wrapped in frustration despite my intense release. My body continues to quake from the aftershocks of my illusion while my mind comes to terms with Sebastian choosing Lydie over me. Tears trickle from my tightly shut eyes that refuse to see the truth. Why can't Sebastian be mine and only mine? Sleep pulls me under and I give in to the peace it offers.

SEBASTIAN

*F*uck... me. Lola still loves me and wants me as much as I love and want her.

My hand fists my thick, hungry cock in time with the rhythm set by her fingers as they pump in and out of her sweet pussy—my pussy. I want this woman more than I've wanted anything in my life. She's mine and I will not stop until she has my ring on her finger and my baby in her belly.

The view of Lola in bed masturbating while she fantasies about me is enough to make me race over there to prove how much I am hers and she is mine. Enough with the games, I will make her mine forever. Fuck Patrick Rockett and Lydie. I won't let anyone come between us again.

A zing shoots from the base of my spine to my heavy balls. My rock-hard dick expands in my hand in preparation to release the orgasm that has Lola's name on it. With one last tug, I throw my head back and roar like a feral beast just as my Petite Seductress screams my name. I nearly fall off the breakfast bar stool when I black out from the intensity of my release. Thick creamy jizz gushes onto my bare chest and abs, then coats my hand. It seeps through my sweatpants as it drips onto my lap. Once the shudders stop and I can see straight, I head to the shower to clean up the proof of my unceasing desire for Lola.

"SEBASTIAN! What the fuck are my cameras doing in Lola's apartment, you asshole?"

What the fuck? Is that Harris bellowing outside of my bedroom? What the fuck is he doing in my penthouse, I wonder as I wrap a towel around my hips.

The door to my bedroom slams against the wall as a livid Harris storms inside. His face is a mask of fury. His gray eyes shoot daggers when he spies me standing in the middle of the room.

"What... the... fuck... are... my... cameras... doing... in... Lola's... apartment... you... asshole?" Harris yells.

Fuck! What made me think giving my family access to my penthouse was a bright idea? He must have seen my laptop in the kitchen, still tuned into Lola's penthouse. Yeah, I didn't quite tell him why I needed the special cameras he designed. Rather, I alluded to needing them to monitor staff stealing supplies.

Lame, yes, but I couldn't exactly tell him it was to watch my ex in her new apartment. The same apartment that I originally bought under a shell corporation to prevent Lola from moving in to it instead of staying at my penthouse. I set up the ruse to prevent her from buying the Sutton Place penthouse when I realized I preferred her here in my bed. It wasn't the owners pulling the penthouse off the market; it was me.

When I realized Lola would not come back, I told Robin to let her know it was available again. I want to keep Lola near. I included the addendum in the contract so I could put Harris' surveillance cameras in the light fixtures to monitor her. I need to determine whether she's dating someone else like that fucker Rockett. Unscrupulous, sure, but I let nothing get between me and something that I want.

"I'm removing my cameras tomorrow, asshole! Don't even think you can stop me," Harris berates me.

His steely gaze rakes over me. His eyes narrow, and he cocks his head, lifting his eyebrow.

"Did you just rub one out while you watched her? Is that why you took a shower this late at night?"

I can only stand there silently as I have no defense; he makes his case.

"What a loser," Harris mutters as he shakes his head. "You're lucky I don't tell Mom. She'll have your balls, creep."

The thought of him blabbing to our mother jump-starts my brain. I draw on my Dom to gain control of the situation.

"Harris, you are right. I deceived you," I start inwardly

relieved when he looks surprised that I didn't lie. "As I told you, Lola is everything to me. I pledged to her I would give her time since she requested it, but know that she is mine. It may be much to monitor her, but you are an Alpha male. Would you not use any means to monitor your woman?"

Fortunately, Harris agrees, but remains adamant about the immediate removal of his cameras. To avoid Lola's suspicions, he'll go under the guise of an inspector sent by the board to ensure the light fixtures remain intact. The task will go smoothly since Robin will assist him by relaying the message to Lola and getting her keys. The arrangements made, Harris leaves with the corkscrew he planned to borrow.

I'm not overly upset by this turn of events. He may have remotely disabled the cameras, but the files autosave to an undetectable backup server. Beyond even his tech savvy self.

A quick conversation with my private investigator replaces the sophisticated technology with old-fashioned footwork and photography. Until Lola is back at my side, I'll prevent anyone else from claiming her.

"Pardon my tardiness. An urgent overseas call delayed me," I say to those gathered in the conference room, but I lock my eyes on Lola.

Her hazel orbs dilate as she unconsciously licks her plump lower lip. I ache to nip and suck it into my mouth.

The memory of her taste fades each day. If all goes as planned, her succulent tongue will dally with mine soon. My dick twitches at the thought of her skillful appendage.

I stride to the table and unbutton my suit jacket. Sliding my hand down the muscular plane of my torso, momentarily hovering over my crotch. I delight in Lola's eyes darkening as her gaze follows the path of my palm. I lick my own full lips as I take the seat opposite my beauty, whose eyes widen when she sees my burgeoning bulge. As our eyes meet, I pin her with my penetrating Dom stare. Lola's sharp intake of air makes me smirk—she's bitten the bait.

Until now, my Retail Properties Division team handled affairs directly with Lola. Out of respect for her time request, I stayed in the background. Although I kept a watchful eye on the goings-on. So, I'm very much aware of each new boutique's property location and timeline.

Relationship aside, it's still all about generating revenue and having the partnership with Lola's Coterie make up for the money lost in the Rockett Construction fiasco. My goal for CEO in just over six months is very much on track.

So far, her New York and Las Vegas boutiques are profitable with expectations of surpassing the initial projections. It's a sound business deal that I will not screw up. I'm living up to the promise I gave Lola when we made a go at a relationship. We even included an addendum to the contract to solidify the partnership. No matter what occurs between us personally, business will continue unscathed.

STEELE Galleria Rodeo Drive is the best spot for her

Beverly Hills boutique since an anchor store recently moved into a freestanding space in one of our West Hollywood storefronts. I held the SGRD specifically for Lola not to curry favor. But for the potential increase in revenue for the site since hers will be the only luxury lingerie store in the vicinity. Our marketing division will work with her team to make a tremendous splash, ensuring a successful opening.

The United Arab Emirates locations in Abu Dhabi and Dubai require a trip to view the three and two spots in each city, respectively, before we make the ultimate decision. Their openings will coincide one week apart for logistical reasons. No need to travel to the other side of the globe unnecessarily.

They schedule the trip for three weeks from now if Lola's time is available. I'll clear my calendar for a chance to be with her on my Gulfstream G650 private jet for thirteen uninterrupted hours.

Lola furtively peeks at me over the course of the meeting. Each time she blushes when our gazes connect. I slowly rub my thumb back and forth over my lower lip, imagining it thrumming her clit.

A thrill runs through me as she sucks her lower lip between her teeth. When she slowly releases her swollen lip and keeps her mouth slightly open, I nearly cum in my trousers. I shift in my seat to adjust my cock discreetly. Zipper marks undoubtedly formed on my turgid length. A look of triumph lights Lola's eyes when she detects my discomfit. I tilt my head in affirmation and curl the corner of my lip in a half smile. She needs to know she affects me as much as I do her.

The meeting continues peppered with our secret fore-play. Lola hastens to gather her personal effects, but I have other plans for my Petite Seductress.

"Lola, a word," I command.

I suppress a laugh when she jumps like a frightened rabbit cornered by the wolf. She's not so far off. My gray eyes are predatory, latched on her. She will not dodge me today—or any day going forward.

"Mr. Steele, I have another meeting—"

"Oh, Lola, I can take it for you. No worries."

I could kiss her assistant, Blair, except that Lola would stab me with her stiletto. Instead, I nod my thanks as Blair hurries from the room. I return my gaze to a shocked Lola, who's staring after Blair's retreating figure as the door closes. No escape.

Instead of speaking immediately, I wait until Lola faces me. I want her full attention.

"Are you pleased with the situation?" I ask, knowing she'll assume I'm referring to our personal relationship.

Flustered, she lowers her head as she places her tablet inside of her attaché.

"Mr. Steele, as you said, 'don't mix business with plea-sure.' So, excuse me," Lola snaps with flashing eyes.

Quickly, I round the corner of the table to block her path to the door. She halts inches from my chest. Another sharp intake of air forces a growl deep in my chest. Lola jerks her eyes to my face. The raw need she sees makes her involuntarily sway towards me. I seize the opportunity to grip the back of her neck to draw her body flush to mine while tilting her head back to swoop my lips onto hers.

The surprise move parts them. I brazenly slip my tongue into her mouth, sweeping around until I catch her tongue and suck it into my mouth. A moan falls from Lola's parted lips as she fists my suit jacket. Our tongues dally just as I planned. We relish the taste and feel of one another.

Reluctantly, I move away. I don't want to push Lola too far. I have to reel her in slowly or risk her slipping off the line.

I take a deep breath of her alluring perfume; hints of tuberose, ylang-ylang blossom, and pear make my mouth water. I close my eyes for a moment to let her scent infuse every cell of my body.

"Have dinner with me now," I tell her, my voice husky with desire.

Lola tries to move away, but I tighten my grip on her neck and tilt her head back up. She's gorgeous with kiss-swollen lips and hooded eyes. Her flushed cheeks mimic the heat on mine. I lean my forehead against hers. We exchange breaths and our souls reconnect.

"You asked for time… Two months, Lola. Have dinner with me," I start, then continue when she softens against me. "Only dinner. We can take it slowly. You can trust me not to take you beyond your limits."

I add the D/s reference to judge her reaction. Against my legs, Lola squeezes her thighs together. Yes, she hasn't let go of her sub needs. I groan and grip her hip with my free hand. Pressed against me, Lola senses the power she has over me. My dick pokes her belly, but she knows it's her choice.

"Let go and just feel," I remind her in a rough whisper as I brush my lips against the shell of her ear.

"Baaazzz…"

Lola's groan reminds me of her in the throes of passion last night. I nip and suck my way from her ear along her jaw and down her throat to travel back up the opposite direction to cover her mouth once again. We gasp when our lips touch. Lola slides her arms around my neck and pulls me down to her. I lift her from her feet and hold her tightly as our kiss deepens. We remained locked together, reacquainting our bodies.

"Say yes to dinner now or it's yes to me feasting on you spread before me on this conference room table," I growl into her neck.

Lola shivers and pants yes. I sense she means the latter, but it will be dinner. Again, a slow pace.

Gently, I lower Lola to the ground, letting her body slide against mine. I hold her firmly by the waist until she's sure on her feet. Once settled, she lowers her head as her cheeks deepen in color. I hold her chin between my thumb and index finger as I bend my knees to align our eyes.

"No need for embarrassment. I miss you, too. A lot," I reassure her with a soft kiss to the tip of her nose.

Her smile makes my heart skip a beat.

Lola finishes packing her attaché. Meanwhile, I send a

text message to my assistants Melody Lawson and Tina Nickles to apprise them of my change in plans for the rest of the workday. I also ask them to have my driver bring the sedan out front. I'm sure they're surprised since I usually leave the office around seven in the evenings. My days are fourteen hours long—a testament to my unwavering dedication to STEELE's success. Since I'm heading out early, I tell them to wrap up whatever they're working on and call it a day.

The sense of being stared at causes me to lift my gaze from my mobile to find Lola peering at me. Her cheeks flush when I catch her hooded stare. A smirk lifts the corner of my mouth—gotcha securely on my line. Defiantly, she tosses her hair over her shoulder and quirks her eyebrow.

"Still cocky, I see," she says to deflect.

I stand from leaning my hip against the table to tower over her. I may have decided to go slow, but I will not allow my Little Pet to sass me. Quickly, I crowd Lola to back her up against the sideboard across from the table. She jumps and squeaks when her plump bottom bumps into the furniture. As I brace my hands against the top on either side of her waist, I lower my lips to press them against rim of her ear.

"Are you ready for punishment so soon, Little Pet? As always, your cocksure mouth needs me to fill it. You realize we do not have to go slow as I originally suggested," I gruffly respond, allowing my breath to tickle her skin.

Lola trembles with pleasure as her next inhalation

catches in her throat. Purposefully, I maintain mere inches between our bodies. The heat building between us is scorching. It radiates between us in waves.

With a sharp nip to her lobe, I pivot on my heel to stride to the door. Sweeping my palm towards the opening, I tilt my head to the side, pinning Lola with my Dom stare.

"Shall we?"

I watch Lola's plump ass and curvy hips in the black-ribbed wool dress molded to her luscious body. The high-heel shoes lift her butt and lengthen her shapely legs. My palm itches to smack her ass to watch in fascination as it jiggles. My dick twitches at the memory of being deep inside of her bottom hole. Fuck, I need her. I shake my head to clear those thoughts and follow Lola like a home-sick puppy. Strong Dom missing alert...

As we walk past the other executive suites, one of my younger brothers Malcolm calls out to us. We detour into his office. At only two years apart, he's my doppelgänger: same six feet, four inches in height; gray eyes; black hair; clean shaven or 5 o'clock shadow covers a firm jaw. As kids, he strove for his own identity, hating being in my shadow. Fortunately, we grew past the teenage angst to develop a close relationship.

Malcolm rises to greet us and pulls Lola into an embrace. He winks at me over the top of her head before giving her a squeeze. A growl falls from my lips and he laughs, releasing her from his tentacles.

"Good to see you again, Lola," he starts with a twinkle in his eyes. "I spoke with Adrienne Anthony, Starr Knight's studio manager. Apparently Starr is out of the country at an ashram in India and unreachable. So, we must connect when she returns."

Again... When the hell did they speak? What the hell is Malcolm talking about? Why didn't he tell me he communicated with Lola? Before I can demand answers, Lola responds.

"It's so good to see you again, too, Malcolm! Thank you for dinner. The—"

"Whaaat???" I yell, my eyes zipping between Lola and Malcolm.

The cool, in-control Dom now completely off the grid. My mind plays a scene of Lola and Malcolm dining by candlelight in a romantic restaurant. Her eyes shiny from the champagne they drink with dessert. He leans over the table to lick cream from the corner of her lips. Lola's laugh rings out. Other men turn to stare jealously at Malcolm. The lovestruck couple leave the restaurant to finish dessert at Malcolm's penthouse in The STEELE Tower. While I lay alone in the big bed Lola and I once shared two floors above...

I snap my head in Malcolm's direction when his words filter through my nightmare.

"—concept could fit well with our latest Jackson Hole venture. New amenities attract unique guests while the regular ones find more reasons to keep coming back to stay. Once I meet with Ms. Knight, I'll fill you in."

As the president of STEELE's Entertainment Properties Division, Malcolm oversees our casinos, hotels, and resorts. His latest project Jackson Hole at STEELE Resorts is in partnership with Lydie and her younger brother Lucien. The concept is members-only, high-end beach clubs for the jet set. It's his second foray with LEVELS New York, Paris, and London BDSM/dine/dance clubs in co-ownership with Lucien. Basically, Jackson Hole is LEVELS on the beach minus the BDSM.

Since a baffled expression lingers on my face when he finishes, Malcolm sighs dramatically realizing that I wasn't paying him the least bit of attention.

"Get your head out of your ass, Baz. Lola and I had dinner last week to discuss business. B-U-S-I-N-E-S-S. Got it?" He admonishes me. "Lola met Starr Knight, the owner of the Beverly Hills-based fitness studio and well-ness center Starr Light Fitness & Wellness. She plans to expand into international fitness retreats at luxury resorts and to add a second center location in the Caribbean. Lola told me about Starr since she had an exceptional experi-ence at her first retreat in Fiji on the private Laucala Island. Are we clear?"

I have to hold back an eye roll getting chastised by another Dom, especially my younger brother. I risk a peek at Lola to find her hazel eyes glowing warmly with suppressed laughter. Malcolm drapes his arm around her shoulders as he joins in her glee. How low can an Alpha male sink?

"Crystal clear, brother. Now, back off my girl. We're going to dinner," I chide to regain control.

Lola's eyes widen. I frown at her, then realize I referred

to her as my girl. Oh boy. Instead of addressing the term of endearment, I grasp her hand and pull her from the office.

"Have fun," Malcolm taunts.

I throw a glare over my shoulder at him as I usher Lola through the door. His booming laughter carries across the office suite. Fucker.

"Possessive much?" Lola asks as she tries to tug her hand from mine.

Not having it. I squeeze her hand and glance down at her. No way am I letting Lola go.

"Yes," I answer definitively.

LOLA

*S*ebastian is definitely trying to get in my good graces and off of my shit list. I acknowledge as I sit oh so comfortably in his Gulfstream G650 private jet on my way to Paris. With a base price of sixty-five million dollars, it's the epitome of luxury travel. During the four months that Sebastian and I dated, we used his jet for frequent trips domestically and abroad. Luc also has a custom model that frequently over the six years we've known each other I've flown in. Of course, he's had a few upgrades as recent ones hit the market. Private jets without a doubt surpass commercial and charters by miles —no pun.

This latest lure comes on the tail end of two weeks of romantic dates, phone calls late into the night, and dozens upon dozens of exquisite Sterling Silver Roses, each with a touching—sometimes lascivious—note. I blush just thinking about the hedonistic pleasures Sebastian promises: lave your glistening pink pussy until you beg me to stop; cuff you to my pommel horse and spank your engorged clit; lock your legs in my spreader bar and plunder your tight ass. My core clenches at the graphic visions. Damn, I miss my man.

Sadly, he still insists that we take it slow. So we haven't had a date at LEVELS New York, yet. How unfortunate, I sigh. Sebastian also refuses to touch me beyond kisses and hand holding. Snooze. I want those full lips suckling my peaked nipples. His enormous hands gripping my hips as he pistons deep inside of me from behind.

Sebastian's denials only make me crave him more. It's probably some Dom-mind trick designed to drive the sub insane with sensual need. Their unsatisfied arousal high, way beyond the pleasurable torture of edging.

Each night, I have to release the pressure built from our dalliances with the help of my new BOB—Battery Operated Boyfriend. Not quite Sebastian in size or sensation. But it gives me a bit of relief. When I teased Sebastian about needing to use it after one of our explicit phone calls, he called me back on FaceTime deliciously naked. His mouthwatering body leaning against the headboard of the bed we shared. That night, both of us eased the load.

The sight of Sebastian vigorously pumping his thick ten-inch girth with his muscular thighs spread wide, his heavy balls hanging between them was something to behold. Particularly when ropes of his creamy semen shot all over his bare chest, his pecs, and abs tight with tension. He threw his head back as he squeezed his eyes shut and yelled my name. My mouth waters just thinking about his taste and the feeling of his girth stretching my throat. Yum.

My Captain Caveman. My Dom. My Baz.

"Lola?" Billie asks. "Luc just called me because you're not answering your mobile."

Damn. I forgot to turn my mobile back on once we were in the air. So busy fantasizing about Sebastian. It's been two hours, so I wonder who else may have tried to reach me. Well... really, I only wonder if Sebastian called or sent a text message.

My mobile chirps with multiple voicemails, texts, and emails. It distracts me from wondering why Luc called Billie and not Blair. I thought they were back on track. I make a mental note to ask Blair after I handle these incoming communications.

Half an hour later, I'm through the backlog. But disappointed not to hear from Sebastian. It's about eleven thirty at night back in New York City. I expected at least a call.

Doubt surfaces at the edges of my mind. Now that I'm gone, is he at LEVELS to ease his Dom and sexual needs truly? Before me, Sebastian was the quintessential Alpha Billionaire playboy who only fucked a woman one time. Then on to the next one whenever the urge arose. He was highly sexual. When we were together, we fucked regularly. As many as four times a day.

I haven't had the guts to ask if he was active these past three months. Really, it's not my place since I broke up with him. Even though it was his fault. That damnable Lydie. Could he be with her now?

I also haven't told him I witnessed their post-sex cuddling in one of the penthouse's guest suites. Yes, I'm a wimp. I like a touch of pain with pleasure. But I'm not a masochist. The answers could only lead to more heartache. Something I have no interest in experiencing so soon. Particularly since Sebastian and I are seemingly working on our relationship.

Although I know trust is the foundation of any relationship and even more so a D/s one, as Sebastian emphasized repeatedly during our lessons, I still wonder. Now, I'm tense and it has nothing to do with sexual buildup.

To avoid going further down the path of madness, I call Luc. It's early morning in Paris, so I'm not sure what could be so urgent for him to call me now. I brace myself since the last time I received an urgent early morning call, the police were at my family's door to tell me a car crash killed my parents. I shudder at the thought and send a loving prayer to them. With trepidation, I tap Luc's number.

"Lola! I've been trying to reach you."

I hold my breath to wait for the dreadful news.

"Splendid news, *petite chérie!*"

His unexpected exuberance forces the air from my lungs. I nearly faint from the rush of blood to my head. Did he really just say "splendid news"? Thank you for that relief.

Luc says he wanted to be the first to tell me ANDAM the prestigious fashion awards nominated Lola's Coterie for the Best Breakthrough Collection. I squeal. In my haste to jump from my seat, I nearly drop my mobile. I barely hear another word out of Luc's mouth as I dance around the cabin.

I put Luc on speaker to share the news with Blair and Billie. They join in my dance, bumping hips and slapping high fives. Once I'm seated again, Luc fills me in on the details. Afterwards, we end the call with plans for a celebratory dinner at Arpège. The three Michelin star restaurant is my favorite in Paris. Luc and I make a habit of dining there for milestones and anniversaries.

My next call is to Sebastian. I'm excited to tell him. Plus, it's the perfect excuse to call. His mobile goes straight to voicemail. I try not to think the worse. It's hard since Sebastian only turns his mobile off when we were having sex or doing a scene at LEVELS.

"Drink up, *Ms. Best Breakthrough Collection Nominee!*" Billie giggles as she hands a flute of Dom Pérignon Rosé Vintage 2005.

Sebastian rubbed it on thick by stocking my favorite champagne on board. Still, at this moment, he's remains on the cusp of my shit list. I'll give him the benefit of the doubt. For now.

With a sigh, I down the entire glass. Billie and Blair exchange glances. I shrug and lift my flute for some more. I might as well, take the edge off with a few glasses of the ambrosial bubbly.

It's refreshing to walk into Lola's Coterie Paris. The flagship location is in the former home of a courtesan to a French king. It was his gift to her after she bore him their first of four children. He wanted them to live royally in the opulent *maison.*

The decor sets the mood with the air of a boudoir: sparkling Baccarat crystal chandeliers; silk wallpaper; scenes of Parisian streets hand-drawn on accent walls; light hardwood floors; vamp and shell pink colors with platinum touches; beveled mirrors. The warm and creamy, sweet and clean, sensual and sophisticated, woodsy fragrance wafts through the hidden atomizers. Soft French background music by Josephine Baker and Edith Piaf delights the ears. Stylish, sexy shopgirls assist fashionable, gorgeous women and men. The boutique invites patrons to relax in an atmosphere of splendor and entices them to indulge their inner sexpot or to gift their lover with pieces.

Standing amongst a gathering of mesmerized fans— patrons and staff alike—stands Leonie. Ever the muse for Lola's Coterie, she wears one of the Las Vegas collection's beaded and silk camisoles, a pair of skinny jeans, and strappy sandals. Her hands move animatedly as she chats with her admirers, the tinkle of multiple bracelets punctuate each word. She offers advice on their selections and tips to look flawless in lingerie. As she shows body angles to highlight curves, Leonie sees me. Her liquid amber eyes and dazzling smile light up the room.

Yes, it's terrific being back in Paris.

"Lola, *Chérie!*" Leonie gushes, rapidly covering the

distance between us as she stalks towards me like the feline she's named for.

"How long have you been here? I'm so glad to see you!"

She pulls me into an embrace as she whispers, "*Félicitations!* Luc told me about the ANDAM nomination."

"*Merci beaucoup, mon amie!*"

We do our little celebratory shimmy—dance in a circle, holding hands, and bouncing on the balls of our feet. Then turn our attention back to the others. They delight in our exuberant reunion.

The most rewarding part of my job is engaging with patrons. So, I take the time for fittings, explanation of materials and care, and gift suggestions. Their feedback whether positive or negative helps me to better my collections. It's all about the wearers. They agree an evening wear line that harkens to lingerie would be favorable. Something I had considered, now I'll make a priority.

Several ideas for fresh pieces pop into my head. I'm eager to put them in my sketchpad. It's as though I'm plugged back into my creative fuel.

After a while, Leonie and I bid them adieu. It's time to get to the business side of Lola's Coterie. We scheduled Luc to meet us in my office in thirty minutes. On the ride in the elevator to the top-floor atelier, Leonie peeks at me sheepishly.

"Gio is in Paris. We haven't seen each other in over a week. He asked me to dinner"—she rushes on when I open my mouth to complain—"But I told him I have plans."

"Good, because I haven't seen you in weeks..." I reply

with a huff. "Besides, I thought you broke up since he was gallivanting with other women."

That Giovanni, such a handsome devil.

I send a silent prayer Leonie doesn't go back on her word about moving on from him. He's nowhere near being ready to settle down. The billion-dollar playboy, an Italian nobleman to boot, attracts women with no effort. They throw themselves at him.

Leonie is the exact opposite. She intrigues him because she doesn't take his shit and has her own millions, fame, and admirers. Giovanni may not settle down now. But when he's ready, I'm sure he would prefer Leonie. If she still wants him by that time.

The elevator doors open to the all-white atelier bathed in natural sunlight from the skylights and oversized windows. The whitewashed hardwood floors and matte-white walls act as the perfect backdrop for any fabric, color, or texture. The open space includes workstations for staff. Glass walls separate my office and a conference room from the primary area. I prefer to sit amidst the action, but have privacy when necessary.

Blair and Billie sit outside of my office at an antique partner's desk. Their mobiles glued to their ears while they type rapidly on their laptop keyboards. They arrived before I did since I detoured to my flat.

Leonie's mobile chirps. Her eyes widen at me and she pulls her lower lip between her teeth when she sees the name on her screen. I snatch it from her with a raised eyebrow. Giovanni, of course. She grabs it back and turns away to respond to his text message. Whatever, she's a grown woman. I'll be there for her either way. BFF and all.

"Lola, Luc's on his way up now," Billie informs me.

I glance at Blair to gauge her reaction since once again Luc contacted Billie instead. Blair refuses to meet my eyes. She pointedly keeps her attention on the monitor. I'll leave it for now since this is work time.

Damn, these girls will drive me nuts with their men issues. Hell, I have enough of my own. Especially since I still haven't heard from Sebastian. Shaking my head, I stroll into my office to sit at my drawing desk ready to put the thoughts of the evening wear collection to life.

The morning is a blur of activity. Once Luc arrives, we have several meetings with vendors and internal marketing and finance teams. Leonie stays for the marketing meeting as her input is invaluable. She takes her role as Lola's Coterie muse seriously. The success is due in part to her representation of the brand.

Before she leaves, Leonie pulls me aside to tell me we're going to a party tonight after dinner. Giovanni invited us and "we can't say no" she insists. I give in, needing to have a distraction. Sebastian is a no show all day despite my messages.

Time to get my groove on. No sitting in my empty flat dejectedly watching my mobile for me. No ma'am!

LONDON IS DREARY WITH RAIN, just like my mood. Sadly, I'm not as wet too.

The past week in Paris may have had my creativity at a peak. But those were the only juices flowing. Sebastian and I spoke briefly a few times. He claims to have had meetings that kept him busy. The time difference didn't help the situation. So no late-night FaceTime sex to stave my needs. And I left BOB in New York. How the hell does Sebastian satisfy his cravings?

I try not to dwell on thoughts of him with someone else —especially not Lydie. Leonie did her best to distract me. Giovanni's party was a blast, after all. He was extremely attentive of Leonie. His possessive eyes never left her as we danced in the crowd. Another upside is Sebastian called me the next day after he saw me on social media and the Internet surrounded by gorgeous men. Jealous much? Well, too bad.

The rain pelts unceasingly on the windows of my office. The leaden gray sky reminds me of Sebastian's eyes when he's aroused. The memory of him staring up at me as he used his skillful tongue to eat my pussy has me shifting in my seat. I close my own eyes to revel in the flashback that plays in my mind.

A chirp draws my attention out of the clouds and to my mobile. The text message from LEVELS London makes me clench my thighs. Tonight is Masquerade Night—how apropos.

Thankful that I upgraded my seven-day guest pass to the New York flagship to an All Access Global Membership, I reply YES to RSVP. With a mask on, I can at least select a black voyeur bracelet. I'll live vicariously through others' lustful encounters…

With more wanton excitement than I've had in a week, I head down to the boutique's couture collection floor to select tonight's attire.

SEBASTIAN

*L*ola's absence is equivalent to me missing a limb. I need it desperately. But it's not there, only its phantom presence tricks me.

For two weeks, she's been in Europe on business and it feels like two months. The only upside is the barrage of unexpected work I've had to deal with dominating my time. I haven't had an idle moment. Otherwise, my thoughts would continuously stray to Lola.

I've only had time for a few brief calls with her. Not enough to have phone sex and definitely not enough for FaceTime fucking.

The five-hour difference makes it inconvenient to connect. By the time my business day ends and I'm crashed on my sofa or bed, it's after two in the morning for Lola. She seemed distracted the last time we spoke, or perhaps irritated. I hope she's not having as difficult of a time with her business affairs as I am with mine.

Somehow an undetermined employee accessed one of our corporate servers to download confidential data on STEELE's global VIP list. They compromised personal information such as names, addresses, and credit card details for high rollers who frequent our casinos and royalty and the über-wealthy who stay at our properties. It was a well-orchestrated job that could involve more than one person from within STEELE and externally.

Harris and Haley's cyber security team detected unusual activity from a non-STEELE IP address. It was their latest security protocol they just implemented across all the STEELE divisions that triggered the alert. The system immediately started the shutdown of the transmission and isolated the source. The process is complex and meticulous. So it will take time. Undoubtedly the Dynamic Duo will resolve the issue.

In the meantime, the handling of the communications with the VIPs lands in my wheelhouse. Our father delegated the task to me even though the division impacted falls in Malcolm's purview. The undertaking is the perfect opportunity to flex my future CEO finesse.

Forget an email or conference call, this demands face-to-face conversations to avoid legal and public relations nightmares. Fortunately, the compromised individuals are only in New York City and London—the total of twenty out of thousands. Thank fuck.

Since last week, I've met with everyone in the city. As expected, they were beyond pissed and threatened legal action. That the security protocol not only interrupted the download, but sent a zap to delete the receiving server's system eased the VIPs' concerns. That along with our legal team's preemptive contract that assures full financial compensation for any damages caused by the breech directly.

Tomorrow morning, I fly to London. The Brits are more stiff upper lip than Americans, so I expect fewer threats of "taking you to the cleaners" and "ruin STEELE forever." Not that it'll be a cakewalk. Shit, I would end STEELE if it were me.

My mobile dings with a Google alert for Lola Lewis. I smirk as I think of Lola asking me if I'm possessive much. Yup. She'd add obsessed stalker if she knew I have an alert for any mention of her name on the Internet.

What... the... fuck!

I damn near crush my mobile.

Lola's shaking her ass dancing in a tight-as-fuck red mini dress. Her toned thighs on full display damn near to her crotch. She was at some party with Leonie a few hours ago—this after the last one of Mattei's. Guys circle around her, reaching out to touch her body in various places—her hand, her waist, her fucking hip. All the while, she's laughing with her arms overhead, twirling, bumping, grinding.

I may very well have a coronary.

I grit my teeth in irritation, pissed that I didn't fully reclaim her from the get-go. Take it slow, I said... Lure her in... Give her the time she needs... Don't rush her...

Fool.

That probably explains her reticence. Lola's mind is on other guys and far from me. Clearly, she fell off my hook.

Would this have happened if I were still a playboy, not spending more than two fucks with various hookups? Absolutely not.

Would I even care? Hell no! My only priority was to give them immense pleasure and to relieve my needs.

Lolas has me all fucked up.

Not giving a damn it's three in the morning, I call her. Furious, I use facial recognition to unlock my mobile. The current scowl that adorns my face renders the capability useless. With a herculean effort to rein in the myriad of emotions roiling in my mind, I set a neutral expression.

The telltale click precedes my finger jabbing at the phone icon. Favorites... Huh. For a moment I wonder if Lola even has me listed in her Favorites. If so, by what name? Baz... Sebastian... Sir... Idiot? Yeah. I continue to seethe while the call connects.

Damn if it doesn't go straight to voicemail. Un-fucking-believable.

At first, I thought it was Lola saying hello, so I started heatedly to demand what she's doing. But no. It's only her message. I end the call even more pissed off than before since she never turns her mobile off.

If she's fucking someone she picked up at that party. Or some schmuck wrapped himself around her hot little body after they fucked, limbs tangled, passed out from the exhaustion of going at it for hours...

Grrrrr!

I scroll through more photos, scandalized as I scan for likely suspects. Shit, it could very well be any of these losers. They're all sniffing around her, jockeying for her attention.

The captions magnify Lola's obvious delight in the men fawning all over her: Lola Lewis lingerie designer flocked by sexy admirers; partygoers can't get enough of the curvaceous Lola Lewis; revelers want more of the lingerie world's top creator, Lola Lewis; known for her sexy lingerie pieces, Lola Lewis looks luscious dancing long into the night. Each picture, not to mention the annoying blurbs, makes me see red.

Gone is the simpering pseudo-boyfriend. The Dom in me takes over. When I see her, I will mark her ass red with my palm prints. Lola will explain why she chose to defy me to mess around with other men. She knows she belongs to me and me only. I just told Lola how possessive I am of her. Yet, she purposefully sought gratification from others.

My mobile dings, again. This time it's a text message from LEVELS London.

Lola Lewis Masquerade Night RSVP YES

A wicked chuckle rumbles up from deep within my chest, bursting past my down-turned lips. Deviously, I narrow my eyes in glee—excellent.

Oh, my Petite Seductress, you will get punished sooner than I expected. You dare go to a LEVELS club without me as your paired Dom, leaving you open to the whims of another to slake your sub needs. Hhhmmm. You forget who's your Dom, Naughty Pet. These transgressions will not go unchecked.

My dick springs to life as it lengthens down my thigh inside my gray sweatpants. The anticipation of Lola naked —except for a mask—with her delectable body strapped to a red leather spanking bench on the main stage at the Cellar with her pink pussy dripping to a puddle beneath her as I spank that ass is enough to cause pre-cum to gather at my expanding tip. The bulbous head as red and angry as the one above my shoulders. Both heads are of the same mind: Lola will learn her lesson at Masquerade Night and be mine fully by the end.

I intend to spank her plump bottom until it's so inflamed, even a feather lightly brushing over its rounded curves will elicit a yelp from her pouty mouth. Then fuck her like a wild caveman claiming his mate until her womb fills with my seed. Every one of Lola's holes will leak with my jizz. My scent permanently fused to every inch of her skin. No doubt will remain to whom she belongs.

Me.

I have to wonder whether Lola is provoking me on purpose. The little vixen loves punishments. With my insistence that we take it slow with only FaceTime for self-induced climaxes, I'm not giving her the satisfaction that she craves. Lola's complained about the lack of intensity from the video calls. Plus taunted me enough with hew new BOB and the vivid details of her use of the fake dick.

Her behavior over these past two weeks may be a subconscious cry for my attention—not for those suckers who are hanging around her. Well, I've got her message loud and clear.

Whatever Lola wants, Lola gets.

LOLA

*T*he sweat on my palms makes it difficult to adjust the red enamel bracelet around my wrist. The clasp is too delicate for my clumsy fingers. The two ends circle my wrist, then slide off before I can attach one to the other. In consternation, I bite my lower lip to make my third attempt. Foiled again.

The last time I was at a LEVELS, I wore a wide, black leather collar with a silver ring for a delicate matching chain to dangle from the collar to Sebastian's hand. At first, my Independent Woman balked at being led around like a dog on a leash. But the sub in me appreciated the collar symbolized Sebastian as a Dom who claimed me as his sub. I was his alone, and he was mine. Not exactly a wedding band, but the meaning was just as powerful.

Now my choice of bracelet color shows my availability to others. I no longer have a Dom. To avoid unwanted interactions amongst club participants, the system requires partnered subs to wear collars given to them by their Dom; partnered Doms wear gold bracelets; available subs wear red; available Doms wear white; voyeurs wear black.

This detail of consensual connections is one of the many reasons I feel safe being a member of LEVELS. They enforce strict protocols members, their guests, and applicants must follow. From nondisclosure agreements to no-names given unless provided by the person to super tight ongoing background checks and other security measures. In addition, no judgement!

As though she senses my nervousness, without a word of annoyance or appraisal, the LEVELS London greeter slips the jewelry from my hand and deftly closes the clasp. She returns my relieved smile with a perfectly brilliant one of her own.

Damn. Every staff member at each of the LEVELS locations looks as though they just strode off the catwalk, I giggle to myself.

With more confidence, I straighten my shoulders before I nod my head at her to signal my readiness to enter Peepshow on the BDSM side of the club.

It's fascinating how Malcolm and Lucien Jackson—I adore that incredibly hot *Sexy Chef*—selected locations for their uniqueness and double entendres. The New York flagship in one of the former warehouses of the Meatpacking District plays on the area's name. Put a club where men pack their meat into willing women and willing men allow women to pack them with their toys, or any combinations or groupings thereof.

For consistency and members' comfort, locations share the same layout:

Main entry foyer has two sides with two greeter stations for access to Dine & Dance levels and BDSM levels, an All-Access member can choose from any of the seven levels: 7th Sky Lounge that offers a bar, restaurant by day dance club by night, coverable pool that's open for the summer, and a glass-retractable roof; 6th and 5th multi-level dance club with two bars and a lounge for food and drinks; 4th Level 4 Restaurant and bar open for breakfast, lunch, and dinner; 3rd has twelve private suites for members to continue their pleasure apart from the BDSM levels; 2nd Peepshow for BDSM with seating alcoves, main stage, performance rooms, and a bar that serves non-alcoholic mocktails; below ground the Cellar BDSM dungeon with mocktails bar. The Dine/Dance members only have access to the party levels—Sky Lounge, Dance Club, and Level 4 Restaurant.

London is the third after Paris of the exclusive, luxury, members-only clubs. Its site is a former bank set in the City of London, also known as The City and Financial District. They use the original vault for private parties. Locked behind its massive, thick steel door, who knows what all goes on inside. This LEVELS is an ode to the debauchery of money and the wealthy who wield it as power over others. How appropriate the Sky Lounge provides an unobstructed view of the Tower of London.

Now it's my turn to enter the beast's lair. Despite my bravado, my heart races uncontrollably as soon as the double doors open to Peepshow. My senses amplify as my mind adjusts to the carnality before me.

The space is dimly lit with spotlights on the main stage and several of the smaller platforms where demonstrations in bondage and Shibari are active. Shrouded in shadows, the seating alcoves cluster along the perimeter. Only glimpses of movement prove their inhabitants' presence. Desirable, sensuous men and women appear in various stages of dress or nudity while they partake in all forms of sexual activity.

The atmosphere is pure bacchanalia. Melodic thrumming of sultry music accompanies the moans and groans of the revelers. While the air is heavy with the mixture of expensive cologne, alluring perfume, and immeasurable arousal. The heady aroma alights on my tongue as I gasp from the thrill of the visions. Unconsciously, one of my hands glides along my hip while the other strokes my beaded nipples. Caught up in the rapture, I seek my gratification.

A third and fourth hand join mine to explore my body. I jump from the unexpected touch as a squeak slips from my mouth. Twisting to peer up and over my shoulder, my eyes meet a pair of ice blue ones framed by an ornate gold half-mask. The gold highlights the flecks in his eyes —gorgeous.

"Pardon my boldness, beauty," he rasps in my ear.

I shiver from his warm breath tickling my lobe and the

deep carnal tone of his voice laced with an ultra-posh Queen's English accent.

His enormous hands slide beneath my much smaller ones as he continues, "But I could not allow you to pleasure yourself. Leave it to me to elevate your arousal."

To emphasize his intent, the captivating man lifts my jewelry-wrapped wrist to match his that bears a white enamel bracelet. He's an available Dom.

"Come, beauty. Tell me what your sexy fantasy entails. Perhaps I may help you bring it to life."

No longer stunned by his assertive appearance, my brain turns back on to release my immobile tongue.

"As much as I appreciate your offer, I only just arrived and haven't navigated the room in my pursuit of a partner," I start re-gaining confidence. "However, should I not engage with a suitable Dom, you and I can meet in an hour at the bar."

Gently, yet with enough force to make my point, I detach myself from his clutches. With a smile and a nod, I saunter away without further engagement. Way too much too soon.

The next hour I roam the floor at Peepshow as I hold off on immediately searching for an appealing partner. It's awkward without Sebastian. Instead, I take in the activities on display in the performance rooms: a male-male-male-female ménage with triple penetration; a Domme, her male sub, cock and ball bondage, and a St. Andrew's Cross; two female subs and their Dom use intense breath control; still others with two men and three women, so on and so on.

Yup, Masquerade Night allows members to sate their most explicit appetites uninhibitedly.

Just as I'm meandering to the bar to meet the bold Dom, I see two familiar forms huddled together near the shadows. I don't want to jump to conclusions, so I move closer, sure to keep others between us. The voices carry over the backdrop of Peepshow—a toe-curling baritone and an annoying lockjaw. Now I'm certain the pair are Sebastian and Lydie.

What. The. Fuck!

I stumble as I pivot on my five-inch mules. A man catches me. But I hurry away for fear the motion will draw Sebastian and Lydie's attention to me. I mumble a hasty thank you and rush to the ladies' room. Once inside, I lock myself in one stall. The blood pounds in my ears. Clutching my chest, I try to slow my breathing like Starr taught me at the Fiji retreat before I hyperventilate. Inhale one. Exhale one. Inhale two. Exhale two. Inhale thr—

That bastard!

No wonder Sebastian was so unavailable and couldn't spare me time but a few minutes. Too busy hugged up with that wench Lydie. A-fucking-gain!

How stupid am I? I broke my vow to never go back to Sebastian. See where that got me... Screwed over, again!

The minutes tick by. I grouse some more, crying then stewing in the stall. The sounds of other members entering and leaving keep me from exiting my temporary refuge. As soon as it quiets down, I'll fix my face. Then get the hell out of LEVELS posthaste. A break in the comings and goings gets me moving.

My face is puffy and red from crying. Fortunately, the waterproof makeup didn't smear. I don't carry a handbag to LEVELS, so I make use of the plush cotton washcloths dampened with cool water. One more dab and I'm out.

The door opens to three women. The first to enter is none other than Lydie with her mask still in her hand. She halts when she sees me. But gets bumped further past the entry by the couple who are more engrossed in each other to notice the sudden tension in the bathroom. A loud moan follows the clicking of the lock on the largest stall at the end. Lydie and I never stop staring at one another.

I refuse to let her see how upset I am, so I stride to the door with my head held high, eyes straight ahead.

"Lola, wait," she says as she catches me by the arm. "We need to talk."

"Fuck you, Lydie"—there goes subtlety—"There isn't shit for us to talk about." I snarl as I yank my arm from her hand.

Instead of letting me go, Lydie tightens her grip, and I jerk to a stop. She is taller than me by a good four inches and surprisingly strong. Damn... I need to add strength training to my running.

I stare up to find her emerald eyes no longer lit with arrogance and disdain as they were every time she and I crossed paths. A quick scan of her face reveals a humbleness that wasn't there previously. I nod my acquiescence as the door opens again to more women.

"Not here," Lydie states.

I follow her down a quiet separate hall to a door where she places her palm on the panel. The door opens with a soft click to a private room. Not trusting Lydie, I beckon her inside ahead of me. A small smile returns her usual self-possessed glint to her eyes. I cock my eyebrow and she raises her hands, palms forward in peace. The door shuts behind us.

"First, I must apologize for my poor behavior, Lola."

I stand still, shocked by her words. With a self-deprecating nod, she continues.

"Yes, I was totally wrong and should never have treated you as I did. Please allow me to explain," she pauses, and it's my turn to nod mutely.

"As you know, Sebastian and I grew up together. Although he is best friends with my younger brother Lachlan, Sebastian and I share the commonality of being the eldest sibling and future leader of our family's company. As we grew older and took over more responsibilities in our business roles, I leaned on him for support. He became my confidante."

Lydie pauses, closes her eyes, and takes a deep breath before she continues.

"My father does not believe a woman can run Jackson Corporation. He wants Lachlan to take over from me despite the successes I've achieved. Lachlan loves me and will do nothing to ruin our relationship. My father's consolation prize is to marry me off to a man from another powerful and wealthy family as a business merger."

My jaw drops and I shake my head in complete disgust. Damn, isn't this the twenty-first century and not the 1800s? Lydie exhales at my reaction.

"Yes, I see you agree with me how ludicrous is his idea. Sebastian became a ray of light for me in that I could marry him, please my father, and with Sebastian's support persuade my father to allow me to run Jackson."

Again, Lydie gauges my reaction. I press my lips together to not comment. She takes that as my permission for her to go on.

"You changed the plan that only I created—Sebastian was completely unaware. He loves you and cares for you unlike any prior woman. You may have changed my plan, but you also changed the flagrant playboy who never dated a woman or spent time with one more than once."

My mouth drops open, again. Whaaat??? But Lydie goes on.

"I'm working with a therapist to deal with my issues and part of the process is to right wrongs. It's selfish of me, but I hope you can forgive me."

The entire time Lydie spoke, my mind was reeling. Sebastian loves me? Then why did they have sex? I demand an answer from her for those very questions. She has the decency to appear sheepish.

"Oh, yes, well, I had a bit too much to drink and after midnight showed up at Sebastian's penthouse professing my love. To which he fed me espresso and crackers to sober my ass up so I could go to bed and leave in the morning. What you saw and heard was him supporting me in standing firm against my father's antiquated belief. And yes, he truly loves you. As a matter of fact, he's here looking for you. But these masks make it pretty difficult." She laughs as she twirls her mask by the string.

I search Lydie's face for the slightest sign on insincerity. But find none. Only relief shows as though a weight is off her shoulders.

Tonight is chock full of shocks. I may need a defibrillator before it's over.

"Okay, I see," I start. "You really pissed me off and caused a hell of a lot of heartache and anguish for Sebastian and me. I could go on, but I have to get to my man. I appreciate your honesty and forgive you." I raise my hand to stop her interruption to continue.

"The Steeles and Jacksons may not share the same blood in their veins. But you might as well, since your families are so intertwined. I plan to be in Sebastian's life, so you and I will have to be amicable. We may not be BFFs, but we will be respectful of one another. Deal?" I ask hurriedly as I hold out my hand, eager to leave.

Lydie's face breaks into the most beatific smile—fuck, she's as gorgeous as everyone else here—and shakes my hand.

"Deal, Lola," she grins. "Now, I am on my own quest to find myself a lover. Another suggestion made by my therapist." Lydie winks and opens the door to a fresh beginning for all of us.

SEBASTIAN

*O*h, well, isn't this just rich…

Lydie is at LEVELS London tonight. Amongst the members, she's spotted me the one second I lifted my mask from my face to wipe my eye. Damn.

I sure as hell hope Lola doesn't happen upon us as Lydie goes on about an apology for her atrocious behavior towards Lola. Good for Lydie she has a therapist to help her overcome her Daddy-approval issues. Hopefully, she has marrying me out of her head, too. No more late-night booty calls by her to my penthouse. So, there's a major win at least. I cannot allow Lydie to fuck up my re-claiming Lola now.

"—understand. So, please forgive me, Sebastian. I never meant to cause you any angst. I was just too blinded by proving myself to my father and thought you would be the match he would approve."

Lydie stops to eye me warily. In response, I nod and

incline my head to tell her I understand and forgive her. But I'm looking for Lola and don't need her seeing Lydie with me. She agrees and excuses herself to the loo.

Finally.

Now I can continue my perusal of the crowd.

I spot a petite, dark-haired woman who has a red enamel bracelet on her slim wrist. If Lola is here seeking a Dom, I will lose it. She better have a black enamel bracelet as a voyeur to observe others' sexual escapades. Especially since Masquerade Night gets wild. Still a safe place with only consensual play amongst adults. But fewer inhibitions because of the anonymity the masks provide members.

As I approach the potential Lola, she turns. Even through the decorative mask that covers her entire face, I can see her eyes are a vivid blue. She peeks up at me and tilts her head in question. Before I can shake my head a definitive no, I glimpse Lydie striding towards me. Beside her struts another little woman with raven colored hair.

This one speeds past Lydie to rush over to me as she snatches her mask off her face.

Thank fuck! It's Lola. My excitement is short-lived as she scowls at me, then jabs her long-manicured finger in my chest. Ow, damn.

"Really, Sebastian! Lydie said you were here looking for me. But ohhh nooo... You're hooking up with someone else. Dam—"

Swiftly I grab her wrist—noting the red bracelet and the punishment it will incite. Then turn her back to my front as I reach my other arm across her torso to grip her opposite hip. Her slight frame pinned to my chest while my growing cock pokes her lower back.

Fuck yeah, it's on. My dick twitches in agreement.

"Hold on there, Naughty Pet," I growl in her ear. "So soon you forget who is the Dom and who is the su—"

"Fuck... You, Sebastian! Naughty my as—"

I swing her around and pepper her plump bottom with a volley of slaps. Lola dances on her toes, shifting her body to avoid the unforgiving blows. Now, that's the only dancing long into the night she will do, and only for me.

I ignore her curses and cries for me to stop. Instead, I lower my hand to spank the sensitive area where her butt meets her thighs. Lola yelps in response. Next, the backs of her thighs receive my unwavering attention. Lola remains unyielding, too stubborn to give in. Fine by me.

"Enough... Sebastiaaan! Ouch..."

"When are you going to learn, Naughty Pet?"

Despite her protests, Lola's body betrays her arousal. The scent of her sweet pussy floats to my nose. I inhale deeply. My mouth waters as the aroma triggers my memory of her delectable taste. I lick my lips, then press them to the delicate shell of her earlobe.

"Do you really want me to stop, Naughty Pet? Before you deny it, think long and hard. Your body tells me otherwise. Tell me, Pet, if I were to slide my finger within your folds, would I find you sopping wet?"

The vixen forgets I know how much she craves punishment. Her body needs it to release tension or to ease her nerves. A kink she discovered a little over a year ago when one of her two lovers who was a Dom spanked her before they had sex.

Her need started us doing an anonymous scene together at LEVELS New York. She was in search of a Dom to relieve her nervousness before her meeting to expand her lingerie company. Of all the available Doms there that night, I'm thankful it was me who saw her first. However, neither of us knew the very next morning we would face each other in a conference room to negotiate a multimillion-dollar business deal. Fate, I wonder.

Now, Lola growls in frustration, knowing I speak the truth. She cannot deny her responsiveness to my touch—be it a caress or a swat—nor the pleasure it gives.

Her little body tightens in embarrassment. But loosens when she feels my fingers slowly stroke down her inner thigh to the hem of her clingy negligee.

The lingerie she wears is enough to make me punish her. Glittery black jet beads form the shapes of flowers, leaves, and vines embroidered on sheer skin-tone mesh. Thin black boning accentuates her narrow waist and the flare of her curvy hips. Lola's blush pink nipples wink at me while her mound hides behind artfully placed beads that form the shape of a vase. Lola's lush body is an Eden I intend to plunder for eternity.

"Oh Baazzz."

My name slips past her parted lips on a long exhale as my fingertip brushes her swollen nether lips.

"Let go and just feel, Naughty Pet. Coat my finger with

your succulent juices," I grunt, my girth trapped in my trousers painfully.

Lola spreads her thighs, raising the negligee higher to give me better access to her ambrosial core. With a slow rhythm, I slide my thick finger in and out before I add a second digit.

"So tight and wet for me, Pet. You do not disappoint your Dom."

Lola purrs in contentedness as she rubs her pussy against my palm. Music to my ears; pressure to my cock.

So infatuated by Lola, I didn't notice the members who turned to watch our impromptu demonstration until their murmurs of approval breach our bubble. The gathered crowd includes Lydie who stands stock-still fascinated by the performance. Her blush deepens to a bright red from her hairline to her bosom when our eyes meet. Slowly, Lydie retreats beyond the circle. This intimacy would never happen between us. I sense she still wants it despite what she says, but acknowledges it will never happen.

I return my gaze to Lola, who leans languidly against my body. Her eyes are half closed and a soft smile lingers on her angelic face. I kiss the top of her head before I wrap my arm around her waist to keep her steady as I lead us to the double doors. Our peepshow ends.

Lola's soft curves press into my side as we wait for the elevator to take us to Level 3 for my private suite. Since I live in New York and frequently visit London for business, I have suites set aside for my personal use only at those

LEVELS locations. It's one of many privileges my investor status affords me.

With Lola in my life and having her flagship boutique in Paris, we'll need a personal suite at LEVELS Paris. I make a mental note to send a text message to Taylor Hunt, the head of membership to make the arrangements immediately. Perhaps Lola and I will take a side trip to select our preferred suite before we return to New York.

The ding signaling the elevator interrupts my thoughts. More members arrive to partake in the festivities. Some men turn their heads in Lola's direction. Her alluring body outlined in her revealing lingerie proves too enticing for them. From behind elaborate masks, their eyes scan her bountiful curves from head to toe.

My caveman instincts kick in. Possessively, I move Lola behind me to protect my mate from the challenge of other males. I stand to my full height of six feet, four inches, a projection of Alpha power and strength. I will fight any man who dares to come between me and my woman. Lola is mine.

Sensing their imminent demise, the men move on in search of easier to obtain playmates.

"Where are we going?" Lola asks as the doors close and the elevator starts its ascent.

I cup her face to tilt her lips to mine as I capture her mouth. She tastes divine. After a mind-blowing kiss, I respond to my Petite Seductress.

"We are going upstairs to my private suite to continue your punishment," I smirk.

Lola's eyes open wide, no longer lulled by the bliss of her orgasm. She raises a perfectly arched brow and cocks her head to the side.

"How presumptuous of you, Sebastian," she retorts.

I crowd her space, using my larger body to push her into the corner. Then bend my knees to level our eyes.

"Really, Naughty Pet? Now you question your Dom?"

"Who says you're *my Dom*? You were just chitchatting with your hookup for the night only moments before I walked over to you," Lola accuses, a flicker of sadness sweeps across her face.

"You are mistaken. I thought she was you with her black hair and petite, curvy frame," I reassure Lola while softly stroking her cheek.

Her ample chest expands on a deep inhale as she considers my words. More emotions from sadness to doubt to hope cross her lovely features.

"I came tonight because I knew you would be here—"

The doors open, cutting off my declaration. I gesture for Lola to go ahead of me. Then take her hand to lead her to my suite. The hallway is quiet because of the plush carpet and soundproof rooms. Low sensuous music is the only testament to what awaits you behind the doors.

At the end of the hall, I place my palm on the panel to unlock my suite. Lola enters ahead of me. I enjoy the sight of her ass as she sways her hips. Her fuck-me heels make her butt sit up proudly, just like my dick.

As though she senses my thoughts, Lola peers at me over her shoulder. Her waist-length hair hangs like a silky curtain. It begs for me to wrap it around my fist and pull on its glossy strands until she arches her back in surrender.

"Sebastian, we need to talk."

The most dreaded words fall from her mouth sufficiently ending my reverie. My heart skips a beat at the thought of her ending any chance we have at getting back together before we can even start.

I gesture for her to sit on the extra-large, hard-carved mahogany wood bed. The only appropriate piece of furniture. A pommel horse and chaise with brass rings wouldn't do for a serious conversation.

Lola perches on the foot of the bed and glances up at me. I incline my head for her to speak first.

"I want your commitment as an exclusive couple. What do you want, Sebastian?"

This is what I most adore about Lola. She is a smart, direct woman who doesn't give a shit about who I am or the size of my bank account. She's about me, not the glamour of being on a billionaire's arm.

With renewed hope, I settle beside her. Then pull her into my arms to hold Lola close to my heart that beats for her only.

"You. I want you, Lola. I want us. Period," I profess. "I promised you before, I'm yours, Lola. Only you."

Lola leans back to stare at my face. Her imploring hazel eyes search for any deception. I open up to her to show my sincerity. Satisfied, she nods, then pulls my face to hers, locking our lips together. Our tongues probe and stroke one another in a passionate tango.

I shift us so she lies beneath me, my body pressing her firmly into the mattress. I want to possess her, mark her as mine.

"I want you, Lola. I crave you."

My whisper hoarse, barely audible as I brush my lips over the soft skin of her delicate throat.

Lola shivers, responsive as ever. I must have her now. I can no longer take it slow or wait another moment.

I stand and strip my clothes off. Lola lies back on the bed with hooded eyes now scanning me with heat. Each article of clothing I remove causes her eyes to spark with blatant desire. Unconsciously, she plays with her nipples, tugging on the taut tips through the material of her lingerie. She draws her lower lip between her teeth and widens her legs to me in welcome.

Fully naked, I stalk over to the armoire. There's a particular toy I need to use on Lola tonight.

Returning to the bed, I make haste removing the negligee that's taunted me with hints of the sinful body covered by it. Unable to resist, I lower my head to her puckered nipple. I latch on to suckle from her plump flesh. Lola bows her body, pushing her D-cups further in my face.

Fuck. I've missed the delicacy that is Lola.

My sensitized dick thumps her thigh, reminding me it's time to reclaim my Petite Seductress fully. I pick up the spreader bar and attach it to her ankles ensuring the fit is secure, but not overly tight. The width prevents her from closing her legs from my entry. But first, I have to be sure

Lola is ready for me. If she hasn't been with anyone since me—as is my hope—I must prep her for the intensity of my thick ten inches.

I trail kisses from her full tits down her belly to her bare mound. I lift her legs over my head to put the spreader bar behind my back. As I settle between her thighs, I take a deep inhale to fill my nostrils with the savory aroma of Lola's arousal. A glance up her body shows she's already in the throes of passion with her head thrown back and her eyes closed. With a smirk, I take my first sample in months of Lola's sweet essence.

My tongue glides along the edges of her labia, teasing her to open for me. As if on cue, Lola whimpers when her juices flow from her core. I use the tip of my tongue to catch each drop, savoring her unique flavor.

Lola's mewl spurs me on to probe past her folds to the interior of her channel. The rough texture of her G-spot demands my attention. I pass my tongue over it again and again, sending Lola into a tizzy. She tries to clamp her legs around my head with her need for release. But the spreader bar restricts her movement.

I don't want to prolong her pleasure, only heighten it to get her loose and sufficiently wet for the pounding that I won't be able to control. It's been too long without her.

I add two fingers to her core as my tongue pulls on her engorged clit. The finger fucking combined with the sucking and laving of her clit shoots Lola into a jackknife. I growl and use my free hand to press onto her lower belly to hold her in place. With a strangled cry, Lola settles back into the pillows, barely able to keep her hips from shifting closer to my mouth.

I continue to eat her pussy like it's the first meal I've had in three months. Which is the case since I haven't had her in all of this time. I more than make up for it as I lick and nip until her juices gush into my eager mouth.

Once I've had my fill and she's ready for me, I slide on top of her pliant body. I disentangle her hands from my hair and hold them above her head in one hand while the other aligns my cock dripping with pre-cum to her channel. Without hesitating, I surge forward to impale Lola on my thick length. She wails in response.

"So tight, baby. Fuuuck… Are you still only mine, Lola?" I demand as I drive my girth deep within her core.

My eyes roll back as the overwhelming sensations of once again being one with my baby course through my body. I shudder and demand she answers me.

"Oh yeeesss… Baz… Only you…. Oh fuuuck… Only you, baby… Aaahhh," Lola moans, meeting each of my frantic thrusts with one of her own.

Our bodies need no further direction as we reclaim one another the way man and woman have known from the dawn of time.

Lola is mine, and I am hers. I satisfy my caveman.

* * *

Lola

I thought the goings-on at Peepshow amplified my

senses, but nothing compares to Baz's ability to heighten my desires. This man brings out every emotion in me—joy, pain, pleasure, love...

Once again I let him win. I let him conquer me. For good.

LOLA

*a*wesome...

The only word that comes close enough to describe the past few weeks with Baz.

All during the night and into the morning of our reunion, he only let me sleep for an hour or less. Each time, I awoke to his lips suckling my nipple, his teeth nipping my clit, or his fat cock stroking my pussy walls. He made good on his promise to fill each of my holes, too. By the time we left LEVELS London, both sets of my lips were puffy, my muscles ached, and I staggered out the door bowlegged.

Baz meanwhile strutted like a peacock, proudly flaunting its feathers.

Instead of returning to the Royal Suite where I was staying at Claridge's for the week, Baz took us to his palatial estate in the ultraexclusive Kensington Palace Gardens. Just as his duplex penthouse in New York City is on

Billionaires' Row, his West London home is on Billionaires' Boulevard. As I always say, there's the rich, and then there's the wealthy…

Baz made it his mission for us to christen each room over the three days we stayed. That was a hell of a lot of christening with at least forty rooms over five floors— including the attic. Let's just say he gave me the grand tour and then some.

A surprise trip to Paris took us to LEVELS in the 7th Arrondissement Palais-Bourbon Le Faubourg. Similar to Lola's Coterie Paris, the club inhabits the former Parisian home of a pampered courtesan to another French king— those randy royals.

The beautiful *maison* on a tree-lined street sits behind duplicates of the original double carriage doors and features a spacious interior courtyard. Baz explained they host grand soirees during the warm-weather months under the stars and strings of fairy lights.

He decided we needed to select one of the private suites for our exclusive use. Baz wants to be sure we have one specific to us since I have my flagship boutique in the city and split my time here. We chose a new decor and our favorite toys. I giggle to consider a room in a sex club a sweet gift, albeit an ultraposh one.

When we finally arrived back in New York, Baz insisted I move in with him. But I declined on the basis we need not rush into living together again. Plus, Billie's words of "why buy the cow when you can get the milk for free" floated into my head. A definite reminder that Baz and I moved in together too soon after meeting. Only a week had passed. I made myself too accessible to him. Even though I enjoyed spending almost every non-work hour with him. This time, it's best for us to have our own space. Breathe a little. My version of take it slow.

* * *

"LOLA, what sense does it make for you to live all the way over on Sutton Place when your Lola's Coterie New York is right below our penthouse?" Baz complains, exasperated since we've been discussing me moving back in with him for the past ten minutes. "And to top it off, by yourself! When you can just move back in here."

Secretly, I'm glad he wants me to move in right away. It proves his commitment to us as a couple. But I have to stand firm.

"No, Baz. I want this to be right. We need to have our own space—"

"That's absurd! We had three months of 'our own space' and quite frankly, it sucked!" Baz erupts. His hands thrown up in irritation as he swipes a thick lock of ebony hair out of his eyes.

His hair already disheveled from plowing his long fingers through it makes him look even more rakish than usual. I'm concerned he may just pull it out by the roots.

At the image, a laugh bubbles past my lips despite my attempt to hold it back.

"What the hell is so funny?" Baz demands.

Baz's reaction makes my giggles worsen. Doubled over, I hold my sides and laugh so hard I snort. That only adds to my mirth. Baz's irritation increases as I continue to laugh harder.

"Oh... So the big bad Dom is a big wimpy baby!" I rib him, catching my breath. "Waa, waa, waa!"

And just like that, Baz turns the tables when he spins me around and spanks my ass.

"You think I am entertaining, Little Pet? Let me show you how hilarious I can be..." He chuckles sinfully at my shock.

* * *

JUST THE THOUGHT of the limitless pleasure Baz gives makes me squirm with need in my seat next to him as we fly to the United Arab Emirates. Besides incredible, non-stop make-up sex daily—even if I go home to my penthouse or he goes to his—we accomplished business-related tasks.

Baz's first order of business was to move my New York office back to the executive floor of STEELE International. I gave in to that move since the suite of offices is larger than the two rooms above my boutique. Plus, the unobstructed views of Manhattan are fantastic from the floor-to-ceiling windows on the twenty-ninth floor.

On the opposite wing from Baz's offices gives him a sense of closeness not afforded him with me living in my penthouse "all the way over on Sutton Place." Not to mention the incredible scenes of secretary and demanding boss we play behind the darkened glass walls of the soundproof offices. Definitely worth setting aside my independent streak for clandestine orgasms.

"Hey, babe, private jokes?" Baz asks, poking my ticklish side.

I pull his hand away from my flank to kiss his fingertips before nipping then sucking them between my full lips. A shudder runs through me when Baz's eyes widen in surprise. The normally flint gray orbs darken to lustful onyx.

"Oh, just thinking about you, Sir." I purr, slipping his thick fingers from my mouth. "And the pleasure you so kindly provide me."

A sharp intake of breath precedes Baz shifting in his seat. My gaze drops to his crotch where a bulge forms from his massive cock awakening at my seduction. Hhhmmm.

"Lola, excuse me. I hate to interrupt."

Disappointed I have to look away from a promising sight, I glance up. Baz reaches for his laptop to cover the burgeoning evidence of his unexpected arousal. Unaware of the sexual tension around her, Blair continues.

"The report you requested just came through and we set the con call to start in fifteen minutes. Would you like for me to set up at the table?"

Thwarted by work, I slip past Baz. Knowing he won't dare do anything in response, I purposefully let my butt glide past his face. Tease, temptation, and a raincheck rolled in one. In frustration, Baz growls low in his chest.

"Until later, Sir…" I whisper in his ear, sure to brush my ample breasts against his arm.

Another growl and I follow Blair to the front of the jet.

Billie stands by the table with her mobile at her ear and her laptop in her arm, ready to get started. I have the best assistants ever. And to think I wanted originally to do everything myself, from the design to the administrative tasks. Luckily, Luc disengaged that madness from my mind. Things are more efficient now. I can focus on the creative side of the business—doing what I love the most.

Before we leave Dubai, we must have another Girls' Night Out. I need to catch up with them on Luc and Patrick. Blair's been mum while Billie regularly gushes about the bonnie Scotsman. Funny how the men appeared interested in me at first. Well, at least Baz thinks both. I still doubt Luc thought of me beyond a mentee. All turns out as it should. A Starr tenet I've grown to appreciate.

"Splendid job! The production schedules for the Abu Dhabi and Dubai collections are on track for the openings," I say happy to have the cultural differences worked out.

"Yes. It's good we had a focus group to determine the female patrons' comfortability levels," Billie adds.

"Very true. Also, your pieces are pretty much worn beneath clothing, so less likelihood of issues," Blair nods. "It's like unwrapping a present to find an exquisite surprise!"

Our laughter carries through the jet. The chirp of my mobile draws my attention. Luc is on the line. I glance at

Blair, but she's busy chatting with Billie. I excuse myself to take the call on the sofa.

"*Ciao, Luc, comment ça va?*" I ask as to his well-being once settled and staring out the window at the expansive sky.

"*Comme ci comme ça, petite chérie,*" Luc responds.

I perk up at his despondent tone and ask him what's on his mind, fluently conversing in French. He has an obligation that prevents him from meeting us in Abu Dhabi tomorrow. He's delayed a day or two and will meet us in Dubai.

"I know how important the location selections are for you, Lola," he states. "But I will make it in time for the Dubai sites. You can send a video of the ones in Abu Dhabi. However, I trust your judgment and I know Steele wants the best for you."

On the tail end of our call, Blair's mobile chirps a text message. Her expression changes from perky to disappointed. I slide into the seat opposite her at the table and look at her questioningly.

"Oh, nothing," she says airily as she flips her mobile face down on the table blocking the screen from view. "Nothing at all."

"So you say, but your body language busts you," I tell her with my eyebrow cocked in disbelief. "By any chance was that a text message from a certain French nobleman?"

Blair swings her gaze in my direction, shocked that I guessed correctly.

"Mmm hmmm... So I thought! You don't have to say anything"—I raise my hand to stop her from speaking—"For now at least. But you will spill when we have a Girls's Night Out before we leave Dubai!"

Billie giggles and prods Blair with her elbow.

"So busted!" Billie grins. "Blair refuses to tell me anything. Now, you must divulge all over cocktails at a club for visitors. We'll need some liquor to get us through this drama!"

The rest of the thirteen-hour flight we spend on more prep work, dinner, and sleeping. Despite the bedroom being soundproof, I just can't finish what I started with Baz while Blair, Billie, and the other STEELE staff members are on board. I blush at the thought.

We land shortly after seven in the morning. Several helicopters wait to fly us to the STEELE Abu Dhabi. The impressive complex comprises four towers that resemble modern sculptures. With varying heights of over 1,000 feet and 80 floors, SAD is nothing less than breathtaking elation as it dominates the skyline. The signature gray glass exterior gleams in the desert sunshine. Two towers offer sought-after residences; one tower features the luxury hotel and mall; the fourth tower provides optimal office space. On the ground level, benches under trees and other greenery with water misters make for a respite from the heat. Phenomenal.

Baz and I take the rapid elevator to one of the Rulers' Suites on the top floor. Blair, Billie, and Tina Nickles, who's one of Baz's assistants, and other staff go to a separate bank of elevators to access their suites a few floors below. We agree to meet in the lobby in ninety minutes.

"This is an incredible property, Baz!" I blurt as soon as we're alone on the elevator.

His eyes light up when he turns to me to respond.

"This project is one of my favorites. Since it covers each of the STEELE divisions being residential, entertainment, and retail, my entire family worked together to make it a success. Not to mention the top-notch security installed to protect the elite clientele."

Baz's excitement radiates on his face. He truly loves his family. A bit of wistfulness strikes me when I think of my parents and how much I miss them. As though sensing my sudden mood change, Baz strokes my cheek before tilting my head back to kiss me senseless.

"They would be proud of you, babe," he whispers while his thumb strokes my cheek. "You're not alone. You have me, and my family is eager to have dinner when we get back."

I can only nod since tears of happiness clog my throat as I lean my forehead against his firm chest. The heady aroma of his cologne fills my nostrils. So I burrow deeper into Baz, gaining support from his strength. Moments later, the elevator doors ding open.

My breath escapes me once again. This time because of the jaw-dropping view. Spread before us is the dazzling water with glittering ripples that reach across to the other shoreline. The megayachts moored at the complex's private marina bobbing on the waves resemble toys from this lofty height. The sandy beach dotted with umbrellas calls to me. With a wistful sigh, my gaze moves to the interior.

The sheer opulence of the suite rivals the panorama. A cue from the family's name influences the decor that features platinum, white gold, and white marble with gray and black veins running through it. They cover the walls in white silk while the ceiling is white-gold leaf with crystal chandeliers and strategically placed recessed lighting. White and dove gray furniture made of silk and leather is throughout the seating areas. The primary space is vast with plenty of sunlight and a light airy feel. I can only imagine the decor for the four bedrooms, baths, dining room, and other spaces must be just as resplendent.

"Come on, Lola, we have little time," Sebastian says as he grabs my hand and pulls me away from the living area. "I have something even more captivating to show you."

ANOTHER NOTCH on the Christened Room Bedpost later, we meet the team in the lobby. Everyone changed into lighter clothing to account for the sultry desert heat. Women opting for loose-fitting cotton shift dresses with jackets and the men swapping their wool suits for linen cotton blends. Sunglasses, mobiles, and attachés abound.

A quick walk through one of the all-glass, air-conditioned corridors that connect the hotel to the other towers takes us to STEELE International, Inc. UAE. Similar to the

New York City headquarters, the executive level is on the top floor and the view again is spectacular.

Seated in a conference room facing the enticing water, it's hard to concentrate on business. But concentrate we must.

Gathered around the table sit staff from Lola's Coterie Paris and STEELE New York and UAE. The opening of my boutique requires members from both companies to work together as one team. LCP marketing, sales, legal, and finance staff flew in yesterday afternoon. Less of a time change accounts for their perkier attitudes.

STEELE's staff in attendance include the same departments less sales. Additionally representatives from retail, design and construction, logistics, security, technology, and cultural affairs round out the group. The talent everyone brings to the table is impressive. I'm confident Lola's Coterie Dubai's success will match that of New York and Las Vegas.

The combined marketing teams discuss their plan including the ad and branding campaigns, magazine and television interviews, opening party guest lists, and invitations to social events that I should attend. Another team covers logistics for travel and accommodations for out-of-town guests and staff along with activities since the event will cover two days in Abu Dhabi. After the lunch break, the STEELE retail team shares an in-depth presentation covering the three available spaces. The rest of the departments layout the agenda for tomorrow's sessions.

I thank everyone, and we end the workday at three due to the eight-hour time difference.

"I'M SO EXCITED! I can't wait to see the stores tomorrow!" I exclaim to Baz as we sit at one of the hotel's three Michelin star restaurants overlooking the marina.

Determined to beat jet lag, Baz and I took a nap when we returned to our Rulers' Suite to give us energy to stay up for dinner. Even Baz was too tired to do more than spoon me against him. A refreshing shower followed. Now rejuvenated, we dine on scrumptious seafood and vintage wine.

Billie, Tina, and Blair went out for dinner and to a club with some STEELE UAE staff. In the morning, everyone will meet in the lobby instead of at the office since it connects the mall to the hotel. The retail team will give us a tour of the recommended stores before we make the ultimate decision.

"I'm pleased with the presentation the retail team made. Those store options are A1 on the scale we use to categorize space," Baz responds. "The anchor location closest to the hotel entrance is my first choice, followed by the one near the street entrance. The one in the middle requires foot traffic directed to it as opposed to an entryway with organic passersby."

"I would love to walk through after we eat…" I offer Baz my most-winning smile.

"Since this is a business negotiation, Ms. Lewis, what

would I get in exchange for granting you access to the mall after hours?" Baz asks with a cocked eyebrow.

"Oh, Sir, I will need your help to reach the top shelves in the stockroom. You see, my manager didn't leave a ladder for me to use. So, I will need to sit on your strong shoulders to—"

"Check, please," Baz calls to a server who passes our table.

SEBASTIAN

ubai is one of my favorite cities in the world and holds a special place in my heart.

After I graduated Harvard Business School with my MBA, my father sent me here as part of the team that managed the opening of STEELE's first office in the UAE. I value the experience as I handled various aspects of the project from site selection to land negotiations to construction plans to the hiring of staff. Hell, even the carpet selection fell in the realm of my responsibilities.

My father wanted me to know all sides of our family's business and how to run it. It was a three-year process that helped to hone my skills as STEELE's next generational leader.

Since SD I's initial opening, two additional towers for a five-star hotel and luxury residences joined the office tower at the original site. SD II's expansion across the street includes a multi-level mall with an office tower above and a residential tower.

The boom for housing and commercial space has exploded over the years. People and businesses from all across the globe have made Dubai their home or established an office. Work and big money requires distractions. Thus the need for high-end shops, top-rated eateries, movie theaters, and concert halls. STEELE provides it all.

I'm thrilled Lola agreed to open Lola's Coterie Dubai. The boutique is perfect to join the other luxury retailers in the SD II Mall. Despite what people may think, the women in the UAE enjoy wearing the latest fashions, including lingerie. I can vouch for their desire to appear and feel sexy.

The two spots set aside for Lola to choose from are the best in the entire mall. One opens directly onto the street with an entrance inside to the mall's interior. The other space is near the office entrance. The presentation the retail team shared with us emphasizes the benefits of both. But I prefer the street-front space since she can showcase her new evening collection in the windows. Modesty is still appropriate in the UAE. So Lola can take advantage of the windows to make passersby aware of the clothing side of Lola's Coterie. Either way, the decision is for her to make.

"Lola, this space offers you the most exposure, even if it's larger than you want."

Luc's voice cuts through my thoughts, bringing my attention back to where we stand in the store available at the front of the mall. I was glad when he didn't show up in

Abu Dhabi. Thank fuck! I'm still working on my trust of his intentions with Lola. Since Lola and I are just back together, I keep my mouth shut. No need to make her jump back into the water just as I reeled her into my boat.

"I don't know, Luc. It's a lot larger than I expected. Bigger than any of my other boutiques, including Paris. Sebastian, what do you think?"

My heart warms. Lola asking my advice after her "mentor" told her his opinion. Big step forward. Perfect time for cool points.

"I agree with Luc," I start, casting my eyes in his direction. He looks shocked by my words. Yeah, grandpa. Take that.

"You can showcase your new evening collection in the windows. With modesty very appropriate in the UAE, you can take advantage of the windows to make passersby aware of Lola's Coterie clothing side. Draw them in with the dresses that resemble lingerie, then get them to buy the dresses and the real lingerie. A win-win situation.," I finish with a nod to Luc. Solidarity, my brother.

"Baz! That's a fantastic idea! So smart!" Lola gushes as she claps her hands. "Then, it's settled. This is the location for Lola's Coterie Dubai!"

A satisfied smile blooms on my face. Score!

"Do I look all right?" Lola asks as we head to a party thrown by some friends I met years ago.

I let my gaze travel over Lola's lush body. She looks like a goddess in a red silk chiffon sleeveless gown with a cape detail that sweeps from the shoulder straps to the floor behind her as she walks. Her full breasts accentuated by the vee front and wrapped waistband make my mouth water. Light through the bottom shows the faint outline of her legs lengthened by the sky-high strappy sandals she wears. Being in the UAE, she modestly covers her shoulders with a glittery, embroidered sheer wrap while we're outdoors. Her hair falls loose in lustrous waves down her back. The rare, red diamond earrings and matching bangles, two on each arm, that I gifted her for the opening of Lola's Coterie Las Vegas shine. I note how they enhance her beauty as we sit in the back of the chauffeured Rolls-Royce Corniche that I keep in Dubai. Gorgeous Girl.

Damn. I can't wait to ravage my Petite Seductress when we get back to the hotel.

"More than all right. You look like a dream," I assure her.

The jewels sparkle as she reaches forward to kiss me softly on the lips.

"Thank you, baby," Lola whispers. "I want to make a good impression on your friends."

She peeks at me from under her thick lashes. I lean my forehead against hers and whisper words that have been on the tip of my tongue for months.

"I love you, Lola Lewis. You impress me and that's all that matters."

Lola's jaw drops and her eyes brighten with tears as

she leans back to study my face. Shit, I didn't mean to upset her. Quickly, I pull her onto my lap to hold her close. I press my lips to the top of her head as I croon to her.

"Lola, baby. I've wanted to tell you for so long. You mean everything to me. I thank my lucky stars that you've accepted me back into your life. I was lost without you, my love. Never for a moment think you are less than. You are my everything."

Lola shudders in my arms. We remain as one until the car stops at the party venue. Lola slips off of my lap and straightens her gown before she dabs her eyes with the handkerchief I handed to her.

Just as the door opens, she puts her hand on my forearm to stop me from stepping out of the car.

"I love you, too, Baz. I've loved you from the start."

My heart melts and I sit back in the seat. But Lola shakes her head.

"Your friends haven't seen you in a while and threw this party for you. We have to go in. If only for a little while," she smiles. Her hazel eyes glow with her love for me.

For me, the Dom playboy who said he'd never fall in love and scoffed at a permanent relationship.

Well, that was before Ms. Lola Lewis... Petite Seductress... Little Pet... Soon-to-be Mrs. Sebastian Steele.

As EXPECTED, Lola charms all the guests. The women flock to her and the men leer with lust-filled eyes. She floats about the room with ease. No one is immune to Lola's wit and grace, I smile proudly to myself.

"Hi, Sebastian. It's been awhile."

The purr comes from Vanessa O'Sullivan the Irish expat I fucked regularly when I lived in Dubai and often when I returned for business. She is not someone I want to deal with now that things are well with Lola. I learned from Vanessa not to dip more than once with a woman— too clingy. Shit.

I scan the room and see Lola speaking with a cluster of women. Perfect. Hopefully, I can get this conversation with Vanessa over with fast.

"Hello, Vanessa," I start only to stop when she slips her hand under my evening jacket to reach for my crotch.

I grab her wrist and pull her hand away. Another quick search around assuages my fear that someone saw her bold-as-fuck move. Deftly, I pull her out of the others' sight. This ends now. No Lydie miscommunication happening again. I will make it crystal clear for Vanessa.

"Vanessa, do not put your hands on—"

"Sebastian, sweetie, I only wanted to greet you properly," she purrs, pressing her body close to mine.

I jerk back, but stand firm. She is not the type to back down if she senses a weakness. The Dom in me takes over.

"Vanessa, you will never touch me again. Not in greeting or for any other reason. Good night."

I pivot and without a backwards glance return to the party, seeking Lola out. I catch her glancing about the room, looking for me. When our eyes meet, her smile lights the room.

Fuck, I'm a goner for this woman.

Once beside her, I bend down to kiss her on the lips not giving a damn what others may think. I need to taste her sweetness to banish the sour thought of Vanessa from out of my mind. Lola sighs softly as she melts against me.

"No need to act all possessive, Steele. We get it, you've got the best girl as usual. No offense to you, ladies."

I laugh as I take my lips from Lola's delectable mouth to bro hug Porter Huntington. As Vanessa was a tryst, Porter was a partner in crime while I was in Dubai. It's been almost a year since we last saw one another.

"Porter, let me introduce you to the love of my life, Lola Lewis. Lola, this is my wonderful friend Porter Huntington."

Huntington ever the Casanova takes Lola's hand in his as he bows and kisses her knuckles.

"A pleasure to meet the woman who has captured the heart of Sebastian *Never Fall in Love* Steele," he smirks at me over Lola's hand.

"*Enchanté*, Mr. Huntington," Lola starts. "The pleasure of Baz's heart is all mine."

With that, the group laughs. Once again, Lola is the one to capture everyone's heart.

"WHAT A LOVELY EVENING! Your friends are so welcoming," Lola smiles as we walk into our Rulers' Suite at SD II.

"Well... Of course there was that dreadful woman who made a grab for your crotch..."

I nearly trip over Lola's cape, so taken aback by her comment. Damn. I didn't think she saw what happened with Vanessa. Sheepishly, I glance at Lola, who's turned to stare me directly in the eyes. My pulse quickens in anticipation of an argument. Blasted Vanessa O'Sullivan!

"For a moment, I thought I'd have to take off my earrings and sandals to handle her myself. Luckily, you moved her aside and corrected the situation pronto," Lola ends with a smirk.

I scan her face and realize she's not angry with me. Thank fuck! Without hesitating, I scoop her over my shoulder in a fireman's carry, swat her plump ass for giving me palpitations, and stride to the bedroom. Time to make love to my girl. Her laughter rings out and fills my heart with joy.

Yup, Lola Lewis Soon-to-be Mrs. Sebastian Steele has captured my heart forever.

SEBASTIAN

"*Y*ou will suck me, Little Pet. Every… Little… Inch."

My hips thrust forward with each grunt as I tower above Lola lying supine on the most recent addition to our suite at LEVELS New York. The adjustable table resembles one found in a doctor's examination room. At the foot of the narrow leather-padded bench, the legs split with suede-lined cuffs at the foot. The midsection hinges to allow an upright position or one angled down to the floor. Arms in more cuffs attached to hinged slabs allow for a movement like angel wings.

Ah, and what an angel Lola appears. My favorite types of fruit cover her supple body. Delectable figs with the downy softness of their skin and their plump bottoms blush violet remind me of Lola's lusciousness after a satisfying spanking. Pears shaped like Lola decorate her thighs. Pomegranate seeds made famous for their temptation and sensuality by Greek literature lead a sticky trail from her neck to her mound. The sight of my massive cock burrowing deeper down her throat makes my balls ache. A zing shoots down my spine, straight to my sac. My dick weeps pre-cum in relief.

"Suck… Me."

My growl makes my Little Pet shudder and amp up her tantalizing ministrations. To reward her, I bend my body over hers to gorge on the abundant cherries, grapes, and strawberries that fill her pussy. It's sweeter than ever. I lap at the juices running down her quivering thighs. Then nibble her swollen lips and clit before I spear my tongue between her folds to withdraw a wet cherry. As I chew the tasty treat, I nearly choke on it when Lola nips my engorged tip.

"Fuuuck!" I bellow.

The hum of Lola's teasing laughter shoots vibrations along my shaft, prompting more seed to fill my heavy balls. To prevent an unwanted early release, I pull my dick from her mouth with a pop as I stand.

"Naughty Pet. I know you nipped me to earn a punishment," I chide with a raised brow as I stroke my length. "I am more than happy to oblige."

Despite the blindfold covering her eyes, I can tell by the bowing of her body that she's eager for a spanking. That pleasure I will not give to her as she has not earned it… yet. Instead, I pull nipple and clit clamps and an anal plug from a drawer in the large, double-door armoire. The treasure chest contains a plethora of our favorite toys—

Wartenberg Wheels, cords, dildos, vibrators, and so much more.

My lips pluck a piece of a peach from her left nipple and pull them both into mouth. I suck her bud until it tightens. The pinch of the clamp changes Lola's soft mewls to a sharp yelp. Now that she knows my intentions behind the suckling, she tenses when my mouth engulfs her right nipple. The licks and nips I make along her pomegranate trail cause Lola to writhe wantonly on the bench. The pain of the clamps forgotten.

The delicious combined aroma of her arousal and the fruit makes my mouth water in anticipation. I lap at her thighs and pussy soaked with the ambrosia until she nears her climax. Her body bows and she tries to push her core further into my mouth as her thighs tremble with intensity. The sudden bite of the clit clamp abruptly stops Lola's pending release. A wail follows a frustrated growl that slips from behind her clenched teeth as she flops down against the buttery soft leather of the bench.

Next I carefully insert the medium-size plug coated generously with lube in her puckered hole—a star twinkling at me. Slow, deliberate pressure applied to her back entrance gives Lola time to adjust to the object. Her protests soon turn to sighs once I fully seat the plug within her ass. The red crystal glitters in the ambient lighting.

Stunning.

My attention focuses on the cornucopian spread before me. I continue my feast. A bite of plum, a taste of raspberries, a morsel of nectarine burst with flavor in my mouth.

When Lola's skin emerges with only traces of fruit juice, I return to her head.

Just the mushroom tip of my dick pressed against her mouth is enough to signal her to envelop my girth. A groan of pure bliss escapes my lips from the warmth wrapped around my length. I rise onto the balls of my feet to gain further access down Lola's open throat. My angel is definitely heaven sent.

"FEEL BETTER, BABE?" I ask Lola, seated in the extra-large claw-foot tub as I slide a sudsy sponge over her bountiful breasts.

Her taut nipples floating on the surface dance in and out of the foam.

Since we returned from the UAE and I reminded Lola about my family coming over to my penthouse for dinner, she's been on edge. Her nerves peaked the closer the day arrived for my family to visit. Their first official meeting has my love anxious. She needed a scene at LEVELS New York to ease her anxiety.

"Ooh yes, baby. Much better, thank you," Lola murmurs contentedly.

She leans her back against my front and widens her legs to allow the sponge to stroke further along her body, dipping in and out of her curves. With her arms draped on the tub's rim, Lola lays herself bare to my sensuous cleaning. A soak in the tub and bathing one another after we play is one habit we established early in our relationship.

We enjoy it as much as our lovemaking. The act of caring so intimately for each other brings us closer.

"I went shopping at Eataly NYC in the Flatiron District this afternoon. They have the best of everything and so fresh from Italy! I know you love when I make saltimbocca. We'll start with Mushroom and mozzarella arancini followed by saltimbocca, a tomato and burrata salad with basil oil. Ooh… And garlic sticks! For dessert—"

"You mean besides you?" I tease her as I nibble the sensitive area where her neck meets her shoulder. She's getting wound up again. Her nervousness making her ramble. So, I distract her.

"You and I will save that for the post-party!" She giggles, tilting her head to the side to give me more access. "A selection of sorbet and gelato to end the meal on a lighter note. After coffee we'll drink Limoncello Gin Collins."

Lola slips away to face me, the amber in her hazel eyes glow with her mounting excitement.

"If you don't mind, I'd like to set up a table on the large terrace off of the living room. We can decorate with strings of fairy lights, bright pillows on the furniture, soft music playing over the surround sound system… Recreate an Italian alfresco dining extravaganza!"

Lola's enthusiasm is irresistible. Hating the loss of her body against mine, I cross the tub and pull her back into my arms. With my face nuzzled in her hair, I can join her glee.

"Whatever you want, my love… Whatever you want."

* * *

I FOLLOW the sound of conversation into the kitchen, perplexed by a man's voice in my penthouse... A man's deep voice engaged with Lola's light laughter bouncing off the walls of my home.

What. The. Fuck.

"—so kind of you to offer... Ooh!"

Lola's startled exclamation spurs me to slam into the kitchen, ready to drop kick some motherfucker flat on his ass. The door bangs into the wall, the sound of plaster hitting the floor makes Lola and the man jump in surprise.

"What the fuck is going on?" I demand as I stride across the marble, eyes blazing. "Who the fuck are you?"

In my periphery, Lola's mouth is a perfect O shape. Her eyebrows reach her hairline as she stands in shock at my entrance and domineering manner.

The man stands his ground. If I'm not mistaken, he puffs up his chest. I narrow my eyes into slits. My fists clench. My body poised to spring at him. Shit, if I can take on Borya, I can take this guy. He's two inches shorter than me and about fifteen pounds lighter. I'll annihilate the asshole.

"Sebastian!"

Lola's cry pauses my forward motion. But my gaze remains steady on my opponent. Obviously untrained in the art of war, he glances at Lola.

"What the fuck are you looking at my woman for? Answer my questions... Now," I say, my voice deadly.

"Hey, man, I meant no harm. I just offered my help," he responds, palms up. "I thought she was the caterer."

"Yes, Sebastian. He's a part of the crew you hired to help set up the terrace for dinner tonight," Lola adds.

"Really? The terrace is about thirty feet beyond that door. So, again… What the fuck is going on?" I demand.

"Is everything all right?"

A woman in her fifties steps through the kitchen door and plants herself between the man and me. She surveys the situation, then turns to face me.

"Mr. Steele. Please allow me to introduce myself and my employee. I'm Mrs. Cartwright, the party planner your assistant Ms. Lawson hired for your dinner this evening."

She pauses and turns her gaze to the man. With a flare of her nostrils, she takes a deep breath and continues.

"This is Blake, a recent hire. I apologize for his behavior and assure you I will deal with him properly. Do you approve of the rest of my team completing the task?"

I rake my gaze over Blake from head to toe before I respond.

"Security will see him off the premises," I give him the once-over again. "Mrs. Cartwright, we would appreciate you finishing the job, thank you."

Lola picks up the penthouse phone to the concierge and asks for security to come upstairs to the kitchen immediately. Her wide-eyed stare stays on my face. Wary of my next move. I don't blame her as I'm wound tight, about to blow.

Moments later, four members of the security staff

stride into the room. Their eyes take in the scene. No doubt sensing the tension in the air.

"Mr. Steele, Ms. Lewis, how may we help you?" The leader asks, flicking his gaze to Mrs. Cartwright and Blake.

"Please remove this man from the premises following the protocol. Thank you," I respond.

"Yes, sir, Mr. Steele."

Blake throws a glare in my direction. But the guards hustle him out, avoiding any further confrontation.

"Mr. Steele, Ms. Lewis, I apologize greatly. We will finish expeditiously. Our services are in kind," Mrs. Cartwright tells us.

I will not allow some asshole's poor behavior to prevent payment. So, I thank her for her offer. But we will pay her as contracted. She thanks us graciously before returning to the terrace.

Now that Lola and I are alone, I brace myself for an argument. My gaze settles on her at last. Still clutched in her arms, a pot top nestled against her heaving bosom. She traps her lower lip between her teeth. Then glances over her shoulder in the direction Mrs. Cartwright left the kitchen. Lola swings her gaze back to me. Her eyes sweep up and down my body as her eyes darken and her breath quickens. I raise my eyebrow in question.

Lola dashes to me, grabs my arm, and pulls me into the walk-in pantry.

"Fuck... That was hot! I have to have you... Right... Now!"

And have me she does. When at last we exit the pantry

and check on the party planners' progress, they're long gone. Mrs. Cartwright left a pleasant note on the terrace table thanking us and apologizing for Blake's unacceptable behavior, again. She promises the servers will be up to par.

Well, I thank Blake for the best *aperitivo* I've ever had in my life.

"LOLA, THIS WAS DELICIOUS!" My mother, Shelley beams. "I feel like I'm back on holiday in Positano at Villa Sogno! That's our home on the Italian Rivera. You must come the next time we're there."

At those words, my mother stares at me pointedly. I press my lips together to stifle a chuckle at her blatancy. Lola, however, claps her hands and bounces in her seat.

"Thank you so much! I was so very nervous to meet you all. But you've made me feel so welcome. Thank you."

She bows her head, then lifts it, smiling at everyone seated around her. The entire Steele clan is present. The elliptical table is the perfect shape to allow all eight of us to see each other. While we enjoy the view through the frameless tempered glass around the edge of the terrace. The many lights of the Manhattan skyline do not compare to the ray of light my Lola projects.

"I propose a toast," Morgan with his Limoncello Gin Collins in hand stands at the end opposite to my mother. "To the first and the last woman our eldest son Sebastian has ever introduced to his family. We welcome you, Lola!"

"Here here!"

"Bravo!"

"*Cent'Anni!*"

"Cheers!"

"*Salute!*"

With my glass raised, I look around the table at my father, mother, sister, and brothers. My heart is full of joy and a peace I never knew could exist ten months ago. My gaze lands on Lola. Her eyes meet mine and her smile brightens even more.

I know she's happy with me and how our relationship progressed these past two months. When my father stated the proposal, it almost made the words "will you marry me" slip out of my mouth.

However, as elated as Lola and I are right now, I never ask a question I may get a no answer. Lola's not ready to tell me yes... yet. So I won't ask her to marry me tonight. Even though the words fight to escape my mouth. I rein them in for a more suitable time.

A time that is without a doubt in the very near future. That is my mission.

LOLA

"*W*e have so much to catch up on!"

Leonie's tinkling laughter floats over our FaceTime call. I've missed my BFF. With both of us super busy at work, we haven't had time for a lengthy conversation since Paris. It's so good to hear her voice.

"*Chérie, tu me manques tellement!*" Leonie exclaims. "It's been forever since we said more than hi and goodbye! Just business-related emails with sketches, colors, fabric swatches... Tell me everything I missed in your personal life."

I laugh at her snuggling back on the settee in her bedroom lifting a cup of tea, ready for the gossip. She wears a Lola's Coterie cream silk dressing gown over the matching tank top and sleep shorts. The color highlights her golden caramel-colored skin beautifully. Her glossy, mahogany hair swept up in a messy bun and her flawless face is bare of makeup. The supermodel lounges at home look at its finest!

"He told me he loves me!" I gush as I almost bounce off of my sofa.

"He who???" Leonie asks as she tilts her head, squinting her eye with a raised eyebrow.

"Baz, girl!! He told me he loves me when we were in Dubai on our way to a party his friends threw for him."

Leonie sputters as the sip of tea dribbles from her open mouth. Her amber eyes widen as she stares at me in shock.

"*Ce qui!!! Etes-vous sérieusement en train de me dire que Sebastian Steele vous aime??*"

I giggle and ecstatically nod like a human bobblehead. Yes, I am seriously telling her he loves me! Sebastian *Dom Playboy* Steele loves me and only me. A thrill rocks my body, shooting from the top of my head to the tips of my red-polished toes. Baz has been so attentive since he uttered those three words. I swoon at the memory.

"*Oui! Il m'aime beaucoup!!*" I whoop.

"*C'était merveilleux, Chérie!*" Leonie smiles with tears in her eyes.

She understands how much it hurt me when I saw Sebastian with Lydie. Damn, I forgot to tell her what really happened at his penthouse.

"Leonie! You won't believe what Lydie told me..."

After I fill Leonie in on the details, her mouth hangs open for a second time. She has to excuse herself to get a refill of tea. As she walks with her iPhone, she shakes her head and mutters to herself in French.

When she settles on her settee, we dissect the entire situation and surmise that Lydie isn't as bad as we thought. She had her reasons with her father's archaic thought process and expectations. Leonie agrees for the sake of my relationship with Sebastian, I should move forward and be cordial with Lydie. No need to prolong the issue. Especially since Baz was not in the wrong.

"And his family is so nice. I cooked an Italian extravaganza for dinner alfresco on the largest terrace at Baz's penthouse," I steer our chat to a more appealing topic.

Leonie's eyes light up as she leans forward expectantly. Her teacup clasped in both hands before her bosom.

"Give me the deets! How did his mother act towards you? What did his father say? Who was there…" She trails off.

We realize at the same time she's thinking about Roger. Her intense ex-lover flew in from Paris to join us. He was pleasant during dinner. But I sensed his thoughts were elsewhere. I really would like to speak with him about his contributions to their breakup. Leonie doesn't want me to speak to Baz either. She and Roger will have to figure out their deal without my interference. No matter how much I want to help.

"Baz's mother is wonderful! Her name is Michelle, but everyone calls her Shelley. She complimented me on the meal and invited me to their villa in Positano. When she extended the invite, she glared at Baz as if she dared him to say no!"

"Really? You must have made an excellent impression

on her to extend an invitation after just meeting you!" Leonie nods sagely.

"I know, right!" I laugh, then add, "His father Morgan even toasted me as the first and hopefully last woman Baz ever introduced to his family!"

"*Merde!* That's fantastic, *Chérie!* I'm so happy for you!" Leonie beams.

"In fact, his sister Haley invited me to dinner tomorrow. La Goulue, one of your favorites," I add smiling back.

Leonie rubs her flat belly as she licks her lips, "Mmm mmm mmm! I'm so jealous. Get the *Moules sauce "Poulette!" Non, non, le Pavé de saumon aux lentils!"*

I laugh and shake my head in disagreement, "Sorry, sweetie! You know I'm rather partial to the House Specialty *Le soufflé au Fromage.* Yummy!"

"By the way, how did you like the designs I sent for your penthouse?" Leonie asks. "Do you like the library?"

We chat about each of the rooms, brainstorm ideas, and timelines. So far, I'm impressed with Leonie's plans. Just like her, the aesthetic is incomparable. We account for her modeling schedule, classes, and travel to showrooms like the D&D Building here. If all goes as expected, she'll finish in two months.

With promises for more FaceTime and a meetup in LA, we end our call.

"SEE, if you lived in our penthouse instead of just spending the night, you could always take our elevator to meet Haley. A total breeze."

I throw a wry glance over my shoulder at Baz as I finish tying the belt on my Diane von Furstenberg wrap dress. For a moment, he tempts me to jump back in bed with him. His sizable frame is all sprawled out on his back with his hands folded behind his head. My gaze travels from his tousled hair, over his gorgeous face with sexy stubble, down his sculpted chest and eight-pack abs. The silk sheet just reaches to the v-cuts of his Adonis belt and emphasizes the outline of his massive dick resting on his muscular thigh. Damn.

"Like what you see, my love?" He taunts while shifting his hips side to side, making his dick bounce.

Baz locks me in his Dom stare as he slides his fingertips down his chest, along his happy trail, and under the sheet to stroke his hardening length. I lick my lips and swallow.

"Are you just using me for the pleasure I bestow upon you, Little Pet?" He croons, stretching languidly.

I flare my nostrils and purse my lips to keep from moaning out loud. No... No... No... I will dine with Haley. Period. Instead of a response, I bend at the waist to wrap the strings of my sandals around my ankles. An added shimmy of my hips precipitates the sound of rustling sheets.

A squeal pops from my mouth as Baz grips my hips and with knees bent thrusts his cock against my ass. His thick thighs bear my weight easily as he lifts me from the floor. Grunts and growls fill the air as he humps me. When his climax nears, Baz lowers me to my feet. I spin around on wobbly legs, eager to see what he'll do next.

His hooded gaze locks on mine. Staggering back, he tugs at his engorged dick as it pulses. Muscles taut in preparation. One last pull. Great ropes of creamy semen spurt from the reddened tip like a geyser. I'm enthralled, unable to take my eyes from the spectacular sight.

Spent, Baz falls back onto the bed with his feet on the floor, throwing his arm over his face, breathing rapidly.

"You'll be the death of me yet, Little Pet," he pants.

I'm listening to Haley.

But I swear, my body is back in the bedroom with Baz. He's the walking personification of hedonistic sex. I can't decide if he's Bacchus, Hedylogus, Min, Freyr, Kuni, Priapus, Cupid, Xochipilli, Kurupi, or every god of love, sex, fertility, and sweet talk in the history of mankind. My womb throbs thinking about him. I'll worship at the altar of Temple Baz for the rest of my life!

I squirm in my seat, excited by his Captain Caveman words he imparted as I untied my dress to switch into a fresh one.

"No, you cannot change your dress. I marked you with my scent on purpose. As you walk past other men and sit in the

restaurant amongst them, intuitively they will know you are taken. And it will remind you that you are mine."

"—his birthday? Since he never plans—"

"Wait, what?" I ask startled out of my reverie by the word birthday.

"Baz's birthday is later this month. What do you have planned? He does nothing for it himself. My mother and I usually throw a party for him. We don't want to conflict with what you have planned."

I stare mutely at Haley for a minute. Damn, all this time and it never occurred to me to ask Baz about the date of his birthday. What a sucky girlfriend...

"You'll probably think I'm the worse. But I didn't know Baz's birthday. We've been so all over the place, I never remembered to ask him," I respond sheepishly.

Haley pushes her glasses up onto the bridge of her nose. Her expressive face can't hide her surprise. Fortunately, she doesn't berate me or look at me with pity.

"I can understand. Don't worry about it. His birthday is on the 30th. We have a few weeks to plan something fun." She looks at me from beneath her lashes. "That is unless you want to have a private celebration."

No way will I isolate Baz's family. This is an important step in our relationship. We have plenty of birthdays ahead of us. I shake my head in response.

"What do Shelley and you have planned? I'd love to be a part of it."

Haley's mobile buzzes on the table. As if by kismet, it's

their mother. A warm smile spreads across Haley's heart-shaped face. Her dimples pop out, adding to her sweet beauty.

"I have to take this call. It's my mom," she tells me.

Before Haley can say hello, I hear Shelley asking her if she's spoken to me about Baz's birthday, yet. Haley peeks over at me and laughs. I join her.

"Right on cue!"

After little to no arm twisting, Shelley agrees to join us for dinner to discuss ideas. Haley and I share things about ourselves as we await Shelley's arrival. Haley just turned twenty-nine, fluent in French, and is fiercely loyal to her family. We share a lot in common from food to movies, even favorite color. It'll be good to have a friend who's constantly in the city besides Blair. I can't be as free with her since she's my employee. I can see Haley and I forming a great friendship.

"Hi, girls!"

Shelley bends over to hug us before she sits in the chair the maître d' pulled out for her. She's a striking woman in her mid-fifties with shoulder-length, wavy black hair and expressive brown eyes. I smile at the Steele Matriarch who I can tell is the boss of the family. As her feisty New Yorker personality affirms.

"I'm so glad you'll let us throw Baz's birthday party with you! Let me tell you, I love my family fiercely and we love to be together for birthdays, holidays, just because. I'm not a smother mother. No! It's their choice. They just love their parents so..."

She tweaks Haley's cheek. A diamond ring mounted on a platinum band catches the light. The stone is so ginormous it reminds me of the stunning engagement ring Elizabeth Taylor wore. Similar to her 29.4-carat emerald-cut diamond she referred to as "My ice skating rink." Shelley's diamond may not be almost 30 carats, but it's not far off. I absolutely adore it!

"Yes, Mom!" Haley turns to me as she laughs heartily. "Lola, don't think we're odd. But we are a close-knit family. We don't pry and we have lives. So no fear!"

"Oh, I don't mind at all. I'm an only child and with my parents gone, I miss having a family," I end wistfully.

Shelley stands and pulls me into a tight embrace. Her genuine warmth brings tears to my eyes and I can't stop a few from falling.

"Lola, darling," Shelley starts. "Baz told us about your parents and how strong you are. You've made an immense change for the better in my son. He's finally opened himself up to love a woman who's deserving of his love. So, when Morgan says we welcome you, we truly welcome you into our fold."

She pulls away slightly to wipe my face before she continues as she stares intently in my eyes.

"He also meant it and we all agree that you are the first and better be the last woman Baz introduces to us!"

Shelley gives me another hug, then bustles me into my seat.

"Now, I say we have it at Villa Sogno. We haven't been there all together in a while. The weather is perfect this time of year. Swim at the beach, go out on the boat, dine alfresco! Lola, have you been to Positano?"

A born and raised New Yorker, Shelley speaks faster than I do. I can only laugh. Happiness replaces my tears. Haley joins in with chuckles of her own. While Shelley stares between the two of us.

"What? What did I say? Oh... Too much?" She laughs at herself.

The server places our meals in front of us. In a comfortable silence, we savor the delicious dishes. I paid homage to Leonie and ordered *le Pavé de saumon aux lentils*. As I eat, my mind processes Shelley's words. Baz spoke of me to his mom and more than likely Malcolm and Roger mentioned me, too. She and Morgan must have been suitably impressed. Good.

"Positano is a favorite spot. I did a photo shoot with Leonie *The Lion* Beaulieu for a collection four seasons ago. Should we make it a three-day trip or is that too long?"

"Darling, that's not long enough! What with the travel time and it being the season... How about five?" Shelley counters.

I can tell where Baz learned his negotiation tactics...

"Then it's a deal!"

"Ooh! What fun we'll have! I can't wait!" Haley claps.

"How was dinner?"

"It was so nice! Haley and I will be BFFs. You guys are lucky to have Shelley as your Mom."

Baz pulls me tighter as we sit on a chaise sipping drinks, a Jackson Scotch for Baz and a Whiskey Sour for me. The Manhattan skyline spread before us. I snuggle against his powerful chest with a contented sigh.

"Yeah. We lucked up with our parents. Don't get me wrong, we argue, have misunderstandings, and all the things any family goes through. But we are loyal, supportive, and love each other dearly. We wouldn't be where we are without each other."

He kisses the top of my head.

"Are you truly happy we're together Lola? Do you mind my parents saying what they did the other night? Be honest."

I stop for a moment to think on it. Then, shift around to peer into his gray eyes.

A vulnerability I never noticed before lies in their depths. It makes me think back on what Shelley said about Baz finally opening himself up to love. He's a confident and experienced son, businessman, and Dom. But he's never had an actual relationship with a woman beyond sex. As much as I'm scared of being hurt. I now realize Baz is afraid of me hurting him, too. We've had enough heartache and anguish.

"Yes, Baz. I am truly happy we're together. No, I don't mind what your parents said. It was wonderful. What about you?"

Baz's gaze intensifies.

"I love you, Lola. I love you more than I ever thought I could love someone outside of my family. So, yes, I'm truly happy we're together. No, I don't mind what my parents said. It was indeed wonderful."

The kiss he gives me makes stars float behind my closed eyes. Stars that rival the ones that sparkle above us.

SEBASTIAN

"*I* saw Rhys Rockett at the club the other day. He wasn't as smug as usual. I imagine word got to him about the deal you completed last week?"

When my father mentions club, for a second, my mind goes to LEVELS New York. A visual appears of my parents in a scene where my mother waits bound to a St. Andrew's Cross while my father brandishes a flogger. It fries my retinas. I shudder at the thought.

I dislodge it from my head with a shake that brings the Union Club to the forefront. The Steele men have been members of the one hundred-eighty plus year old, exclusive social club since its founding as the first of its kind in New York City. Despite being notorious for denying membership to sons, they have always accepted us. A Steele as a founding member helps.

"When he first entered the squash courts, he almost turned tail seeing me standing there with Benson," my father continues. "He tried to save face by greeting us. But the cocky grin disappeared."

Morgan despises Rhys more than I loathe his eldest son, Patrick. Morgan never divulged what took place years ago. But I have a sense it was because of a woman. Perhaps my mother, who's just as evasive about the disdain my father harbors.

"Good. The sly bastard. Excellent job, Baz," Malcolm nods his head and tips his glass of Scotch at me in salute. "I saw Alastair last night at LEVELS parading a sub around the Cellar. Since he's a member, I was cordial. But didn't strike up a conversation."

I snort into my rocks glass as I stretch my legs out. We're on board Morgan's G650 headed to Naples, where we'll board *Serendipity* the megayacht he gave to Shelley for their thirtieth wedding anniversary.

Gifts and anniversaries prompt me to glance back at Lola where she sits chatting animatedly with my mother and Haley. My heart soars at the happiness on her face. I knew she needed more women in her life who would give her the comfort of a supportive family. Every time I think of how strong Lola is in the face of losing her parents at barely eighteen, encourages me to make up for it.

I jump around when something hits my chest. Harris tossed his stress ball at me. Fucker.

"Good grief, Baz... You just can't stop peeping at her. She's still there, Lost Puppy."

He and Malcolm make goo-goo eyes and clutch their

hearts. Loud guffaws fill the cabin. I cringe, but couldn't care less. That's my girl.

"Leave your brother alone. You two need to settle down," Morgan admonishes them. "I remember the first time I saw your mother where she worked as a shopgirl at one of our men's clothing stores. She was the most beautiful woman I'd ever seen. Immediately, I knew I had to make her mine. I stare at her every chance I get."

At the suggestion they settle down, Malcolm and Harris zip their lips. Malcolm preoccupies himself with refilling his drink. Harris checks his newfangled gadget.

Right.

"I'VE BEEN on some of the most renowned yachts in my life. But this… this is beyond exquisite!"

Lola and I stand on the sixth deck of *Serendipity* watching the sunrise over the Gulf of Naples. She was too excited to go inside of our suite. I can't blame her. *Serendipity* is a majestic boat. The largest megayacht in the world has a length of six-hundred feet, nine inches. That extra nine just to nudge past the next yacht down. At least for now, *Serendipity* holds the record since everyone competes for the prize of the biggest on the water. There are already rumors that a Russian oligarch contracted a prominent builder specifically to outsize *Serendipity*.

It's definitely a beauty to behold. The all-white, sleek design boasts seven decks. The top for the bridge; the sixth for four palatial suites where my parents, Malcolm, Haley, and I stay; the fifth deck for four suites where Roger and Harris and up to four close friends stay, plus our private library, office, family and dining rooms with galley; the remaining decks accommodate twenty-four guests in staterooms, quarters for eighty-eight crew, helicopter pad, submarine and water vehicles and toys garage, swimming pool, spa, gym, barbershop and salon, disco, living and dining areas, and an entertainment deck with a bowling alley, cinema, pool room, cards room, and game room. The open-air decks hold chaises, beds, tables, televisions, and dining spots. *Serendipity* is a floating haven for rest, relaxation, and partying.

When we arrived on board, everyone went to their suites to rest until we reach Positano. The vibrant colors of the rising sun playing on the Tyrrhenian Sea's crystal blue surface awed Lola. So, we detoured to my favorite spot on the fifth deck near my suite.

"My father bought her for my mother as a thirtieth wedding anniversary. They keep *Serendipity* here during the season. Then transport her to the Caribbean for the fall and winter months."

"Your dad really does it big! Your mom's engagement ring is as incredible as her boat!"

Lola's laugh tinkles in the air before ending on a yawn. I scoop her up and carry her to our suite.

"Time for bed."

Her giggles continue as I take her dress off, then tuck her in bed. She hums a striptease between yawns as I undress, making me wish we weren't so tired. Instead of ravaging her, I slip under the covers and pull Lola into my arms.

"Sweet dreams, princess," I whisper into her hair.

A FEW HOURS LATER, I wake before Lola and lie on my side watching her sleep. A slight frown furrows her brow as she murmurs. The gentle pressure of my kiss smooths her scowl. On an exhalation, Lola sighs my name. Still asleep, her lips curl up into a smile as she reaches for me. Denial is impossible. I slide my body closer to hers, resting her cheek on my chest. It's my turn to sigh.

While I embrace Lola, my fingertips trace along her naked back. Her warm skin is soft. I could lie here all day, but I know we should approach Positano any moment. We need to disembark for Villa Sogno. Based on Lola's excitement about the boat, I'm sure she'll want to see the spectacular sight of the colorful hillside town at our arrival.

"Babe, wake up," I briskly rub Lola's back while I kiss the top of her head. "We're not far and you'll want to see the landscape."

"Mmm… Mmm… Mmm."

Lola arches her back and stretches like a cat, lifting her arms overhead. Her more-than-a-mouthful boobs appear from beneath the sheet.

I can't stop myself from pulling her plump nipple into my mouth, suckling on her tit. Lola's coos stiffen my cock. A quick roll and I pull her under me, settling my hips between her warm thighs. My mouth still on her breasts

169

alternating between the mounds, I cup her ample ass to angle her entrance to prepare for my dick.

"Ooh… Baz. You're so big, baby…. Damn… ahhh," Lola hisses as my girth expands her pussy.

My lips continue to ravage her breasts, knowing my ministrations will stimulate her core to release her juices. Lola's luscious body creates generous amounts of lube naturally. She is the most responsive woman I've ever been with, and I play her body like a fine instrument. Her high notes of pleasure music to my ears.

"Yaaasss! Right there. Right there! Yes… Yes… Yes…" She stutters with each powerful thrust.

Nothing is more important than Lola's climax. I continue to pound into her, circling my hips and changing my angle to spur her release. My dick pulses when her inner muscles grip it greedily.

"Cum on my cock, Lola. Cum for me now!"

Her body spasms as she comes undone, her mouth open in a silent cry.

One orgasm is never enough. My thrusts continue until I've wrung multiple climaxes from her core and she begs me to stop. Only then do I chase my release. I flip her onto all fours and slam into her from behind. The force shifts her towards the headboard. I grip her hip in one hand and her hair in the other, bowing her body to gain better access. Lola screeches and writhes, tilting her pelvis to open further for me. A few spanks to her butt cheeks make her explode. Her whimpers beg me to cum.

"Fuck, Lola! You… feel… so… fucking… good! No need to beg, baby. I'm right… with… you!" I roar my release.

Stars dance before my eyes and my thighs shake. Unable to squat any longer, I collapse onto her back, then roll us to the side. I spoon Lola while our breathing returns to normal. I give a silent thanks for the soundproof walls.

Freshly showered and dressed, we stand beside my parents at the front of the sixth deck. This spot offers the best vantage point to see the town as we pull into the coastal waters off the Positano shore. Everyone else headed to the third deck. The crew prepares the tenders to take us to the marina, where we'll drive up a hillside road to the villa.

"The early light's beauty drew me here for the photoshoot. That campaign was one of the most popular we ever created. Leonie channeled Sofia Lauren. Everyone loved it," Lola shares.

"I adore it here. It brings such wonderful memories," my mother responds, as she gazes with affection at my father and squeezes his hand in hers. "When we came as part of our honeymoon, we knew this would be a regular spot for the two of us, then our family."

Morgan stares down at my mother with such love in his eyes. I want the same with Lola.

"Villa Sogno is a gem! You'll love it!" My mother continues dragging her eyes from my father to the approaching shoreline.

Moments later, we disembark and climb into the Mercedes-Benz G-Wagens my parents keep at the villa.

Roger arrived yesterday, so my parents and Malcolm ride in the SUV Roger drove down to meet us. Harris and Haley hop into the back of the one I drive with Lola in the passenger seat.

During the two-mile ride, Haley and Lola chat about their favorite places to eat while Harris and I chime in on our preferences. It's great everyone has claimed Lola as part of our clan. Being the first child to bring home a partner puts pressure on me for Lola to get along with my family. Both are important. So, I prefer we like each other, rather than to be at odds or merely polite.

All talk stops as we approach the gates to Villa Sogno. As Shelley said, it's a gem set atop the highest hill. An abundance of flowers covers the lower stone wall surrounding the base of the property at its perimeter. Their beauty welcomes you with vibrant colors and fragrant aroma. At once, your mind is at ease, ready for the dreamlike atmosphere.

We pass through the wrought-iron gates and climb further up the hill past terraces for gardens and lemon trees, seating and entertainment areas, and the swimming pool and cabana. The property covers several acres in a prime location, the real estate developer in me notes every time I arrive.

I pull into the motor court next to Roger to the side of the villa. Lola hops out first and claps her hands at the incredible cliffside views of Positano and the rugged Amalfi coastline this vintage retreat offers.

The sun sparkles on the azure waters of the Tyrrhenian

spread out into the distance. *Serendipity* appears but a miniature version as it floats amongst other boats below us. The marina, beaches, restaurants, and shops line the streets. Other villas, residences, and hotels pack the cliffs. The view is second only to the villa itself.

The staff greets us and unloads our belongings. I take Lola by the hand as I stride along the path lined with potted flowers and plants to the portico. A mosaic floor leads to the double wooden doors framed by terra-cotta urns with miniature lemon trees. Their citrusy scent reminds you of being in Italy.

Once inside, we walk the terra-cotta floors beneath colorful frescoes and dramatic Renaissance paintings. The spacious, airy main floor has the living room, family room, study, bathrooms, dining room, and kitchen among other rooms. Several outdoor areas including loggias and balconies are perfect for reading a book or watching the sea as the sun goes down. The second and third floors have twelve oversized bedrooms with en suite bathrooms and sitting areas. Villa Sogno has occupied this land for years, and my parents did a magnificent job of respecting its history while bringing it into the present. It has a modern Baroque style.

"This has got to be the most spectacular estate I have ever seen aside from Luc's ancestral chateau. The view... the fragrance... the peacefulness... the home... Words can't describe it," Lola exclaims.

"Darling, I told you you'd love it! You can stay as long as you want. Or come back anytime. Perhaps a part two of your photoshoot?" Shelley responds, pleased Lola is so taken by the villa.

"That would be delightful! Thank you!" Lola smiles graciously, then beams at me with her hazel eyes shining. "Yes?"

I squeeze her hand back and nod.

Damn. My throat too clogged with emotion won't vocalize an answer. Maybe I am a wuss after all.

LOLA

"What do you think of this?"

Haley and I stand in a fine watches shop perusing at a selection of vintage Rolex, Patek Phillipe, Audemars Piguet, and Vacheron Constantin. I know they're more than likely overpriced, being sold in a jet-set spot. But I couldn't find anything that resonated with me in New York at the auction houses or dealers.

Baz collects vintage timepieces, so I want to be sure it's one he'll cherish since it's the first birthday gift I've given him. A smile lifts my frown as I think of the future we can now have together.

His family is amazing and accepts me as one of their own brood. Yesterday, Morgan and I had a lengthy conversation about some ideas he has for Lola's Coterie. He's a no-nonsense, straight shooter. His wealth of knowledge comes from his years of running the retail stores division for STEELE to prove his mettle for the CEO role, as Baz is doing now.

The Steele Patriarch is a handsome, distinguished older man who's the mold for his sons. Their unmistakable similarities in height at six feet, four inches, black hair with Morgan's salt and pepper strands cut short, piercing gray eyes, and fit physique. Judging by his authoritative manner and Shelley's reactions to it, he passed his Alpha Dom gene to his sons, too. Funny how Baz's parents remind me of us. Except his father is more of a player being ten years older than Shelley!

I chuckle to myself just as Haley points to an Audemars Piguet that looks as powerful and dominant as Sebastian, and just as complex.

"That's it!" I proclaim triumphantly. "Thanks, Haley!"

"An extraordinary piece," starts the salesperson who presented us with the tray of watches. "This is the limited edition Titanium Grand Complication watch. Only three made. It features a 44 mm black clay bezel titanium circlet and croon posh pieces. The ceaseless almanac shows the durations in a fractional second chronograph, minute repeater, day, month, and year..."

He croons on and on about the watch. Magnificent, yes. But okay already. I pick it up with the soft, white gloves he provided to Haley and me before he allowed us to touch any of the fancy dancies. I use my discerning designer's eye to check for any imperfections. None found, I stop him.

"I'll take it. Please gift wrap it with the certification and original box, thank you."

"Of course, madame. Excellent choice! He will enjoy it immensely," he pauses to gaze at me. "It's $778,000 plus applicable taxes. How would you prefer to pay?"

As I said, this is my first gift to Baz. It has to be special. With all the lavish presents he's given to me, this ranks with them. Not a competition or you bought me, I owe you situation. Every occasion he glances at the time, I want him to think of me and his birthday celebration here. With that thought in mind, I happily hand the salesperson my Black AMEX Centurion Card.

"Sebastian will love it!" Haley claps gleefully before pulling me into a tight hug.

While they wrap the watch up, we stroll through the shop. So many beautiful pieces. We pause at the collection of diamond rings. They're all drool worthy.

"Your mother's ring is far superior to these trinkets," I tease. "I wonder why she's not wearing it now. I would wear it every day for the rest of my life if it were mine!"

Haley ducks her head, causing her hair to fall across her profile like a curtain. She refuses to glance my way. Then walks at a clipped pace to the other end of the store. Odd, I think. I hope I didn't sound nouveau riche. Elizabeth Taylor is an icon to me. Shelley's ring reminds me so much of Liz's many pieces. I follow Haley.

"Haley," I touch her arm as she stands in front of the cuff links' display case. "Please forgive my lack of tact—"

She cuts me off with a wave of her hand, "No, no. You did nothing wrong or distasteful—"

"Madame, your gift is ready."

The salesperson hands the discrete package to me with a flourish. I glance back at Haley, who has an expression of relief on her face. Despite what she said, I wonder if I didn't offend her.

We thank the salesperson and I link arms with Haley to walk a few streets over. We promised Shelley we would pick up Baz's cake from her favorite bakery in town. She stayed at Villa Sogno to manage the party decorators and caterers and the villa's staff for the influx of guests, some of whom will stay at the property.

As the head of STEELE International, Inc.'s STEELE Foundation that builds and manages attractive, affordable housing for urban, lower-income families, Shelley grew accustomed to throwing elaborate galas and events. She's the family's go-to party planner. Haley convinced me it's best to leave Shelley to her task.

Haley doesn't broach the subject of Shelley's ring again. Instead, we chat about what we're wearing tonight for the party and who's coming.

I agreed with Shelley we should invite their cousins the Jacksons and some of Baz's closest friends. Lucie Jackson, their family's Matriarch, is best friends with Shelley. As Baz explained the women spent most of their adult lives together when Lucie moved to New York alone. After meeting, they formed a closer bond than they had with their families. It remained strong even after marriage when they went from a shopgirl and a bartender to socialite wives of multibillionaires.

Lucie and Connor drove over from their nearby villa. Lachlan flew in from Aberdeen, Scotland, where Jackson Corporation has their UK headquarters. Baz sent the helicopter for Lucien, who's at his villa in Monte Carlo. Laurent, the youngest of the siblings, sent Baz a vintage lacquer humidor filled with Jackson Cuban Cigars since he's unable to make it. I give a silent thanks Lydie declined because of a business conflict.

Baz's Harvard roommate Scott and his wife Lauren with whom we had dinner several months ago at Le Bernardin in New York arrive later today. Some of his friends from Dubai and London flew in this morning for a few days. They round out the list to twenty.

"I've not met the Jackson parents nor Lachlan. What are they like?" I ask Haley.

At the mention of Lachlan's name, Haley stumbles.

"Are you all right? Did you trip on something?" I ask, glancing over my shoulder at the ground.

Haley pushes her glasses back up the bridge of her nose. Her eyes dart away.

"My foot caught on a crack," she shrugs. "Anyway, here's the bakery."

Again, she avoids my eyes and waltzes ahead of me through the door.

"IT IS such an absolute pleasure to see you again so soon, Lola. You look ravishing, luv," Porter Huntington kisses my hand as he greets me on the terrace.

Baz's party begins on a terrace one level below the villa. The view at night just as spectacular with the lights of the villas and hotels along the cliffside, the waterfront restaurants and shops, and the boats moored at sea or docked at the marina. The breeze is warm with the ever-present fragrance of flowers and lemons wafting through the air.

Shelley did a fantastic job with the transformation of the terrace from a lush verdant space where you can unwind to a festive party spot. The decorations, musical quartet, and bar service keep the guest in lively spirits. One of Lucien's two Positano restaurants catered the dinner and provided the servers. The cocktail hour gives guests time to arrive, Porter being one of them.

"You are too kind, sir," I respond with a dramatic curtsy.

"Sir?"

A shiver runs down my spine at the sound of Baz's commanding voice spoken against the shell of my ear. His unexpected closeness sparks sensuous thoughts.

"Really, Little Pet?"

"Aah… Correction… Fine gentleman," I babble.

"Better… However, you will correct yourself on your hands and knees later," he finishes with a nip to the delicate shell.

I cover my yelp with my hand and blush, avoiding Porter's quizzical gaze.

"Well, here's the birthday boy!" Porter claps Baz on the back in a bro hug. "And this gorgeous creature hasn't abandoned you, yet! Well done, old chap!"

"No, if I have my way, Lola will never leave me," Baz responds.

"Hey, hey! Happy birthday, man!"

The three of us turn towards the deep voice. A striking male strides over. He resembles a movie star. His fit, six-foot-four-inch frame topped by a face so incredible it takes your breath away. Blazing green eyes lock in on you as your gaze takes in his thick, dark brown hair slicked back from his chiseled cheekbones and strong jawline. The cleft chin adds to his Cary Grant vibe. Wow.

"Thanks, Lach. Glad you could make it after all," Baz grabs his outstretched hand as he pulls him into a bro hug.

"Of course! It wouldn't be a party without me," he teases, green eyes dancing in delight.

"Babe, this is Lachlan Jackson. Lach, this is my girl Lola," Baz introduces us.

"So nice—"

"Finally, I get to meet—"

We laugh at the exchange. In my periphery, I notice Haley watching Lachlan's every move. Hhhmmm. Now I know why her "foot caught on a crack" when I mentioned his name earlier. She's attracted to him. This family and their love lives. I'll suss out this one later. With hope faster than I have Leonie and Roger... But right now, it's all about my love life.

The evening is a success. Delicious dishes with ingredients fresh from the Tyrrhenian Sea dazzled our palates. Flavorful wines and Prosecco from their cellar fill crystal glasses and flutes. The camaraderie enhanced by everyone's love for Sebastian. My heart is full as I hand his gift to him. I have the honor of presenting last.

"Thank you, my love," he smiles as he kisses my lips tenderly.

The ambient lighting from clusters of torches set about the terrace sparkle in the gray depths of his eyes when he shreds the wrapping paper from the wooden, hinged box. Then widen in surprise at the magnificent watch nestled in the soft leather lining.

"Lola," he breathes out.

My insides melt at his awed expression. The sound of the others' ohs and ahs fill in the silence. I can only smile, thrilled that he's so taken by his gift. Perfect.

"Put it on already, Sebastian! Don't just slobber all over it," ribs Scott.

Baz laughs and slips his platinum Rolex Day-Date watch off his wrist. That little number is a beauty, too, with its unique meteorite and diamond-set dial bezel on a President's bracelet. He swaps one handcrafted piece for another. Then holds it aloft for all to see.

"This is an exceptional timepiece, Lola. I know my watches and this is—"

I press my fingertips to his lips as I shake my head.

"You are priceless to me, Sebastian. Nothing in this

world or beyond compares to you. Think of my love whenever you glance at the time," I respond.

Baz presses his lips together as his gray orbs moisten. He clears his throat and closes his eyes for a moment to collect himself.

I press my lips to his as I murmur, "I love you."

Baz exhales and opens his eyes to stare into mine.

I smile slightly, shaken by the intensity of his gaze, and raise my eyebrows in question. The room is silent and feels tense suddenly. I bite my lower lip as my nerves tingle.

Baz inhales deeply, then exhales slowly. He reaches into his pocket and slips off his chair to drop to one knee in front of me. My heart stops as I see a small, black box in his hand. My wide eyes fly back to his as my mouth drops open. No way!

"Lola. Marry me. I want it all with you, my love. And I want it now."

Before I can answer, Baz opens the box, takes my hand in his, and places the ring on my finger. Then, he pulls my hand to his lips to kiss the ring.

The ring that's his mother's diamond engagement ring I lusted after from the moment I saw it on her finger at La Goulue. Tears form in my eyes as I peer up to search the group for Shelley. When I spot her wrapped in Morgan's arms, she smiles and wipes tears of joy from her eyes. With a nod, she kisses her fingertips and blows it to me.

I'm so choked up with emotions I can only nod wordlessly in response to Baz.

"Words, Little Pet. I will have your words," Baz rasps just as full of emotion as I.

My pussy clenches and my nipples pebble as my Dom-cum-fiancé commands me.

"Yes, Sir," I answer, my voice low and throaty with love and heightened desire.

I smile through my tears of joy as my ice skating rink glimmers in the light.

SEBASTIAN

"**Y**ou are doing well, son. STEELE exceeding revenue projections for three consecutive quarters. Your impressive leadership of your division, the company, and of your younger siblings. Now, a lovely fiancée to settle you down—start on heirs to continue our legacy," my father looks at me pointedly with a cocked eyebrow. "You make your mother and me proud, Sebastian."

My gaze flicks to Lola, who's floating in the Tyrrhenian with Haley, Lauren, and Huntington's date. It's our last day in Positano. Our favorite spot to soak up the sun and to swim in the crystalline waters is at beautiful Fornillo Beach.

It's a little hidden secret in Positano on the Amalfi Coast. Unlike tourists, those in the know spend time here. The overcrowded hot spots hold less appeal. The small, pebble stone beach sits at the bottom of the plunging cliff face below the town with an unobstructed view of the sea. Two ancient stone watchtowers flank the ends of the beach. A bathhouse with lounge chairs and a restaurant provide amenities for beachgoers.

Shelley and Lucie shopped with their friends. While Malcolm and Lucien drove to a potential site for some new venture they plan. Roger, Harris, and Scott eat at the restaurant. My father, Connor, Lachlan, Porter, and I sit on lounge chairs near the shoreline.

"I had urged a more permanent alliance between the Jackson and Steele families. Sebastian and Lydie would have made an excellent strategic match," Connor harrumphs.

My Limoncello Gin Collins chokes me. Lachlan glances at me apologetically. My father releases a barely audible sigh.

"Our combined businesses would increase revenue and monopolize the markets," Connor continues blatantly unaware of our reactions and silence. "I told Lydie a marriage would be conducive to both company's bottom lines."

It's unbelievable he would voice such inane thoughts on the heels of my proposal to Lola. No wonder Lydie bowed out of attending my birthday party. She probably guessed Connor would say something ridiculous. More than likely, he berated her for not closing his deal.

"Father," Lachlan starts before my father or I can speak. "With all due respect, Lydie and Sebastian are not chess pieces. I say the best of luck to Lola for agreeing to stay with this guy for eternity!"

He raises his tumbler in a toast.

"Here's to a long life and a merry one. A quick death and an easy one. A pretty girl and an honest one. A cold beer—and another one! Cheers!" Chimes in Porter with his glass of Guinness stout.

"Agreed!" Morgan adds with his eyebrow cocked as he stares at Connor.

"What are we toasting to?"

Our heads pivot to see Lola and the girls approaching. Her curvy body makes the innocent pink seersucker bandeau bikini sinful. She stressed about wearing a swimsuit that wasn't too revealing since we were going to the beach with my father and Connor. But damn. There's not much she can do about her luscious body. Fuck. I'm thankful.

She slips onto my chaise and gives me a chaste kiss on the cheek. Then takes my drink for a sip.

"Aah... Refreshing! Cheers!" She laughs.

Everyone can't help but join her infectious happiness. Even Connor, who offers a small smile with a shake of his head. Undoubtedly wishing it were Lydie beside me.

"Oh, just wishing you and Baz the best. Really, you!" Lachlan roars heartily.

"Whatever, jerk," I throw my towel at his head.

Deftly catching it, he stands to offer it to Haley.

"Here, Haley. Your brother's aim is off. I'm sure he

meant to give you a towel to dry yourself off..." He adds rolling his eyes at me over his shoulder.

Haley fidgets with her bikini top, then blushes as she peeks up at Lachlan. She stammers a thank you and something about going to the restroom. Then rushes off, wrapping the towel around her body.

"Maybe there's hope, yet," murmurs Connor.

I shift my gaze to Lachlan, whose sharp, green eyes follow Haley's retreating figure, oblivious to his father's remark. Lola didn't miss a thing. She nudges me and goes after Haley. Lachlan must sense my stare because he turns to me with a smirk.

"Race you to the pontoon, lovestruck!"

Interesting.

We climb onto the deck and settle on an empty spot facing the beach. My muscles appreciate the hard swim since the only workouts I've done comprised wrestling Lola beneath me. I stretch my shoulders and turn to Lachlan.

"Spill," I demand.

Lachlan jerks his head in my direction, his eyes scan my face for my mood. I maintain a neutral expression. He knows he better tread lightly regarding my sister.

"What?" He rejoins.

"Do not fuck with me, Lachlan," I threaten.

Wasn't he just sitting there listening to my father speak of my leadership of my siblings? He knows me well enough after these years, I'm difficult on fuckers messing with my kid sister.

"Sebastian, fuck off."

"Ciao, ragazzi."

Two leggy Monica Bellucci lookalikes stand over us. Their minuscule bikinis barely cover their abundant assets. One reaches for Lachlan's cheek and the other grins at me.

Lachlan and I glance at each other. A nod sets our squabble aside to avoid a bigger one if Lola sees a woman flirting with me. Without hesitation, we dive back into the azure waters.

Lola waits for me at the shoreline. I grab her by the waist and toss her into the surf, diving in after. I've got a Siren to conquer. Lachlan and his bullshit can wait. For now.

* * *

"I WAS WONDERING why Haley acted weird when I mentioned your mom's engagement ring the other day. I thought Haley reacted to my comment about the size of the diamond."

Lola tells me as she stares at her ring with a broad smile.

"I told them when we had our first dinner date it reminded me of Elizabeth Taylor's famous Ice Skating Rink Ring," she continues. "You realize I'm a huge fan of hers since she inspired me to create Lola's Coterie after seeing her in *Butterfield 8* as a young teen."

"Yes, babe, I noticed," I answer with a smirk. "You've

told me about your fan worship of your idol only a million times..."

"Whatever, Baz," she retorts with an eye roll and smirk of her own.

I spank her ass, admiring the way her tanned flesh jiggles and reddens. Then pull her squealing onto my lap. We're alone aboard *Serendipity* on the fourth deck. The party is over, and everyone heads back to the actual world from Villa Sogno. But my dream rests comfortably in my arms.

"I'm glad you like it," I tell her as I lift her hand up to watch the diamond sparkle. "It's a family heirloom passed to the first son to his first son for generations. My mom recognized one day it would go to my wife. When I asked her for it, she told me she's glad it's you."

Lola spins around to face me with tears in her eyes. Her arms wrap around me as she buries her face in my neck. Her body trembles with each sob.

"Shhh, please don't cry, my love. Tell me, what's wrong?" I ask as I rub her back to soothe her.

Lola's cries continue unabated by my soft caresses. My heart breaks as my mind jumps to the loss of her parents. It must be hard to not have at least one parent for thirteen years. The death of both at the same time is unimaginable.

Now, it's her wedding. Lola won't have her mother to help her pick out a dress or her father to walk her down the aisle.

My parents understand her situation and told me they

would step in. I'm not sure how Lola will react. But I expect she'll be gracious.

"I miss my parents, Baz," she whispers.

"Ba—" My voice catches in my throat. "Babe, I know. I know."

I pull away to lift her face so her eyes meet mine.

"No one can replace your parents or their love for you," I gaze into the depths of her sad hazel eyes. "My mother told me to let you know she'd love to help you select your dress and plan our wedding. My father said he'd walk you down the aisle."

She speaks. But I kiss her lips softly to stop her.

"You don't have to decide now. Just realize they... Hell, we all love you and want our wedding day to be one of joy. Whatever you want. However you want it—"

I stop her again so she hears me correctly.

"But... We're getting married after your Dubai boutique opening."

A beat passes. Lola's emotions play across her face like an exaggerated cartoon character. Sadness; confusion; shock; indignant. The firecracker is lit. I hold my breath for the bomb to detonate.

"Hold on... Did I hear you correctly?"

I pull my lips over my teeth and raise both eyebrows with a nod. 10... 9... 8... 7

"Whaaaaat?" She screeches.

Lola momentarily forgets her tears as she jumps to her feet and glares down at me. Her hands on her hips and her feet in a fighting stance. Lola is ready to rumble.

"You cannot be serious, Sebastian! That's only eight weeks from now!"

She pauses to stare at me for verification. I nod again. She throws her hands up and paces the deck, muttering. Every few steps, she turns to look at me and I nod.

"Lola. Did I not say 'and I want it now' when I proposed to you?" I remind her. "What did you think I meant?"

"Oh, no you won't! You will not turn this around on me, Sebastian Steele!" She growls.

It's difficult. But I hold back my laugh at the petite pistol starter. A neutral expression drops over my features. I have to win this negotiation. Funny how it always comes down to a deal with us.

First at LEVELS New York, I had to persuade her to allow me as her Dom that night. After the initial meeting for her expansion plans, she gave in to my offer of teaching her the fine points of a D/s relationship. Her move into my penthouse instead of a rental proved a very satisfying repartee on the kitchen banquette. I intend to win this bid, too.

"Lola, why forestall the inevitable? If it is the work, hire as many planners as you need. Unless you are not sure…"

She stomps her feet. Then shadow boxes while growls and curses fall from her lips. I can't contain my chuckles any longer. Lola has exploded.

My sides hurt from laughing so hard. Lola dives on top of me, knocking me back onto the sunbed. We wrestle and she ends astride me. Her fiery core grinds on my dick. Oh,

I get it. My Petite Seductress thinks she can use her feminine wiles to change my mind.

Not going to happen.

"Baz, baby, you realize I love you and have absolutely no doubts about us. None... what... so... ever," she purrs, circling her hips with each word. "So what is another six months, hhhmmm?"

My dick protests. But I lift Lola off of me and sit up straight with her beside me.

"No. You had your way for three months. Unnecessarily I might add since I had done nothing wrong," I cock my head at her as I drop the gauntlet.

A beat passes as she glares at me, and I raise my eyebrow at her. 10... 9... 8... 7... 6

"I cannot believe you're only giving me two months to prepare for our wedding, Sebastian!" Lola wails as she flops back on the sunbed.

Success!

LOLA

*S*ebastian knows, and I do. He didn't persuade me to have our wedding so soon. I want it as much as he does. Well, he was eager to put a ring on it. And boy did he with this super stunner! I laugh to myself as I wave my left hand in the air à la Beyoncé.

"Okay giggly goo, we have work to do you know."

I glance across the immense table strewn with bridal magazines, legal pads, colorful stickies, fabric swatches, and other wedding prep items at Shelley. Haley was correct. Leave Shelley to her world of party planning. She's a firm taskmaster and the epitome of organization amid craziness. And this right here is insanity… eight weeks. No, seven weeks, three days to be exact. Good grief.

Not to mention my upcoming trip to LA for a few days; finalization of the Abu Dhabi and Dubai boutiques' collections and pre-opening party tasks; everyday responsibilities of running my company. Oh, and the redesign of my penthouse that Baz recommended I turn into a corporate apartment since I'm moving in with him to "our penthouse where you belong." He wasn't having it when I told him my plan to stay on Sutton Place so we could savor the moment I move in after the wedding. "Not happening, Lola!"

Which is exactly why I took him up on his suggestion to hire as many planners as I need. With Shelley spearheading the operation, Baz is right, it won't take long.

Haley, Leonie, two wedding planners, and I sit in Shelley's home office in her STEELE Tower duplex penthouse on the fifty-seventh and fifty-sixth floors floors. If one considers three generously sized rooms an office. An anteroom for two assistants' desks, a sitting area, and a bathroom, a conference room, and her inner sanctum with en suite bathroom comprise Shelley's version of a home office. She runs her private activities from here and her foundation work from that office on the executive floor of the corporate office.

She and Morgan live on the top two floors. Baz and I are below. So it's convenient. Some women may find living so close to their mother-in-law a nightmare. But Shelley is not the meddling type. Plus, I don't mind the company of an older woman in the absence of my mother. Not that Shelley is an old woman. She's a sexy vixen! And it's obvious Morgan can't get enough of her.

Blair has a conference call she can't reschedule and Billie joins us via video conference from Las Vegas.

"Right! Return to Earth, girl. Time is precious," Billie teases me in her Southern drawl.

"*Oui, Chérie.* Get it together. Tick Tock..."

Leonie chartered a private jet to New York as soon as I told her about my engagement. In her excitement, she dropped her iPhone and lost the FaceTime call. I tried calling her back, but didn't get an answer. My consternation ended when she called me from the tarmac at Le Bourget Airport to tell me she'll see me in a few hours and to have bottles of Dom Pérignon Rosé Vintage 2005 Champagne on ice. That was last night. Now, it's time for work.

"Yes, yes, sorry," I smile apologetically for my wandering thoughts.

"I understand your distraction, which is why you have us to keep you focused," Shelley smiles warmly. "With all you have going on you need not get bogged down in the minutiae. We'll narrow the choices to a few based on what you prefer. Then you make the big decisions like your dress, bridesmaid dresses, colors, invitations, flowers, venue, food, cake. Sebastian will handle your honeymoon. Sounds good?"

This is a monumental relief. It's my wedding, so my involvement is paramount. But I acknowledge I can't do it all. With a light heart, I return Shelley's smile.

"Thank you so much! You do not understand how stressed I've been in just a few days," I respond. "Eight weeks to plan a wedding..."

Haley laughs.

"Girl, you must know by now when Baz wants something, nothing will stop him!"

"You speak the truth!" We crack up.

Tap. Tap. Tap.

Sergeant Shelley raps her Montblanc champagne gold rollerball pen on the surface of the table. Once all eyes fix on hers, she clears her throat.

"Ladies, shall we begin?"

"Yes, ma'am!" We salute.

The other night Baz and I discussed key decisions for the bridal party. We prefer an intimate number of our closest loved ones. Leonie as my maid of honor paired with Malcolm, Baz's best man. Haley as my bridesmaid paired with Lachlan, his best friend. Then Blair and Billie paired with Roger and Harris, respectively.

Leonie and I spoke of her concerns about being with Roger if he were a groomsman. But I assured her Baz understood and chose Malcolm as best man since he's the oldest brother of the three. She's still nervous to interact with Roger. So, I told her I was fine with Giovanni as her plus one. My BFF's happiness is just as important as mine.

Haley was just as pensive as Leonie when she agreed to being my bridesmaid. I want to include her since she's my future sister-in-law. Also, I genuinely adore her. We've grown close over the last five weeks. She confessed to me she's had a crush on Lachlan since she was a kid. But not ready to move beyond family friends. Particularly since he's Baz's best friend—her ultra-protective eldest brother. I promised her I won't mention anything to Baz. Not that I'm keeping secrets from him. Rather, I'm maintaining her privacy.

For their dresses, we let them choose gowns in the wedding colors and that complement their bodies. They vary in height, but all curvy. So, what flatters most.

"Ooh, Haley and Billie! A designer friend of mine just sent photos of his latest formal dresses to me!" Leonie exclaims. "Here. Scan through these. I saw a few that could be *parfait*! Billie I'll text message the link to you now."

She nods while Haley eagerly swipes through the photos on Leonie's iPhone. Their ebony and mahogany heads bob yes and no over the mobile.

"These two would look great on you," Leonie states.

"And this one... Ooh, no that one for you!" Haley adds.

She turns to me and says, "Leonie and I will go over the dresses with Billie and Blair. Then show you our selections by tomorrow."

"Excellent!" Shelley claps. "Now for you, Lola. What are you thinking for your gown?"

My gown is a whole other story. I know I want three— for the ceremony, dinner, and after party. I'm not the princess type. Instead, the mermaid or sheath styles suit me best. I like a little vavavavoom action. Baz will love to see my curves accentuated by the flattering fit.

"I have little time for a custom gown," I lament with a sigh. "I never dreamed of my wedding dress like most little girls. I always sketched the lingerie trousseau! But I want a special gown so I can see Baz's eyes light up when I stand at the top of the aisle."

Shelley nods, "Don't you fret, darling! One of the most important things I learned by being Morgan's wife is a billionaire's influence goes way beyond the norm! I'm sure Baz told you whatever you want, you will have, unquestioned."

She and the planners make notes to book appointments starting tomorrow with designers in New York City in person and virtually for Paris. She's as determined as me to find memorable dresses.

As for the colors, Baz and I are strong, bold individuals with a flair for the unexpected. Our palette has to represent us well. I'm partial to orange and fuchsia. Hues on the same side of the color wheel work well together. Their undertones will act as a seamless gradient rather than two contrasting shades. I opt for neutral supporting colors to ensure the vibrant shades pop wherever they're featured. A striking, winning combination of a dynamic couple and their wedding colors.

The guests are the next item to tackle on Shelley's master to-do list. My side comprises Luc, Leonie, Blair, Billie, Starr, and some friends I've gained in the industry— about forty. Baz, thus the Steele clan, has a much larger list. It accounts for our wedding being the family's first. The need to invite family, friends, society members, business associates, and political figures increases their number significantly. I understand and leave it to Shelley to decide. Truly, the only person I need there is Baz.

As though we drew her in through telepathy, Shelley's assistant announces the invitation company rep's arrival. Shelley uses them for her most important events since their unparalleled designs are exceptional. We spend the next hour discussing my preferences and reviewing options. Then plan to provide her with the final number tomorrow.

Sergeant Shelley maintains her Double VIP list by guest category for such occasions as an unexpected party or event. So a day's notice poses no problem.

"The venue is up to you, Lola," Shelley starts. "STEELE has the best in the city, well honestly anywhere. But do you have a preference?"

I remember how STEELE42's beauty impressed me when I attended a charity gala there with Baz the first month we met. It's one of their award-winning entertainment venues that specializes in weddings, parties, and galas for society's best both in the United States and abroad.

It was a bank. When STEELE refurbished it, they strove to keep the integrity of the space with the original columns, teller windows on the sides, the vault, and more original details. I was most awed by the vaulted ceiling that twinkles in the dim lighting with a replication of the constellations. Since STEELE42 is one of Baz's favorite venues, I ask Shelley to plan for that space. She smiles delightedly and agrees it's perfect.

"Now, on to the most appetizing part!" I shimmy in my chair.

My girls laugh. But don't deny it. Women after my heart.

The food and drink tasted so divine at the gala I ask for Lucien to cater the wedding. For the cake Shelley insists we use her good friend Sylvia Weinstock. She's *The Queen of Cake* whose delicious confections cross the lips of high society, celebrities, or anyone who can afford her chefs d'oeuvre. Who am I to argue? I can't wait for the cake testing set in two days. Yum!

Flowers play a major part in our relationship. The endless vases Baz sent to my suite at STEELE Monte Carlo, the everyday bouquets he sends to me at the office and home, the exquisite Sterling Silver Roses he used to entice me back. They're small tokens that bring a lot of happiness. I want the venue decked out in them. Not one to waste, we'll donate the flowers to the nonprofit children's hospital for which Baz is a patron. Shelley's florist joins us virtually to discuss ideas. We schedule an in-person appointment before the cake tasting.

Shelley confirms what Baz mentioned to me the other night. The official press release announcing our engagement and upcoming wedding will be distributed in the morning. She needed the details we worked out today to complete the announcement. She warns me from her experience with Morgan to expect paparazzi, the nosy, and jealousy. Suddenly, it becomes oh so real. Despite what may come, I wouldn't have it any other way.

"Here's to an exceedingly productive day, Ladies!" Shelley toasts with more of my favorite Dom Pérignon.

"Cheers!" We chorus as we raise our Waterford Crystal flutes filled with the tasty champers.

I send a silent toast to my parents, who I know watch on with love.

* * *

"Shelley is wonderful! You're lucky to have such a nice mother-in-law, *Chérie*," Leonie clinks her flute to mine.

We parted from Shelley and Haley with hugs and kisses a few hours ago. Now, we're ensconced on a terrace at my STEELE Tower penthouse sipping more Dom P. Hell, we're more than sipping, we've finished two bottles.

I wanted her to stay here. But she declined, preferring to stay at my Sutton Place penthouse to "get a true feel for the space." I believe she wanted to avoid being in the same building as Roger. After I told her he's in Paris, she agreed to spend time here after the wedding prep session. Her expression went from guarded to relieved. Now, it's blissfully happy from the bubbly.

"How are you and Giovanni?" I ask since she hasn't mentioned her on-again-off-again lover after I extended her plus one to him.

She stares beyond the glass surround at the city view for a moment. Then shifts in her chaise to face me.

"Oh, *Chérie*, I just don't know if I want to—"

Abruptly, she sits up and swings her feet to the floor, staring with wide eyes over my shoulder. Surprised by her reaction, I turn to figure out the cause for her concern.

Roger!

Fuck!

He's striding over to us with that intense gray-eyed gaze of his pinned on Leonie. I hear her quick inhalation of breath and turn to face her. Her normally golden-caramel complexion is ashen. Her mouth opened in shock.

What. The. Fuck.

I jump to block his path to her. He will not hurt my best friend again. I don't give a damn what I promised her.

"Stop!"

I put my hands up and glare at Roger and at Sebastian, who I notice stands behind him.

"Leonie doesn't want to see you. So, please go," I tell him. Then forcefully I add, "Now, Roger!"

He blinks away from Leonie. His eyes cut to mine. I don't waiver before him. I meet his stare with my own hazel eyes blazing.

"Roger, bro, you need to slow down," Baz tells him, putting his hand on Roger's shoulder to pull him back. "You're freaking them out. Not cool, man."

The air is tense until I hear movement behind me. I peer over my shoulder to see Leonie putting her shoes back on and gathering her things. She's a bit wobbly from the champagne, but determined to leave.

"Lola, I have to go. I'll call you later," she whispers in French.

I know she's upset because she rarely calls me Lola.

"No!"

We jump around to stare at Roger who raised his hands palms forward in surrender. His stare less intense, but still focused on Leonie.

"Please, Leonie, I just want to speak with you. Just for a

moment... Please," he beseeches in a voice rough with emotion.

Collectively, we hold our breath for Leonie's response. She sighs again, but nods her head in acceptance. I start to speak, but she shakes her head. I sense she's trying to control her emotions, so I give her the space she requests. The glare I give Roger would set him on fire. Sebastian turns to Leonie and asks if she's comfortable speaking with Roger. She nods, again. We leave them on the terrace and head to the living room.

"What the fuck, Sebastian?" I round on him once we're out of earshot. "I told you Leonie was here! Why did you let Roger come over without telling me? You said he was in Paris!"

"Whoa, babe," he responds with his hands up in supplication. "He told me he needed to make things right with her before our wedding. She wasn't answering his calls or text messages. He had no other choice."

I narrow my eyes at him, not assuaged by his answer.

"Fuck that! If Leonie wanted to speak with him, she would have answered. To put her on the spot is unacceptable," I retort.

"I'm sorry. I should have told you so you could have prepared Leonie. But he's sincere. Trust me. I know my brother. He won't hurt her. Besides, they're adults and capable of working out their love life. We did, right?"

I give it to him. Baz is so good. He easily flipped the conversation to make me focus on us.

"Okay, you're right. But she's my best friend. I will

allow no one, and I mean no one to cause her pain. She's a kind, loving woman who deserves respect. I don't care if Roger is your brother. He better not fuck up, Sebastian."

He enfolds me in his muscular arms, pressed firmly to his chest, and kisses the top of my head.

"He won't, my love. He won't."

Roger better not, I think to myself as I allow Baz to lead me to the sofa.

I tuck my legs under me, angled to see through the glass wall onto the terrace. On the chaise I vacated, Roger sits forward with his elbows resting on his knees, his hands clasped together. Leonie returned to her chaise, perched on its edge with her hands folded in her lap. At first they stare at each other, apparently waiting for one to speak. Roger breaks the silence.

We can't hear what's being said. However, Leonie's response to Roger's lengthy utterance has her hands moving rapidly in agitation. Roger shakes his head, speaking again. They exchange words for some time before Leonie nods and stands, a sign she's ended their conversation.

I rise, too, but Baz grabs my arm to stop me from going onto the terrace.

"What?" I ask, throwing him a glare over my shoulder.

"Wait a minute, Lola. Give them a moment," he responds, then points his chin in the terrace's direction.

Roger rose to stand before Leonie much as I blocked him earlier. He cups her face in his hands, then tips her face up towards his. Leonie's body shudders in response when he slants his mouth over hers in a scorching kiss.

Well, damn.

The intensity of their passion makes me blush and turn away. Baz pulls me onto his lap, and I can't help but peek at them again. Leonie clutches the front of Roger's shirt in her hands as she swoons from his embrace. Roger's mouth moves to trail kisses along her jaw and throat as he murmurs words only she can hear. She trembles, then pulls away, shaking her head while her hands no longer hold him, rather they push him away. Startled by her abrupt reaction, Roger loses his grasp on her. Leonie spins around, scoops up her belongings, and rushes to the door, swiping her face. Coming upon Baz and me, her eyes widen and she covers her mouth on a sob.

"*Merde*," she whispers.

"Leonie!" Roger calls to her as he strides through the open door. He too pauses when he sees us and wipes a hand over his face with one hand and attempts to adjust his pants from the not so discreet enormous bulge at his crotch.

"Fuck," he mutters.

No one moves until Leonie tells me she's leaving as she hastens to the front foyer. I follow her this time, not letting Baz stop me.

"I'm coming with—"

"*Non, non... Je vais bien, mer—*"

I cut her off, not believing for a moment she's fine. I grab my handbag from where I left it on the entry table before I turn to tell Baz. He and Roger stand watching us. Baz nods in understanding. Roger shakes his head dejectedly. I purse my lips and take Leonie by the hand as the elevator doors open. She squeezes my hand in response as she smiles through her tears. I understand exactly how she feels: wanting him, but not wanting the pain.

"Time for something a little more potent than Dom P., *oui?*"

Leonie's snort of laughter starts us on a fit of giggles.

She'll be just fine.

LOLA

*I*nstead of returning to Paris, Leonie continued on with me to Beverly Hills earlier than we planned for some much-needed girls' time before business meetings start.

The night she spoke with Roger on the terrace, we went to my Sutton Place penthouse. She admitted she still loves him, but is afraid of being hurt again. She assured me he had said nothing untoward. She was overwhelmed.

While we drank shots of tequila, Roger called and sent text messages she refused to answer. Until his last voice-mail when he threatened to come over to see her in five minutes. She promptly called him back.

He apologized for upsetting her. His agreement not to pressure her and to give her space made Leonie feel better. For the sake of peace at the wedding and out of respect for Baz and me, they decided to hold off on any further conversations.

I wonder at his reaction when she arrives with Giovanni. Two Alpha Males, one lioness…

"Lola… Hey girl… Lola?"

Once again, Starr's gentle voice pulls my mind from rampant thoughts distracting me from my meditation session.

Focus, Lola! Like Baz said, Leonie and Roger can figure out their relationship without my interference. Well, at least I hope so.

I shake my head to clear my ruminations. Then open my eyes to see not only Starr's angelic face, but Leonie, Haley, Blair, and Billie peeping at me. My cheeks redden as I laugh in embarrassment.

"No judgement… But again, Lola!" Starr's dimples appear as she joins in.

The first stop to jumpstart our girls' time was to Starr Light Fitness & Wellness Beverly Hills for yoga and meditation classes. The concentration vinyasa requires prevented my mind from wandering. Instead, I tuned into my breath and the sequence of challenging asanas Starr used in the flow. The vigorous physical and mental workout was just what I needed as opposed to the slower pace of a Hatha class. Starr's dynamic teaching style made it fun.

After a few minutes in the steam room and a quick shower, we head to lunch at nearby Crustacean Beverly Hills. The modern Vietnamese fare specialties include delicious seafood that's the perfect light meal after yoga.

We settle on the gray suede seats at a banquette near the

Walk on Water. The path runs from the front door through the restaurant between tables. Interspersed with wood and weight-bearing glass, the water below appears to offer a glimpse of the ocean's depths. Aside from the cuisine, the path is the eatery's highlight.

When the server arrives, we order An Sum—Crustacean's version of dim sum—to share and salads for our meals. I haven't spoken with Starr in a few months, not since her return from the ashram in India.

"Have you spoken to Malcolm Steele, yet?"

"No, we keep playing phone tag. Right now he's it!" She laughs. "I was unreachable in India, then traveled a few more weeks. He was away on business followed by holiday in Italy."

I forgot I hadn't told her about my engagement. That's where Malcolm was recently.

"Oh, well, you see…"

Exaggeratedly, I brush my left hand against my cheek. I removed my ring for the class and locked it in the safe at the center. Now, Starr's eyes bug out of her head as the light bouncing off of my rink nearly blinds her.

"Holy shit! Are you serious with me right now? That's humongous!"

Her quiet calm, namaste, om, center your mind blown clear out of the water. We giggle at her reaction. The server places our drinks on the table with a smile, enjoying our mirth.

"Here's to the woman who got her man!" Starr raises her sparking water in a toast.

I smile graciously at my friends as they raise their glasses to my happiness. Just as glad they like one another. My little circle expands nicely.

"*D'accord*, where do we go for our Girls' Not Out?" Leonie asks.

"The latest hot club to open is the Remy West Hollywood," Billie who knows all the West Coast happenings responds. "Their It thing is dancers bound by ropes Shibari style suspended from the ceiling. It has a BDSM vibe if you know what I mean."

She giggles and lifts her eyebrows up and down.

Leonie and I glance at each other, then snort. If only she knew we're All Access Global members of LEVELS. But then I remember Patrick Rockett is AAG, too. She's probably been there plenty of times with him. Holy shit we're all kinky! I laugh uncontrollably.

"What did I say?" Billie asks, confused.

"Oh, Billie, nothing! It's aah… How do you say… graphic!" Leonie giggles. "Let's meet at eleven in the lobby. *Oui?*"

Billie nods, accepting Leonie's save.

"What are you wearing?" Haley asks. "I have a black mini dress or a light blue sequin romper."

Fortunately, the conversation switches to a safer topic. Blair chimes in on how well the light blue would contrast with Haley's gray eyes and ebony hair. Meanwhile, Leonie's eyes still twinkle with glee.

"What the—"

I screech when enormous hands grab me from behind as I walk into my Penthouse Suite at the STEELE Rodeo Drive, an iconic property at Wilshire Boulevard. As a scream rises in my throat, a hand covers my mouth and the other wraps around my waist locking my back to a massive chest. Fuck me!

"Surprise, Little Pet."

My legs give out. But for Baz's arm banded about me, I would have crumpled to the floor. My pulse races as the adrenaline pumps through my veins. My armpits tingle and my palms are damp. I close my eyes.

Once Baz lowers his hand, I take a deep inhale. Which serves to push my breast into his hand that slipped inside of my dress. My breath catches when he pushes the lace of my bra to the side and tugs my nipple into a turgid nub. My pussy clenches.

My head lolls to the side as he plants open-moutheded kisses along my neck. A nip followed by a long suck forces a hiss from my lips. His new habit of marking me with "Baz Love Bites" starts my juices to collect in my core. The combination of the nipple tweaks and mouth assault drives me wild with lust. I rub my thighs together, hoping for some kind of relief.

"You cannot cum until I give you permission, Naughty Girl," Baz chastises me as he plunges two thick fingers past my G-string into my wet, aching pussy. My inner walls greedily suck the invading digits deeper into my channel.

Blatantly disobeying Baz, I rock my mound against his palm in sync with his thrusts as he finger fucks me.

WHAP... WHAP... WHAP WHAP

"Naughty... Naughty... Naughty Pet," Baz punishes my pussy with slaps that coat his hand with my juices. "You want me to put you over my lap to spank... this... round... ass."

He couples each word with a thrust of his groin against my bottom. I writhe and moan my response. My orgasm is so close, so close. I'm delirious with need.

"Aaaahhh, Sir... Please may I cum..." I beg pitifully.

Baz flips us around, braces my palms against the suite's door, and kicks my legs apart. The sound of his zipper opening makes my pussy quiver in anticipation. I don't have long to wait.

The force of his thrust as his enormous dick slams inside of my pussy lifts me to the balls of my feet. My calves strain to hold me in position.

His pistoning strokes intensifies as I feel him expand in size. His snarls and grunts trigger my release as I wail with relief. Baz effortlessly lifts me from the floor with one hand hooked under my thigh, opening my core to his brutal thrusts. My pelvis slams into the hard, wooden door. I fear the hinges will break from his power.

I love it! I slap my palm against the door as I throw my head back.

"Yaaaasssss!"

"You want my fat cock to fuck your tight, juicy pussy,

Naughty Pet," Baz grunts in my ear. "Your pulsating heat around my dick. Take it! Take... every... fucking... inch!"

My pussy spasms with wave after wave of my third orgasm. I can't even think straight anymore. I can only respond with grunts of my own.

"Uh... Uh... Uh... Uh!"

My inner walls clamp down hard on Baz's dick. He roars and jackhammers my pussy. His thick length swells, stretching my channel to the point of pain. His tip hits my cervix and I cry out.

"Fuuuck!" I scream. "Oh... Fuuuck, Baaazzz!"

His cock unleashes ropes of creamy cum deep within my core. Bathing my pussy with his seed.

Another orgasm rocks me. I'm too spent to utter a sound. I lean heavily against the door and let Baz pump into me until every drop of his cum empties within my womb.

"Lolaaaa... Fuuuck!"

My body shivers at his primal call. My mate claims me again.

* * *

SEBASTIAN WAS NOT THRILLED I left him after hours of making love to go to a club. But, hey, he came two days early... literally.

My girls and I sit in the VIP area of the Remy West Hollywood. Billie was right. This is a hot spot. The Shibari tied dancers hover inches above the crowd. The colorful silken cords artfully swathe their long, toned limbs. They blindfolded some. While others stare boldly at the revelers. The dungeon-like atmosphere adds to the BDSM theme. It's a nice attempt at a sex club. But it doesn't compare to the LEVELS locations.

I chuckle as I lift my Manhattan to my lips, thinking of how discerning my sexual tastes are now. Eleven months later, and I'm no longer the novice ashamed of my sub inclinations. I proudly embrace my Independent Woman and submissive.

RAWR, Sir!

"Time to get our groove on one more time, Ladies!" Blair announces as she pulls Billie to her feet. "Let's go. No time to decorate the banquette!"

She's right. We've been dancing and drinking for the past three and a half hours. It's about that time. Besides, I have an even hotter fiancé in bed waiting for me. Girls' Night Out is fun. We enjoy each other's company and our drinks. But, hey... I finish the last of my cocktail and join my friends on the dance floor. One more shimmy and I'm out.

The DJ's music and callouts have everyone bouncing to the beat. I throw my hands up and shimmy in my gold backless, strapless mini dress. It's one of my latest designs for the evening wear collection. A band at the top connects to the front panel that circles around my rear, dipping dangerously low to the crack of my ass. The chain-mail material shimmers in the lights. Leonie already requested one for a movie premier she's attending in a few weeks.

I shy away from a guy who's dancing too close only to bump into another one who's behind me. I slide away. But he slips his hand around my waist. Turning to face him, I peer up into Baz's smirking face. The devil!

He bends to reach his lips to my ear as he whispers, "I will wrap you up in my silks, Little Pet. Then fuck you as you swing from the ceiling."

Damn!

Baz twirls me around and with bent knees, he grinds his pelvis into mine. The sensation of his hard dick against my soft mound breaks goosebumps across my skin. We move as one for a few songs, glued at our groins. Our foreheads pressed together. My arms draped around his neck with my fingers gripping his hair. His hands clutch my hips possessively. As the next tune begins, he whispers in my ear.

"I am not staying. Just reminding you what you are missing, Little Pet…"

With his mission complete, Baz strides away. He leaves me standing with my mouth hanging open, pussy wet and wanting. Torn between my man and my friends, I hesitate.

"Go! Be with your boo!" Billie laughs and shoos her hands at me.

Leonie, Haley, and Blair nod, giving me the thumbs up as they continue to dance.

I only hesitate a moment. Blow kisses to them. Then rush after Baz, pushing my way through the pulsating crowd. He's so tall I can spot him ahead of me. I slip my hand in his and he smiles down at me.

"Excellent choice, Little Pet," he whispers against my ear.

Excellent choice indeed, I smile.

"*W*e're a family and we support one another, Lola."

Morgan says to me with a fatherly smile that makes my heart soar.

Baz and I just arrived at Meridian Teterboro the deluxe FBO at the private jet airport. It surprised me to see the entire Steele clan other than Roger aboard. I guess he'll meet us in Abu Dhabi since he's in Paris.

Blair and Billie left two days ago to coordinate with the STEELE teams. Leonie and Luc flew in yesterday. Ever the supermodel, she wanted to acclimate to the environment before interviews and the red carpet.

An unexpected fitting for my wedding dress delayed my departure by two days. However, Blair and Billie assured me they would handle everything in my absence. I'm confident all will be well. They've proven themselves more than capable with the New York and Las Vegas boutique openings.

"Morgan, thank you so much! Everyone being there means so much to me," I smile warmly at him.

Shelley stands from where she sat with Morgan and takes my hand, "Lola, darling, come! Haley and I must brief you on the latest updates."

I cast a glance over my shoulder at Sebastian. He and Morgan chuckle as they salute Sergeant Shelley. I can't complain. My future mother-in-law has morphed into my fairy godmother. She meets all of my needs even before I voice them. When Baz and I return from our honeymoon —destination still unknown to me—I'm taking Shelley and Haley on an in-laws' getaway to thank them for all they've done. They more than deserve it.

Settled at the conference table, Haley's fingers fly across the keyboard of her laptop. Without moving her gaze away from the screen or slowing down, she nods in greeting.

"Right on time! You can view the latest program on these tablets. I'll make adjustments to the master file from my laptop. Take a moment to review it. Then we can go into details."

Haley is a genius. She created a cloud-based software program and coordinating app to compile each component of my wedding into one user-friendly, easily accessible and updated organizer with virtual assistant. Shelley insists Haley patents and sells licenses of it.

I agree. Brides, planners, vendors all will benefit. The Steele family knows how to generate more wealth!

"Haley, this is fantastic! You've done so much more

since I last saw it," I exclaim, slapping high five with Shelley. The girl is good.

Shy Haley blushes as she pushes her glasses up the bridge of her nose. Well aware of her brainiac intelligence. But not one to boast, she gives a self-deprecating shrug.

We jump into wedding planning mode for the next few hours. We set the date for a week after Lola's Coterie Dubai opening. Baz gave into an extra week to give me time to address any unforeseeable issues. He refuses to let post-opening situations delay our wedding. He won't let me forget canceling the Cabo San Lucas getaway he surprised me with after the Las Vegas party. I more than made up for it by treating him to a spa day. I gave him the best happy ending ever!

Once the press release went out, my publicist moved into overdrive funneling appropriate interview requests and television appearances with local, national, and international media. The gossips' tongues can't stop wagging. They proclaimed I snagged the most eligible and lusted after bachelor in the world. Some implied my non-existent pregnancy spurred the quick nuptials. Others speculated I married him to benefit Lola's Coterie.

Social media accounts and bloggers devoted to us popped up overnight. The monikers *Couple of the Century* and *SeLo* trend on Twitter and Instagram. Major topics: What's Lola wearing today? *SeLo* Spotted! Lola's Baby Bump! *SeLo* Breakup Countdown! Whether the posts are true or false, the likes, reactions, shares, and comments are off the charts. Celebrities and the wealthy are uppermost in people's minds.

Baz doesn't have a social media presence other than the STEELE corporate handles. I have mine on Instagram to post behind-the-scenes photos and my activities and on Pinterest some boards for my favorite foods, recipes, and inspiration. Nothing particularly personal, just enough to keep people interested. My follower count rose from hundreds of thousands to millions. The comments now include snarky haters. Funny enough, my loyal fans defend me. I stopped reading them. Better for my wellbeing, Starr told me.

My marketing team had to add three people to handle the increase in demand for Lola's Coterie social media and public footprint. The vice president told me the number of Google Alerts increased over two hundred percent and the languages are no longer predominately English and French. The Asian and South American countries increased their coverage of Lola's Coterie, Baz, and me. Marketing monitors Baz from a business standpoint. But when I started dating him, I set up alerts to keep track of his name and what he was up to in the news. #NotAStalker

Shelley's warning was correct. And every day it increases. It's sheer madness!

"I'm sorry I missed your last wedding ceremony dress fitting, Lola."

Haley's voice brings me back to the planning. Another Shelley prediction rings true for my wedding dresses.

Each of the designers we met with were eager to create

my dresses even with less than eight weeks to finish. I narrowed them down to Mr. Valentino, Reem Acra, Naeem Khan, and Amsale. After reviewing the sketches, I fell in love with the exquisite long-sleeve, lace mermaid gown with a cut-out in the back by Mr. Valentino. The elegance, drama, and sensuous lines made it the clear winner for my ceremony dress.

For contrast at the reception, I chose the Reem Acra sleeveless, deep-vee sheer mermaid gown overlaid with hand-stitched flower appliqués and a silk satin belt with a diamond brooch. It harkens to our theme of abundant flowers.

In the end, I opted to alter dresses from my evening wear collection for my rehearsal dinner and post-reception party dresses. Baz made the point with all the photos picked up by media. It would be an organic way to promote my new line.

Mr. Valentino and his team brought my gown to New York since I couldn't make it back to Paris for the last fitting. It's just as well since the dress needs to be there for my return from the UAE. No worries of it going missing. It's now safely ensconced with my other dresses in my new temperature-controlled walk-in closet in our STEELE Tower penthouse.

"No worries. I'd rather everyone see it when I walk down the aisle," I wink at Haley.

"I'm sure you look stunning," Haley smiles.

"Oh, indeed! She looks divine!" Adds Shelley, who I was

happy to have there for her support. "All three gowns and her rehearsal dinner dress are sensational!"

"How do you feel about your bridesmaid dress?" I ask Haley.

Leonie already told me she's ecstatic about her Elie Saab custom creation. Since he has a studio in Paris and is her good friend, he made her gown specifically for her matching our color palette. It's a dreamy strapless column of silk organza layers in various shades of the orange and fuchsia hues.

Haley also chose one of his designs. Her halter-top column dress follows the same layers as Leonie's.

"I love it! So light and moves beautifully," she exclaims. "Very dreamy and romantic."

Blair's and Billie's dresses suit them perfectly and match the color theme. Blair chose an orange empire gown that accentuates her lithe figure. Billie opted for a fuchsia gown with a draped neckline and body skimming silhouette.

Baz and the groomsman will wear classic, bespoke tuxedos in black with boutonnieres.

Our updates move to the RSVP list. The final total of three hundred people may seem astonishing. But it's not out of the ordinary, Shelley assures me. She whittled it down from the original four hundred after Morgan and Baz added their lists. As long as everyone enjoys themselves and the delectable dishes Lucien crafts and the yummy cake Sylvia Weinstock makes, I'm happy.

Now, I'm sketching some exclusive designs for the

Beverly Hills boutique. The anchor store location at STEELE Galleria Rodeo Drive is optimal. Spread across three levels in the open-air mall, two above ground facing the Drive and the interior courtyard and one below grade with a glass wall and double doors opening onto the courtyard. Passersby from all directions can access the entrances.

The windows will display the glitzy gowns and luxury lingerie perfectly. The opening is just in time for awards season. With Leonie's advertising campaign highlighting the evening wear, I'm positive celebrities and Hollywood's elite will order the custom creations.

Baz was smart to wait for my boutique to fill the retail space. Lola's Coterie Beverly Hills will be the only luxury lingerie store on Rodeo Drive. The lack of competition combined with my unique pieces and our joint marketing teams working to hype up the launch will ensure significant exposure and traffic. Thus impressive revenue gains. My man, the future CEO of STEELE International, Inc.

I lean across the armrests to buss his cheek. Startled, he jumps in his seat, his hands fumble with the tablet he held.

"Sorry, baby!" I giggle.

I can't resist his gorgeousness—I'm engaged to a stud. I pull his face to mine and kiss him silly. Once we come up for air, I rest my forehead against his with a sigh. I love him so much and cannot wait to be his wife, Mrs. Sebastian Steele. Independent Woman or sub, I'm old-fashioned. I intend to take his name, Lola Steele.

"I love you, too, babe," he murmurs, so attuned to my

attitude he knows without me speaking a word my state of mind.

For the rest of the flight, I cuddle against his side in total bliss.

* * *

"Luc!" I cry as I rush over to hug him. "I've missed you so much! I have a lot to tell you."

We're having lunch at one of the hotel's restaurants at the STEELE Abu Dhabi complex. I left Baz in our Rulers' Suite so I could have some private time with Luc. I know they only tolerate each other for my sake. My wish is for them to be more friendly. They're both important to me.

Luc's been my support for over seven years, stepping in as a mentor and father figure after losing my parents. Fortunately, now that he's put a ring on it, Baz has relaxed his stance on Luc secretly crushing on me. My Captain Caveman may still growl, but at least he won't bite.

"Oh, *petite chérie*, it's so good to see you!" He responds holding me in a tight embrace. "I guess as much since I saw a certain article in the *Financial Times* about a pair dubbed the *Couple of the Century*. Or perhaps it was the *International Herald Tribune*? Oh no, it was *The Asahi Simbun*."

Laughing, we settle at the table, and I hold out my left hand to him. His smile is genuine as his eyes brighten with unshed tears.

"*Félicitations pour vos fiançailles!*" He says. "Steele is a man of honor after all. Are you truly happy, *petite chérie*?"

I nod enthusiastically, *"Bref, je crois que nous sommes, sans l'ombre d'un doute, amoureux!"*

No doubts whatsoever. Baz and I love one another, I smile happily. Luc nods, satisfied with my response.

Sitting up, I reach for his hands. Surprised, he lifts his gaze to mine.

"Luc, for over seven years you have been my rock. A staunch supporter of my business endeavors, financial guru, and father figure," an emotional hitch catches my words.

I clear my throat to start anew.

"Luc, it would lift my spirits if you would walk me down the aisle and sit in the front row beside the chairs reserved for my parents' memory. Then at the reception, thank guests for coming and give the toast in place of them. I would also love if you would dance with me."

The unshed tears well in his eyes, turning the stunning dark blue orbs black with unbridled emotion. Luc squeezes my smaller hands between his larger ones and nods, too emotional to voice his answer.

We sit quietly for a moment. Then he squeezes my hands again. His emotions back in check.

"Steele couldn't find a bigger ring to profess his love for you, *petite chérie*? Ah, the cheapskate!"

Luc's joke instantly shifts the somber mood to a light one. I snort loudly and cover my mouth with my hand. My ice skating rink dazzles Luc with its brilliant light.

SEBASTIAN

*M*y woman stuns on the red carpet. The paparazzi flashbulbs shimmer against the metallic material of her mauve, one-shoulder, ankle-skimming gown. When she walks, her toned legs peek from behind a hip-high slit that meets the ruching on one side of her waist. The strappy sandals that match the color of her dress make her petite frame taller. Shimmery metallic eye makeup stresses the golden flecks in her hazel orbs. For added drama, her glam squad crimped her hair, flowing down to her waist in a raven arrow aimed at her luscious ass.

In celebration of this opening party, I gifted Lola a pair of pink diamond chandelier earrings to grace her swanlike neck. Never jaded, she whooped and smothered me with so many kisses she had to reapply her lipstick and I had to wash the dusty pink color off of my face. I can't wait to see my dick tinged pink when as she promised to "thank you properly later, Sir." My length twitched.

I step back to allow the cameras full access to her beauty. Lola poses and smiles radiantly. My ring shows big and bold on her hand, placed sensuously on her hip. Turning her megawatt smile in my direction, she beckons me like the Petite Seductress I first nicknamed her at LEVELS New York that fateful night twelve months ago. Unable to resist her call then or now, I stride over to take my place by her side. A gentle kiss to her upturned pouty mouth seals the deal.

Yup. *Couple of the Century*.

"Lola!"

We pivot to see Leonie stalk the red carpet towards us. Another irresistible beauty. *The Lion* commands the crowds' attention without even glancing their way. Their shouts of her name only elicit a brief smile as she's determined to reach her best friend.

Leonie captivates in a burnt-orange sequined one-sleeve, fitted gown that reaches one knee then flares at the other like a mermaid's tail to angle down to the top of her foot. Her long legs make quick work of the red carpet in open-toe stilettos. Each sway of her hips reflects the light of the incessant flashbulbs. Her signature mane piled in a bedhead tousled style.

A flicker of irritation shoots through me when I see she's accompanied by Giovanni Mattei. For my younger brother's sake, I'd hoped Leonie would arrive alone. I glance around, but don't see Roger. Good, I'll warn him.

"Lola! *Chérie*! How marvelous you look!"

The BFFs hug and the paparazzi start their blitz again. Now that she's caught up to her friend, Leonie affords the press her full attention. She and Lola pose together and apart, ensuring their best angles. Meanwhile, Mattei and I stand to the side. I shoot a quick text message to Roger to let him know not to freak out and to maintain his cool. Mattei is no chump, so it could get ugly real fast. I await Roger's response when I see the three dots show he's answering right away. As expected, he's pissed, but promises not to start shit. Good.

Lola calls to me, and I join them for more photos. Fortunately, Mattei keeps his distance and doesn't join us in the shots. As I stand between the two of them, the crowd goes wild. In my periphery, I see Roger walking on the red carpet with Malcolm, Harris, and Haley. I call them over to get in the pictures. The rarity of all the Steele siblings in one frame will make for excellent social media posts and traditional media coverage.

I don't hesitate when I refer to all of us as Steeles, since I have a feeling Roger won't let Leonie wander much longer. After his drunken confession to me last month, it's only a matter to time.

As they approach, I feel Leonie stiffen and shift to move away. I won't let her. I tighten my hold on her waist. The professional in her won't cause a scene, so she relaxes at my insistence and beams for the cameras. Roger doesn't hesitate to stand beside Leonie and place his arm around her possessively. He didn't even acknowledge Mattei's existence. Now fully assembled, the flashes nearly blind us as the paps go crazy for the best shots.

"Luc!"

Lola calls to her mentor as she waives him over to us.

I've cut him some slack. Particularly since Lola is officially mine. He smiles at her with the affection of a proud father. So that helps. I'll do anything to make Lola happy. I clap him on the back and invite him to stand on Lola's other side. Luc nods in acknowledgment of my olive branch and we pose for more shots.

"Lola, Leonie, Sebastian, Luc, you have news crews to speak with," Billie says as she steps behind us.

"Thank you, Billie! You look gorgeous!" Lola says enthusiastically.

And she does. Lola has some attractive friends. But no one compares to my love. I slip her hand into mine and follow Billie to the awaiting crews. Lola winks at me. Her eyes twinkle brighter than the pink diamonds that adorn her ears.

Just inside the boutique, I spot my father deep in conversation with some prominent businessmen from the UAE. Their wives peruse pieces from the collections while engaged in conversation with my mother. They exemplify a power couple I hope to replicate with Lola.

We finish the interviews that interspersed questions on Lola's Coterie collections and rapid rise to success to details on our upcoming nuptials. Lola answered the business-related questions with gusto. But deftly avoided substantial responses on our personal lives. She kept it simple with we're in love and look forward to our future together.

The less fodder given to the media, the better. As with most old money families, the Steeles like media coverage to further our business gains, but prefer intimate aspects to remain private.

"Honey, how are you holding up?"

My mother materializes next to me. I smile down at her and wrap my arm around her shoulders. She's an inch taller than Lola and fits under my chin with her heels on.

"Good, thanks Mom. How are you? You've been so busy with our wedding plans. Thank you so much," I squeeze her close.

I love my mother dearly. She's grounded since she didn't grow up wealthy and made sure we were, too. She always has our best interests at heart and loves my father passionately. Shelley's the epitome of a dedicated wife and mother. I hope that Lola and I can have an amazing family, too.

"Now you know I don't mind at all. You're our first baby to marry. We have to be sure everything is perfect! Your father and I are very proud of you."

She pauses as her eyes mist with tears. She takes a deep breath and I squeeze her again. Her words make even the Dom in me blink back tears. I strive to make my parents proud of me. It's so good to hear it from both of them.

"We're very pleased with Lola, too. She'll make an excellent wife for you, smart, independent, loving. She's not after your name or wealth. She reminds me of myself," she laughs. Then adds, "Although I was a shopgirl, and she owns the shops!"

We crack up over her joke.

"Yes, well, each generation improves upon the prior one," she smiles as her gaze lands on Lola who's charming a group of guests, mainly men.

My mother must sense me bristle because she laughs and pushes me in Lola's direction.

"Go! You and your father are so alike! Possessive Alpha males," she shakes her head.

"—the truth! You have the figure for modeling your designs—"

"What did you just say?" I demand, moving between Lola and some git flirting with her.

He backs up, locking eyes with me. He's about my height and broad. Not that it matters. I'll still knock him on his ass.

"You... Come with me."

I hear Malcolm. But don't see him since I refuse to take my gaze from the fucker. Without waiting for his response, Malcolm takes him by the arm, and Roger flanks him. Quickly, they move him through the clusters of guests.

A small hand slides along my back. Instantly, I'm soothed by Lola's touch. I take a deep breath and pull her into my arms, nuzzling her hair. Her seductive perfume fills my nostrils. She's a balm for my agitated psyche.

"Thank you for protecting my honor, Captain Caveman," she murmurs, suppressing a giggle.

I chuckle against her hair. Then flip it because I can, and Lola loves it.

"Are you being a smartass, Naughty Pet?" I demand, pulling back to pin her with my no-nonsense Dom stare. "You know, I can always take you to the stockroom to administer a proper spanking for your sass, Little Shopgirl."

A shudder runs through my sub-cum-fiancée and her pupils dilate. The tip of her tongue darts out to moisten her lips as her eyes scan the guests, wondering if they overheard. When they alight on mine, I nod with a smirk. Right.

"Okay lovebirds, I need Lola."

Another man trying to monopolize my woman's time. With a sigh, I relinquish her to Luc, who laughs good-naturedly at my obvious annoyance.

"Don't worry, Steele, I won't keep her long. There are some business associates who want to meet her. You're welcome to join us."

I decline again, mending fences with Luc. I'll give him a chance to earn some of my trust. I leave them to it and network with other guests.

"Do not even think about it."

Haley jumps when I come up behind her and take the sheer negligee from her hands. Her face reddens and her glasses slip down her nose.

"Dammit, Sebastian! Stop being a jerk!" She retorts, shoving her glasses back in place, glaring up at me. "You're not my father, you know!"

I have to hold back a laugh. She's been repeating those same words to her four older brothers all of her life. If I wasn't so protective, I would feel sorry for her. Oh, well. It is what it is. Which reminds me.

"What's going on with you and Lachlan?" I ask, narrowing my eyes at her.

Haley sputters, and her blush deepens. She's so flustered she can't speak.

"Sebastian! Are you pestering your sister?"

Again Shelley materializes out of thin air, this time to admonish me. For a moment, I'm transported back in time to when Lachlan and I were sneaking out of my room to go to a party. Unbeknownst to us, Haley who was forever tagging along followed. But tripped on the rug right outside of my parents' room. They woke from her cries and reprimanded Lachlan and me.

"No. She doesn't need a piece like this see-through negligee," I answer, then glance around and hold up a more modest piece. "This is better."

Haley snatches it and puts it back.

"Bugger off, Sebastian!"

My mother and I watch as she storms off. Then we glance at each other and laugh. As she dabs the corners of her eyes, my mother speaks first.

"Leave your sister alone, Sebastian. She's a grown woman, Big Brother."

"Yes, Sebastian, let her be."

Lola slips her arm around my waist as she stares up at

me with a raised eyebrow. Outnumbered, I acquiesce... for now.

"Fine. Let's get back to the party. Shall we?"

I offer my mother and Lola my arms to escort them to where my father stands talking to some people Lola should meet. The light in Morgan's eyes when he sees my mother approach is like glancing into a mirror. I feel the same way about Lola.

She's the light of my life and I'll forever be happy to have her at my side.

SEBASTIAN

"*Spasibo* for the trip, Steele. Now let's see if I can knock you back to the Big Apple, *da?*"

I have more pent up energy than release options. Sparring sessions with Borya is just what I need.

It's been a week since the Abu Dhabi opening. Rather than returning to New York, we spent some days in Abu Dhabi. The usual post-opening work preoccupies Lola. More media coverage interviews, photoshoots with Leonie in the desert and around the city, in-boutique private parties for the city's wealthiest women. Lola's exhausted.

Leaving me to my own devices...

Borya flew in three days ago to Abu Dhabi, then traveled with us to Dubai. We train twice a day before my workday starts and in the evenings before dinner. I can't let my mind wander to my blue balls when I have the fist of a giant Russian coming towards my face. Lola thinks my slightly crooked nose that broke in a fight as a teen gives me a more edgy and less pretty boy appearance. Well, I don't need for it to happen again. Borya would smash the bones to bits. Forget crooked. He'd decimate my nose.

Roger flew back to Paris after Abu Dhabi to avoid drama with Leonie and Giovanni. Everyone else stayed and worked from the STEELE offices in Abu Dhabi and now Dubai. It's good for employee morale to see New York flagship executives in the branch offices. Morgan especially inspired them since he stays in New York or travels to London and Paris.

We've had meetings, lunches, and dinners with our respective teams and top-level leadership. It's good to hear their feedback and address their concerns in person. One of my goals as CEO is to spend three days in each office every month.

Tonight is the opening party for Lola's Coterie Dubai, so Borya and I hit the mat early. I'll have time to grab a protein shake, take a shower, and get dressed. Lola's booked until ninety minutes before we leave. My poor baby. She'll get to unwind soon.

"Privet, mal'chik!"

Whap Whap Whap!

An unrelenting succession of blows to my torso reminds me to refocus or risk permanent body damage. I pivot to the right and land a few punches to his flank. Quick to recover, Borya roundhouse kicks at my retreating form. I fake left and jab right. The action of our session is intense. We go at it for an hour before we stretch and cool down.

"Good job, Steele. You should join me in a double MMA match, *da?*" He claps me on my back when we head out.

"Nah. Gotta look pretty for my girl," I respond, reminding him of his taunts to me about my obsession with Lola.

A grimace appears on his face, the closest to a smile that his lips can create. Followed by a deep, rumbling sound that's his version of a laugh booms around the boxing gym at STEELE Dubai I.

"*Veselaya*, Steele!"

We leave the gym floor and head over to the juice bar for our shakes before returning to the hotel.

"See you tonight. Maybe a girl will find you pretty too, Alexeyev," I smirk, patting his cheek.

"*Veselaya*, Steele!" His laugh follows me as I stride to the elevator bank for the Rulers' Suites.

As expected, our suite is empty. I checked my mobile on the elevator. Other than business communications and a voicemail from my mother, I didn't hear from Lola. I open my calendar app and filter today for her schedule. She's in a meeting with a textile vendor who specializes in fabrics by local artisans. Impressed by the samples he sent, she was eager to meet him. She considers the cloth incorporated into the UAE collections a friendly gesture of inclusivity and respect for the culture. The STEELE UAE cultural affairs team agreed.

I shoot a text message to tell her I'm back. Then strip out of my hoodie and shorts. I close my eyes, as I duck under the spray from the multiple shower heads and tilt my head back, bracing my hands on the marble wall. The warm water sluices down my rock-hard body. The ache in my muscles from the strenuous workout lessens. I drop my head and roll my neck, getting the kinks out.

Thoughts drift to Lola—my luscious beauty. I groan as my dick lengthens, and the girth thickens. What I would give to bury myself balls deep in her tight, wet heat. I groan again when I think about how we haven't made love in days. Days... Damn.

My hand slips from the steam slick wall and slides down between my eight-pack abs, the well-defined ridges taut under my fingertips. The texture of the trail of hair leading from below my navel to my groin contrasts with my bare skin. I suck in a ragged breath at the vision of Lola naked on her knees before me with her eager mouth open wide to receive my ready rod. Her hooded eyes bore into mine, filled with lust.

They're her full lips that wrap around the base of my dick, not my hand, as she takes me down her throat. My ten inches fill her cavity. Her gag reflex spasms sending a zing to my heavy balls. I squeeze my eyes tight, not wanting to lose the vision before I can blow my load.

A cool breeze touches my warm back. A small hand covers mine. My eyes fly open, but the steam fills the glass enclosure, hampering my sight. But my sense of smell recognizes my mate—Lola. Here in the shower with me, not in my head.

"Please allow me, Sir."

Her soft, wet curves meld to my back as she slips her

hand under mine. I drop my forehead to the slick wall and brace myself on my forearms for what promises to be a leg wobbling experience.

Lola does not disappoint.

As she trails nips followed by kisses along my back, one hand massages my sac and the other grips and tugs my turgid cock. The rhythm she sets alternates between gentle and painful, keeping a delicate balance that has me close in moments.

"Fuuuck… Lola… Shit, that feels so good," I grunt as my palms slap the wall.

A pinch to my tip sends me rocking onto the balls of my feet, driving my hips forward to pump against her hand. Lola senses how close I am to release, so she speeds up her pace.

"Lolllaaa," I roar as my dick jumps in her hand and ropes of creamy cum splash onto the wall.

My hips move on their own since my mind left. Lola snakes her hand that was on my balls up my torso to pinch my nipple.

Dayummm!

My cock hardens again and I grab her wrists to pull her in front of me, facing the wall. I bend her ninety degrees and put her hands in place of mine on the marble. I grip my dick and line it up to her slit, then check in with her.

Lola flicks her long raven hair over her shoulder and lifts her heated gaze to mine. She licks her lips and nods. Without breaking eye contact, I slam into her tight pussy. Her inner walls greedily suck me in deep. Lola mewls and lifts to her toes, bowing her back to grant me better access.

I grip her curvy hips tightly and piston into her, chasing our climaxes. I ride Lola and she bucks against me, meeting each of my thrusts with her own. The sound of our wet skin slapping against each other reverberates in the shower.

I bend my knees and tilt her body back towards mine to change the angle. As I hit deep within her, Lola screams her release, her pussy clenching my dick like a vice. I roar and continue my onslaught. She writhes wantonly, demanding more. With unimaginable joy, I give her what she wants—whatever Lola wants, Lola gets.

Our bodies continue the feral dance of the ages until I wrench three more orgasms from her core and she's begging me to stop. Only then do I release my load with a roar of her name. Sated at last, we slide to the floor of the shower. I pull Lola between my still quivering thighs and wrap my arms around her, nuzzling her hair.

"Thank you, my love," I murmur.

Lola's contented sigh makes my heart swell more than her lush body makes my dick grow.

"I'm sorry I've been so busy, baby," she says as she shifts to peek at me. "I promise after this opening, I'll make it up to you at our honeymoon—destination still unknown to me... Okay?"

"I know, babe," I respond sincerely. "You know I respect your company and your work ethic. I want you to succeed and achieve your goals."

I lift her chin to kiss her lips softly, then continue, "How could I want less for you than I do for myself?"

"Thank you, my love," she whispers as she smothers me with heartfelt kisses.

"FUCK YOU, YOU SLIMY DICK!"

CRASH!

Roger? What the fuck is going on!

I spin around to see him and Mattei exchanging blows in the middle of the fucking party. The opening night party for my woman's boutique in a STEELE property. Not happening.

I beat security to the fray. Malcolm and Harris grab Mattei as Luc and I grab Roger. Roger struggles against our hold as does Mattei who tries to shrug my brothers off. Roger and Mattei are bulls in a lingerie shop that knocked over two mannequins.

Suddenly, they stand stock-still when my father storms over. He is pissed.

All eyes turn to Morgan, including that dickhead Mattei. He must have done some shit for Roger *The Responsible* Steele to lose control. And at a highly public event— never. That goes against every cell in his physiology.

"You will cease this outrageous, infantile behavior at once and apologize to Ms. Lewis and her guests. Then leave. Do… you… understand?" Morgan issues his edict.

His Dom stare knocks Roger and Mattei down several notches. In fact, they're below ground by the time he finishes his chastisement of them. Everyone else stands in silent awe of his power.

Roger gains control first and turns to seek Lola out in the crowd gathered around. I too scan for her, hoping she's not as upset as I imagine. I spot her standing between my mother and Leonie. Haley, Blair, and Billie stand near them. All have shocked expressions on their faces. Damn.

Mattei tries to walk to them. But Malcolm puts his hand on his chest to stop him since Roger headed their way already. Mattei has the sense to back down.

"Lola, I apologize for my poor behavior. Please forgive me," Roger beseeches.

With grace, she nods her head and accepts his outstretched hand. Her eyes meet mine and I offer her a consoling smile to which she nods.

"Mother, Leonie, I ask for your forgiveness, too," Roger says to both of them, but his eyes lock on Leonie whose amber gaze shies away.

I can see his shoulders rise and fall on a disappointed sigh in response to her reaction. Then, he turns to the guests and apologizes to them before he excuses himself from the event.

As he passes me, I squeeze his shoulder to offer my support. He nods without breaking his stride.

Next, Mattei apologizes. The Italian nobleman exudes charm as he bows to the women and to the crowd. His accent laid on thick as he issues his apology like a statesman at the Colosseum.

He takes Leonie's hand in his and kisses it with a flourish. She won't meet his eyes either. Then he speaks in her ear. But she shakes her head. Denied, he pivots and struts out the door without a backwards glance.

Good.

"Now, let us return to the celebration of Lola's Coterie Dubai. As a token of STEELE International, Inc.'s gratitude for welcoming our newest partner to the UAE, we gift each guest twelve hundred Emirati Dirhams for use at her Dubai or Abu Dhabi boutiques."

Morgan speaks into the ensuing silence while holding Lola's hand in unification.

The crowd cheers and raises their glasses in salute.

"Enjoy!" Lola exclaims as she beams at the guests then up at Morgan.

Crisis averted, I join them as my mother slips her arm around Lola and whispers in her ear. Lola nods and turns to me.

"Well, as they say, 'all publicity is good publicity.' Your name in people's mouths is what you want. So don't worry," I say.

"Oh, I know. I'm more concerned about Leonie."

She thanks Morgan, gives me a hug, then excuses herself to go talk to her best friend. Leonie looks shaken, but brightens when Lola reaches her. They speak briefly and head to a private corner.

"Talk to your brother, Sebastian. Or I will. He knows better than to act boorishly, particularly at one of our business functions."

I follow Morgan's directive and step away to call Roger. He answers on the first ring.

"Sorry. That was a shitshow Lola did not deserve. Does she really forgive me? Are you going to kick my ass?"

He sounds like a wreck, so I don't add to his ill ease.

"Yes, and no. Dad gave the guests gift cards. What the fuck happened?" I ask.

Roger clues me in on the details. I tell him I understand. But remind him to keep his shit together in the future. Then tease him about not being responsible. Roger grouses over the gibe. We hang up with a reminder about breakfast.

LOLA FELL ASLEEP QUICKLY after all of tonight's drama and the long week she's had with both boutique openings. I watch, mesmerized by the woman I love more than life. Thankfully, her sleep is peaceful.

I bend over my sleeping beauty and inhale her natural scent, a combination of her lavender bodywash, shampoo, and luscious Lola.

"Sweet dreams, princess," I whisper into her hair.

Then leave the bedroom, closing the door softly before I exit the suite.

Until tomorrow, Mrs. Steele. Until tomorrow.

LOLA

*M*mmhhhhmmm.

As I waken, last night replays behind my closed eyelids. Roger, his face flushed red and intense stare locked with unrestrained anger on Giovanni before he punches him in his face. Giovanni falling backwards into mannequins that crashed to the floor. Gio charging Roger. Then Sebastian, Luc, Malcolm, and Harris holding them apart. The guests shocked speechless. Hell, I froze, too.

Thank God for Morgan. He prevented a catastrophe. I felt sorry for Roger and Giovanni after he castigated them. Oh, well. The gift cards… Brilliant.

Poor Leonie was too distraught. I had to console her. We still don't know what caused the battle of the Alpha males. Ever the professional, she refused my offer to go back to the hotel. *The Lion*—brave woman—continued on until the end.

I agree with Baz about any publicity being good. Still, I shudder to read the event's report from my marketing team.

This bed is so comfy, I could stay in it all day. In fact, that's exactly—

My fingers brush over cold sheets and not the hot torso of my fiancé. Sitting up, I notice Baz's side of the bed remains untouched. Weird.

"Sebastian?"

I call as I sit up, holding the sheet to my bare breasts. A scan of the bedroom proves it empty, and the door shut. No sound comes from the bathroom or walk-in closets. What the fuck?

As I reach for my mobile on the nightstand, my gaze lands on a single Sterling Silver Rose next to a white linen envelope—Baz's personal stationery. Curious but hesitant, I open it and pull out a handwritten note.

My Dearest Lola,

I know how strongly you feel about tradition, so I cannot wake with you held tightly in my arms this morning. But every morning after this one, the sun will rise with you wrapped in my loving embrace.

Each hour until I see you walk down the aisle to me, you will receive one Sterling Silver Rose. As these twelve months have shown, my love for you knows no bounds. Tonight we become one, Mrs. Sebastian Steele.

Love your Husband & Dom forever,
    Baz

My vision blurs as tears fill my eyes. Several times I have to swipe them away as they fall before I can finish reading Sebastian's note. Is he serious? The aisle? Tonight? He can't possibly mean we're getting married in Dubai now and not next week in New York.

With trembling hands, I reach for my mobile and tap his number.

"Good morning, my love."

I can only sit on the line as my sobs increase just from hearing his deep voice so full of love for me. Lightheaded, I fall back onto the fluffy pillows, clutching the mobile to my breasts.

"Lola? Baby? Are you all right?"

I take a deep, cleansing breath. Then bring my iPhone back to my ear.

"Fuck… I think she's fainted."

"Whaaat?"

"Call Mom! She'll get her!"

"No way, bro! You scared her off."

"Shut the fuck up, Harris!"

A vision of the Steele brothers worried running around in circles reminds me of the Three Stooges and their antics. Except there's four of them. Hysterical laughter bubbles out of my mouth, followed by uncontrollable snorts.

"Fuck! Now she's laughing hysterically! Lola! You're freaking me out now, babe!"

More suggestions filter through the mobile. And my snorts turn to cries of joy. We're getting married tonight!

"LOLA, darling, you had Sebastian and the boys ready to run to the suite! Sebastian was beside himself! He told me, 'damn tradition!'"

Shelley laughs as we sit in the STEELE Dubai I Spa waiting for our manicures and pedicures to dry. After a full day of beauty treatments, they have pampered us into silky smooth, ultra-relaxed, glammed-up dolls. Just what I needed after the shocks of last night and this morning.

"Yes! Luc called me hyperventilating!" Chortles Blair. "I thought we'd have to ring for the medic to resuscitate them!"

I give her the eye since she's been quiet about their status. She giggles.

Leonie, Haley, and Billie join in on the laughter. We're loud as our voices echo around the nails room. But it doesn't matter since Baz reserved the entire spa just for us. He wanted me to unwind with my girls and his mom undisturbed.

In fact, he bought out the entire hotel for our three hundred guests. They were in Abu Dhabi for the last two days at the SAD hotel and arrived here this morning. He didn't want me to see anyone and become suspicious. So he kept them there, being entertained with an assortment of activities. So clever!

"Pardon me, Ms. Lewis."

One of the spa aestheticians stands at the door. A Sterling Silver Rose wrapped in white silk held in her outstretched hand.

As promised, Baz sends a single rose each hour. I smile happily and beckon her to bring it to me. It smells divine. I add it to the vase filled with four others I've collected since we arrived.

"How romantic," sighs Billie with a wistful look in her big green eyes. "I'm so happy for you!"

"Shelley, you raised a good man," Blair chimes in.

"Thank you, Blair," Shelley responds and lifts her glass of citrus-infused water in toast. "May you all marry your romantic, good man!"

She smiles and glances at each of us. But she winks at Leonie, who blushes and averts her eyes. Which makes me wonder if Shelley knows about Roger and Leonie's *coup de foudre* relationship.

"Ladies, we hope you enjoyed your spa sessions! You seem sufficiently rejuvenated! The restaurant awaits you!" The manager announces.

"Excellent, right on schedule," Sergeant Shelley responds. "We'll have your bridesmaids' luncheon. Then you can rest for two hours before the glam squad arrives."

My heart leaps with joy.

"I cannot wait to become Mrs. Sebastian Steele. The countdown continues!"

Shelley smiles and the girls cheer.

The nail technicians return to help us remove the toe separators and to add moisturizing oil to our cuticles. We chat about my upcoming nuptials as they finish. Then head to our private changing rooms.

I STEP into the lobby first and spin in a circle, feeling carefree in my bohemian-style silk-crepon mini dress in a cornflower floral pattern. The plunging vee-neckline draws the eye to the flattering waist cutouts and flowy tiered skirt. I swept my hair up in a messy bun to showcase the lace-up open back. Paired with flat sandals and a straw top-handle bag, it's a breezy relaxed outfit. Perfect for my bridesmaids' luncheon.

"Don't you look so cute!" Billie declares as she joins me.

"Thanks! As do you, lovely!" I respond admiring her silk halter-back maxi dress. The yellow color makes her green eyes pop.

Once everyone appears, we head to the restaurant. As we walk through the lobby, I recognize some of our guests. They stop to offer their congratulations and express their gratitude for an exciting trip. I thank them for joining us in our celebration and tell them we'll see them soon.

Shelley introduces me to some guests unknown to me. Everyone from prominent politicians to business tycoons, to celebrities eagerly extend their best wishes and delight at being a part of our nuptials.

The five-star treatment continues when we arrive at the restaurant and sit at the best table overlooking the dazzling water. More guests stop by to introduce themselves to me. The buzz is palpable. Shelley was correct again—our wedding is the most talked about of the decade.

"I want to thank all of you for all that you've done to help me with my wedding and for being such a supportive mother-in-law and friends," I tell everyone after we place our order. "I have special gifts for you. But I didn't know this was happening now. So they're in New York. I promise to give them to you as soon as I return."

Just as I finish, an attendant appears at the table with a basket filled with the gifts. How in the world? I swing my gaze to Shelley, who claps her hands and smiles in excitement.

"Oh, darling! We knew your wedding would be here all along. So we planned for everything to be in Dubai. Plus, your bridesmaids' gifts!"

My eyes tear and I wave my hand in front of my face to stop the flow. Damn! I'm so emotional recently.

"Thank you! Thank you!"

I rise and hug Shelley. Then hand out each of the gifts. The girls oh and ah over the diamond drop earrings that they'll wear to complement their dresses.

"These are absolutely exquisite! Thank you!" Blair exclaims hugging me fiercely.

"OMG! They're the most gorgeous things I own!" Billie adds as she circles her arms around both of us.

A teary Leonie holds her pair up to sparkle in the light. They're bigger than the others since she's my BFF and maid of honor. Instead of one drop, hers has three.

"*Merci, Chérie,*" she whispers as she hugs me close.

The last gift is for Shelley. Baz had to help me with hers since it's hard to shop for a woman who has so much. Her grounded personality and intense love of her family dictated her present.

"Lola… This is so thoughtful… Thank you, darling," she says, holding back her tears. "This will sit in the center of the living room table amongst our photos."

I crouch beside her chair and hug her tightly. So happy that she likes the handmade Buccellati Rose sterling silver framed photo of Sebastian and me, a photographer friend of mine captured in honor of our engagement. Baz knew she'd love it and place it with the rest of their family snap-shots—her way of welcoming me into the Steele clan.

"Shelley! Lola!"

I glance up to see Lucie and Lydie Jackson approaching us. Lucie beams and Lydie smiles softly.

"Congratulations, Lola," Lucie hugs me. "We're so pleased for you."

The Jackson Matriarch like Shelley is in her mid-fifties and a dynamo. Her black, wavy bob highlights her angular cheekbones and hazel eyes. The silk wrap dress fits her curves and the strappy sandals show off her long legs. At five feet, eleven inches in her heels, she's six inches taller than me in my flats. We became acquainted in Positano. She's fun-loving and feisty. The perfect mate to bristly Alpha Connor.

Lydie pulls me into a hug, too.

"Yes, congratulations to you!"

"Thank you! So good to see you again," I tell them. "You should join us. They can make room for two more!"

Today, my happiness knows no bounds. They decline. But magnanimously, I insist. If Baz can extend an olive branch to Luc, I can do the same with Lydie. Shelley smiles at me knowingly.

The servers add place settings for them and they give their orders. We hold ours until theirs are ready, instead nibbling on appetizers. I have a form-fitting wedding gown to don in a few hours. So my meal comprises grilled chicken breasts... no carbs... no bloat. Leonie nodded sagely when I told the server my selection. She's in complete agreement and chose the same.

"Where are you going for your honeymoon?" Lucie asks as she sips her champagne.

I throw my hands up and shrug. Baz still hasn't told me our destination or for how long. Every time I mention it, he just smiles and tells me not to worry. When I told him I need to know what to pack, he smirked "nothing." I've given up asking.

"I have no clue and Sebastian is mum. I don't even know what to pack," I lament. "Do you know, Shelley?"

She's the taskmaster. So if anyone knows, she does.

She smiles mysteriously and swipes her fingers over her lips to zip them closed.

No such luck.

"Well, honey, don't worry. Sebastian has excellent taste. He won't disappoint you," Lucie pats my hand and glances at Shelley.

She keeps smiling. But shakes her head.

"I promised Sebastian I wouldn't tell. Sorry, Lola, darling," Shelley responds.

"I trust him. So it's all good," I admit.

The luncheon moves to us swapping stories about relationships we've had and Lucie and Shelley's words of advice for a successful marriage. I take note since they're married for over thirty years. Particularly their counsel on handling possessive Alpha males, and I'm certain in both of their cases Doms.

"Always listen more than you talk so you can understand how to respond if you have a disagreement," offers Lucie.

Shelley nods and adds, "Don't lose yourself in their lives. Maintain your friendships, work, activities."

"Yes, and your personality. If you were feisty and independent when you met, don't change. That's what attracted them to you. Don't simper like women who clamor for their attention," Lucie says.

"Oh and most important, be a proper lady in public, but a sex kitten in the bedroom! Pleasure them in the way they love the most regularly without fail!"

Shelley and Lucie burst out laughing as they high five each other. Shelley dabs the corners of her eyes. She's laughing so hard she cries. Lucie covers her mouth with her hand and giggles some more. Clearly, they have private jokes.

"Mom!"

Haley and Lydie call out in unison. Haley's face reddens in embarrassment. While Lydie covers her ears, shaking her head.

"What?" Shelley asks, hitching her shoulder.

"You're grown women. You know what we mean!" Lucie declares.

The rest of us join in their glee, and our laughter fills the restaurant.

Yup, I knew it. Shelley and Lucie are Independent Women-cum-subs like me.

We continue to enjoy ourselves through the rest of the luncheon. More guests drop by with Shelley providing introductions when necessary. Attendants bring two Sterling Silver Roses in mini vases for my collection. We decline dessert and end with tea.

"Lola, time to rest before getting you ready," Shelley announces with a raised eyebrow, tapping the bezel of her Chopard L.U.C. XP Esprit by Fleurier Peony watch.

"You look so beautiful, Lola!" Leonie gushes as she touches a handkerchief under her teary eyes. "*Tu es magnifique, Chérie!*"

"Oh, how absolutely stunning and sexy!" Haley exclaims.

"Simply divine," sighs Blair.

"Sebastian will snatch you away before the ceremony even starts!" Laughs Billie.

I feel all that they say and more as I stand before the full-length mirror in the dressing suite beside the ball-room. Mr. Valentino outdid himself. Before joining the other guests, he came by to ensure my gown fits perfectly. It does.

The sensuous lines hug my curves and dramatically flare into an elegant, cathedral-length mermaid train. I peer over my shoulder at the cut-out in the back that makes it as much of an exit dress as the deep-vee in the front makes a statement. The fitted long sleeves add a touch of the demure to the provocative gown. The impec-cable detail of the lace exemplifies the craftsmanship of his atelier. It's a masterpiece.

The traditions continue. My mother's diamond earrings adorn my ears as something old and to have her close to me. My gown represents the new. Shelley lent Sebastian's grandmother's cathedral-length silk tulle veil to me as the borrowed. My face will remain symbolically covered for his eyes only until Baz lifts my veil at the altar. I custom designed a lace G-string for the blue—perfect for fidelity.

So we don't see each other before we exchange our vows, we set our photo session for after the ceremony while guests enjoy the cocktail hour. We even signed the marriage license separately. I'm not risking a single thing.

"Lola?"

The photographer and videographer call for me to pose alone and with my bridesmaids, then with Shelley. They followed us discreetly throughout the day, capturing candid shots. Baz has a set following him, too. We want to see all that happened while we were apart.

One of the wedding planners enters the suite to tell us it's time.

My heart jumps. I hold back the tinge of panic with deep breaths. Starr came by earlier and we mediated before I put my gown on. Opening my eyes, I ask for a moment of privacy. I need to speak to my parents. Everyone nods and Shelley lingers to check on me. But I shake my head. I walk to the glass wall of windows and look to the heavens, feeling the warmth of the sun on my face. I close my eyes and whisper a prayer of love and thanks. Then a moment of silence as I feel their love wrap around me.

One more deep cleansing breath and I walk to the suite door. Luc waits just outside. He scans my face with concern. I smile and air kiss his cheeks to let him know I'm all right. When I pull back, his eyes shine with tears. He takes a moment to collect himself. Then extends his arm for me to hold.

Leonie hands my bouquet to me and gives me air kisses, too. She adjusts my train behind me and fluffs my veil into place. Luc and Leonie, my support for over seven years by my side once again.

I love them dearly.

We line up behind the rest of the bridal party at the side of the open doors to the ballroom where the ceremony will take place. The second ballroom will host the reception. The harpist plays the processional music. The sound pure and light. The groomsmen and bridesmaids pass through the doors and make their way down the aisle. Leonie glances over her shoulder at me with a smile before she too glides down today's catwalk. The doors shut for my grand entrance.

"Are you ready, *petite chérie*?"

I smile up at Luc, full of confidence, "Yes."

He nods and we walk forward. The wedding planner smiles and wishes me luck. Then opens the doors.

There are three hundred guests. But my eyes only see Sebastian at the end of the aisle, waiting for me before the altar. He stands tall like the powerful man he embodies, be it Dom or future CEO. The expression of love on his face fills my heart with bliss.

Yes, without a doubt I am ready to become Mrs. Sebastian Steele at last.

SEBASTIAN

"*N*o way, bro! You scared her off.*"

Harris' lame ass joke hit me harder than I admitted to my brothers. Even though I know it's not true, his words have been on repeat in my mind all fucking day. Beyond satisfying a woman sexually for a night or two, I've never been in a relationship. I never had to worry about her leaving me.

Lola left me twice.

The first time after an argument—true, I was a dick. The second time over a misunderstanding I wasn't even aware happened. Lola just left... Poof... For three months. Despite the promise we made to talk things through before doing something we'd regret.

We're stronger now. But it wouldn't surprise me if she pulled a Julia Roberts and turned into a runaway bride. That would be a tough scenario to recover from.

After an early morning sparring session with Borya and

a run on the treadmill, we met my brothers, Scott, Porter, Lachlan, Lucien, and Laurent for breakfast. Bro Bonding, as Laurent calls it. The youngest Jackson is their company's director of cigars and a rebellious playboy who loves to party. He's game for any opportunity to drink and have fun.

While at the table, Lola calls me. She went from silent, to sobs, to hysterical laughter. She freaked me the fuck out. I wasn't sure if she was angry I surprised her with our wedding here in Dubai or if she changed her mind. Even the Dom in me lost control and couldn't demand her words.

Finally, Lola spoke. Relief flooded my body. The adrenaline slowly drained from my veins. Hell, I was about to race back to our suite to get her to answer me. Damn not seeing her before over vows.

Once again level-headed, Roger *The Responsible* suggested I call our mother. She stepped in and met Lola at our suite to take her for the spa day I arranged. Text messages from her assured me Lola wasn't doing a runner. Thank fuck!

"I know you're not still thinking Lola's ditching you. Are you?"

Fucking Harris. At it again.

"No, you ass. And she's not ditching me," I respond, glaring at him as we sit in my office.

I had to keep my mind busy and couldn't take another grueling session with Borya. Tina scheduled meetings for me with some wedding guests who have been waiting to get on my calendar. So, it works out well. Except for Harris.

When we finished breakfast, everyone continued their own way. Borya had friends to catch up with. Malcolm and Lucien took an appointment for a potential restaurant/club. Roger met with planners for a new residential tower complex. Lachlan settled into one of the guest offices with his laptop. Scott and Porter returned to their wife and date, respectively. We left Laurent flirting with two wedding guests.

Harris… He's in his little brother mood and bugging me to death. Stretched out on the sofa, typing on his laptop.

"Well, you've been reading the same paragraph for the past five minutes," he answers with his eyebrow raised.

"How the fuck do you know what I'm doing on my laptop?" I demand. "You better not have some high-tech gadgetry hooked into my system."

His guffaws fill the air. Then he wipes his eyes. Everyone is hysterical today…

"Bro, you are so lame! You *are* still thinking about Lola! You might as well admit it," he chuckles.

"You did not answer my question, Harris. How the fuck do you know what I am doing on my laptop?" I repeat, giving him my Dom stare.

He only laughs some more, grating on my sensitive nerves.

"Oh, don't pull that Dom shit with me, Little Puppy."

I sit back in my chair and tent my fingertips as I continue to stare at him.

"Okay, okay already," he throws up his hands. "I don't have any 'high-tech gadgetry hooked into' your system."

He stares back at me, "It was a guess... an intelligent guess I might add. Your eyes were spaced out. Obviously not seeing what was on your screen. Rather, what's playing in your head."

Harris sits back triumphantly and folds his arms over his broad chest with a smirk. His eyebrow cocked in challenge.

Damn. Busted.

With a sigh, I close my laptop and pace the floor.

"See that's why I came to hang out with you. You're too uptight. Relax, Baz. She loves you. We all can see it. Don't let the blips of the past fog your bright future."

I stop, shocked. When did my kid brother grow up? He's dropping advice like he's our father. Impressed, I turn to him.

"Thank you, Harris. That means a lot to me," I smile, feeling better now than I have all day.

Recharged, I return to work and Harris clicks away on his laptop. He even stays during the meetings. Periodically, I'll glance his way to see him studying me to be sure I'm all right. It's different since I'm usually the one watching out for my siblings. I smile, nodding my head, grateful for his support.

When the last meeting goes longer than intended, Harris stands up.

"Excuse me. The groom needs to return to the hotel.

Tina can schedule a follow-up appointment. I'm sure you understand."

I hide my chuckle with a cough and rise from my seat at the conference table. To confirm the meeting ended, I shake his hand.

"Congratulations again, Sebastian. My wife and I offer our best wishes to you and your beautiful bride."

"Thank you and we'll see you at the reception," I respond, clasping both his hands in mine.

As soon as he leaves, Harris circles his fingers in the air, signaling I need to wrap it up.

A flare of nerves hit. But I think of how peacefully Lola slept as I watched her this morning. I take a deep breath—Lola taught me to channel my inner calm.

We're good, we're good. I exhale the mantra that replaces Harris' earlier words. We're good, we're good.

THE AIR RUSHES from my lungs when the doors to the ballroom open and my bride stands at the top of the aisle. Lola is an absolute vision of elegant beauty. Her enchanting smile teases me from behind a blusher that reaches her hand holding her bouquet. The long, sheer veil modestly covers her curvaceous body clothed in an extraordinary lace gown.

The fit accentuates Lola's greatest assets. The curves of her generous breasts peeks from the plunging neckline. Her narrow waist tapers to her rounded hips. I'm confident the back of the gown cups her full bottom.

The seductiveness of her body balanced by the delicate floral-patterned lace, long sleeves, and flare of the gown's shape below her hip bones. Her regal carriage enhances the graceful style. Lola is the embodiment of a sensuous, classic beauty.

As she nears, I can't help but match her smile that sparkles more brilliantly than the diamonds in her ears. She's stunning. Shelley told me Lola's gown didn't call for jewelry other than her mother's earrings. So I didn't gift her a suite of diamonds as I intended. Her wedding ring and hand harness will make up for it.

They're walking so slowly, I'm tempted to snatch her before she makes it to me. Malcolm must sense my urge. Discretely, he places a restraining hand on the back of my arm. I nod and practice another deep breath. Relax!

Luc smiles at me and agrees to give away the bride. Lola beams at him. Then turns her loving gaze to me.

My heart skips a beat.

I clasp her small hands in my larger ones as soon as she gives Leonie her bouquet. Everyone laughs at my eagerness. I shrug. I don't give a damn.

As we face each other listening to the officiant, the room fades away. We're lost in our own world, filled with love and joy. No one can touch us.

A soft cough brings us back to the room. The officiant awaits the exchanging of our vows.

I clear my throat, and with a loud confident voice I declare my eternal love for Lola. Tears glisten in her eyes. But her voice is clear and carries through the ballroom.

Malcolm opens the jewelry case. The lights hit the enormous diamonds of Lola's custom hand harness and her band. She gasps, as do the bridesmaids. Her wide eyes fly to mine and I smirk. Yeah, no one will miss you being mine, Little Pet.

She lifts her hand to admire the harness. A chain of diamonds connects to her eternity band on her middle finger to a pear-shaped diamond that rests atop her hand connected to a diamond double bracelet. Her engagement ring sits on her ring finger. The harness is removable. So she can wear her band and ring together.

The guests murmur, suitably impressed. Point made and duly noted.

Grinning, Lola places my classic platinum band on my finger. She holds my gaze as she flicks the tip of her tongue across her plump bottom lip. Then brings my hand to her mouth to kiss my ring.

My dick twitches. Fuck me.

The officiant pronounces us husband and wife.

With a smirk, I lift her veil and kiss Mrs. Sebastian Steele silly.

The guests stand, clap, and whoop.

I end the kiss with little nips to her swollen lips; she mewls. Damn. We may not make it to the reception.

Leonie places Lola's bouquet in her hand and fluffs her veil and gown as we turn to our guests. Their cheers follow us as we saunter hand in hand down the aisle.

As soon as we clear the double doors, I pull Lola to the side and kiss her again, cradling her lush ass. My hard length grinds into her soft mound. We groan, full of desire heightened by our newly forged bond. Like a caveman, I want to claim my mate.

She pants, pressing the full length of her body against mine. Lola is as desperate as I am eager to consummate our marriage.

"Oh, Baz, baby," she groans against my lips.

"Ahem."

Malcolm and the rest of the bridal party stand at the doors, blocking guests from witnessing our PDA.

Lola giggles and wipes her lipstick from my mouth.

"Later," she purrs.

My parents and Luc appear. One glance and my mother knows what we were doing. She smiles and shakes her head.

"Photo time!" She says gaily.

Everyone laughs and heads to the atrium. Fortunately, it doesn't take long since we had photo shoots solo and with our parties separately. With the family and group shots complete, we go to the second ballroom for the reception. The wedding planner tells us the guests finished the cocktail hour and sit at their tables awaiting our entrance.

The hair and makeup teams touch up Lola and the other women. Once they're primped, we head en masse to the reception.

I notice the awkwardness of Haley and Lachlan. Once more I wonder what's going on with them, if anything. I haven't broached the topic with Haley since the Abu Dhabi opening and Lachlan since Positano. It's on the top of my list now we finished the wedding.

Lola assured me Giovanni wasn't coming. I was adamant. No one fucks with my family. I don't give a damn if Leonie wants him here. No. The way she glances sideways at Roger and he stares at her adds them to my list.

Now that I've opened my eyes, blinded by jealousy, I observe Luc's interest in Blair. Based on their brief exchanges, it's clear they've had something going on for a while. Good.

My mega concern lies with Billie and Rockett. When Lola asked if I would accept Rockett as Billie's plus one, my head almost split. I asked her when the hell that happened and she told me a few months ago.

They met at some club when Lola went partying with her girls. She claims it was accidental and Rockett didn't know Billie worked for her until later. I told Lola he's full of shit and using Billie to get information on Lola's Coterie and subsequently STEEELE. She agreed she thought the same thing, but Billie signed an airtight nondisclosure and noncompete agreement. Plus Lola asked Billie outright, and she swore her loyalty to both of us. Funny enough, Malcolm says he's seen Rockett at LEVELS New York with the petite beauty. Lola just laughed when I told her.

He's here at our wedding. But I said one wrong move, and he's out. Period. Billie who came to me after Lola spoke with her agreed.

"Ready, Mr. Steele?"

Lola's sweet voice pulls me back from my musings. I

kiss her lips softly and murmur yes. She nods to the wedding planner, who opens the double doors.

The emcee announces, "Ladies and gentlemen, presenting Mr. and Mrs. Sebastian Steele!"

Lola gazes up at me with such love my breath catches. She tips her chin up for another kiss to seal our final deal. Happily, I oblige my wife. The guests stand to applaud as we enter the ballroom.

We make our way to the dance floor for our first dance. Another surprise for Lola is our song. It symbolizes all that I feel for her and want to give her. As the strains of Adele's "Make You Feel My Love" begin, Lola's eyes tear.

When the live voice of the songstress carries over the sound system, Lola's eyes zoom to the stage then back to me. She trembles in my arms, the emotion too much. I pull her as close as two can be without further intimacy. I rock her as I whisper the words in her ear. Her tears make my eyes prick with moisture. I press my face against the top of her head. Cocooned in our love, we let our bodies speak to each other.

As Adele's mesmerizing voice sings the last word, I kiss Lola, and she melts against me. I hold Lola in my arms as I smile my thanks at Adele. She nods and continues with another of her soul-stirring ballads as Lola and I take our seats to prepare for Luc's message and toast.

I wrap my arm around Lola's shoulders and hold her close. Her emotions have been high and Luc stepping in for her parents is difficult for her. She nuzzles her head against my neck and links her fingers with both of my hands.

Luc's speech is passionate. He too gets caught in emotions. Unashamed to let his voice thicken with the tears that stand in his eyes, he does well by Lola. She rises and they embrace. Her little body quivers and I ache to hold her to my chest. But I know she needs her time with Luc. He whispers in her ear and she nods. Then they smile at me, and I stand to welcome my wife back into my arms.

"I love you, baby," I murmur as I hold her close.

"I love you, too," she whispers.

While the meal begins, Lola excuses herself and goes with Leonie to freshen her makeup. When she returns, she stuns me again. Her latest gown shows more of her voluptuous figure. Still a mermaid fit with a deep-vee front, but sleeveless. Delicate flowers cover the sheer material. A belt cinches in her waist while a diamond brooch glitters in the middle. It reminds me of a garden of pure pleasure.

"You like Mr. Steele?" She asks as I take her hand and twirl her around.

"Absolutely, Mrs. Steele," I tell her, bobbing my eyebrows as I gaze at her mouthwatering breasts.

One false move and she'll spill out. Then Borya and I will have that double MMA match he asked me about to fight every man off of her.

"Abso-fuckable-lutely," I purr in her ear.

Lola giggles, "Come on, Captain Caveman. Time to mingle with our guests."

She takes my hand, and like a Little Puppy I follow her, tongue hanging out.

We spend some time circulating amongst the guests as

they eat their seated meals. Lola enchants every one of them. Her elation is palpable. She always touches me on my hand, my cheek, my back. Each time, a thrill runs through me. Soon, I'm pulling her into a closet somewhere.

The wedding planner steps over to let us know it's time for more toasts. We settle at our table and prepare for words from our family and friends.

Leonie stands before us like the Queen of the Savannah. She exudes feline grace. Her toast is touching with a story of how she and Lola first met and now are sisters for life. Lola dabs her eyes and blows kisses to her BFF.

Malcolm steps beside Leonie and pulls her into an embrace as her emotions overwhelm her. I chance a peek in Roger's direction. As I guessed, his face resembles stone and his intense stare riveted on Malcolm. Who's now rubbing Leonie's back and whispering in her ear. Oh shit.

Fortunately, Leonie collects herself and disentangles from Malcolm's arms. She returns to the table. Roger's gaze tracks her every move. When she's close, he stands and helps her into her chair. She touches his chest and briefly leans against him. The relief on his face is clear. Perhaps I can check them off my list.

Malcolm's voice cuts through the murmuring as he regales us with a fairy tale story of my miscreant behavior until the Lovely Lola saved me from imminent doom. The guests roar with laughter. I roll my eyes at the charmer. He laughs, and the meal continues.

Right before the parent dances start, Morgan stands to face us.

"Lola, we welcomed you into our family once. But now we embrace you as our daughter-in-law and daughter of our heart. Your love for our son is true as his love for you is infinite. You will forever be a Steele."

Lola sobs softly in my embrace, and I kiss her temple as I rub her arm.

"Sebastian."

I raise my gaze to my father.

"As we tell you often, you make your mother and me proud. The eldest child who cares for and supports your siblings, they admire and respect you. As a dynamic leader in our family's company, our employees and business associates accept and appreciate your guidance and skills."

He flickers his gaze between Lola and me.

"Sebastian, now that you settled down with a woman who matches and complements you personally and professionally, I officially hand over the reins of CEO and Chairman of the Board of STEELE International, Inc. to you. You will lead our family's business into the next generation and your children after you. You earned it on your own, son. Here's to your success."

The room explodes in thunderous applause. My siblings whoop and holler the loudest. My mother claps with tears in her eyes. Lola hugs me close and whispers how much I deserve it. I'm stunned—months earlier than expected.

My father beams at me and nods.

I stride over to him and we embrace. As he pats me on the back, he tells me he's so very proud of me and he expects great things from me and Lola. A power couple like him and my mother, he adds.

At his words, I choke up. That's exactly what I hoped to replicate with Lola. My father sees it in us. I'm beyond words, and can only nod. Now I understand how Lola feels when she's too caught up to verbalize a response. The thought makes me chuckle and clears my head.

"Thank you, Dad. I will make you proud."

"I know you will, son. I know you will."

The band starts the music, and he pats me with affection on the back.

The partner dances begin with Lola and Luc, then my mother and me, followed by the rest of the wedding party. I'm happy to have Lola back in my arms. She sings along happily as we dance amongst the guests.

After a while, she tosses a bouquet—she's saving her original—that Billie catches. I toss her garter—no revealing of my baby's leg, so it's at her knee. Porter swats it away from him, so it falls into Lachlan's hand, who also looks dubious. They don't know what they're missing; I chuckle.

Not one to behave like a child, I feed the forkful of cake into Lola's open mouth. Her seductive hum vibrates through the fork straight to my dick. My hooded eyes lock on her lips and I lick the frosting stuck at the corner. Yum.

She feeds my bite to me and licks her little pink tongue across her full bottom lip with a smirk. She is so not getting away with teasing me all night, I whisper in her ear. She shivers and her hazel orbs darken with lust.

Leonie comes over and whisks Lola away before I can

make good on my promise. They return just in time for her favorite artist Beyoncé's first song. All the single ladies jump up. Lola struts her stuff in a shimmery metallic purple fitted slip dress with black lace bra cups from her evening wear collection. Sky-high strappy sandals lengthen her toned legs. She's shaking her ass like a matador with a red cape before a bull.

I give her three songs, and I snatch her from the floor.

"Time for the first consummation of the night, Mrs. Steele," I say huskily in her ear.

She purrs in response, the vixen.

LOLA

This morning I awake wrapped in Baz's arms just as he promised me. And I'm Mrs. Sebastian Steele...

"Ooohhh..."

Baz's dark head rests between my quivering, spread thighs. His muscular arms wrap around them with his firm hands holding me in place.

I'm locked in position, unable to shift my body. Only accept the onslaught of his lips sucking on my engorged clit, still sensitive from his ministrations into the early light of dawn.

"Fuuck... Baby... So good—ah, ah, oooh..."

As my hundredth climax rips through my pussy, it wracks my body with uncontrollable spasms. Baz continues to lave my seam, causing a second orgasm to follow the first.

It's too much.

My fingers tangled in his thick strands attempt to push his voracious mouth away from me to no avail. He's a tyrant, demanding more as a third wave crashes over me. My eyes roll back as I thrash my head from side to side. Unsure if I want more or if I want the extreme sensations to cease, I push and pull at his head. He chuckles knowingly against my lower lips.

"Baz... Please no more..."

My pleas fall on his deaf ears covered by my thighs pressed against his head.

His slate-gray eyes watch my pitiful struggle as his tongue flicks lazily over my distended nubbin.

Unable to look away from his intense stare, I watch helplessly as Baz settles deeper between my legs. His wide shoulders push my sore thighs further apart.

Another round... Fuck...

His fingertips slide over my pussy lips to part them. Warm air blows across the sensitive flesh.

I shiver in response as a smaller orgasm massages my inner walls. My mind floats on a cloud.

Gentle licks stroke my core, bringing me back to Earth. Kisses trail from my inner thighs to my calves to caress the arches of my feet lightly.

At last, Baz sits back on his haunches. My juices cover his nose, mouth, and chin. My core clenches at the sight.

He lowers his head to form another path of kisses up my legs, over my belly, to suckle my pebbled nipples.

My body bows off the bed in ecstasy.

Wet, open-mouthed kisses climb up my slick chest to

my neck where powerful sucking marks my heated skin. Satisfied with his claim, Baz brings his swollen lips to mine and I taste myself on his insistent tongue.

"Mmmmmm..."

"Good morning, Mrs. Sebastian Steele. I love you, baby."

I wrap him in my arms, pulling his massive torso to cover mine, enjoying the pleasure of being beneath his muscular body. His biceps bulge as he lowers from his hands to his forearms, holding my face between his hands reverently.

My pelvis cradles his as I double wrap him with my thighs. His enormous cock nestled between our steamy bodies.

"Good morning, Mr. Steele, Sir," I purr, my lips pressed to the shell of his ear.

His deep chuckle reverberates through us. A quick shift of his hips and he grips his thick length before sliding it between my swollen pussy lips.

"Aaahhhh... So big... Oh yes... Ssir!"

The bed rocks with the force of Baz's thrusts. I can only hold on tight while he chases his release. Always determined for me to find my pleasure before him. Now it's his turn.

If this is what he meant by me waking every morning in his arms forever, an abso-fucking-lutely good morning they will prove to be.

Moments pass before either of us can move. Limp from

the exertion, we rest, allowing our bodies and minds time to come down.

With a contented sigh, Baz rolls onto his back, carrying me with him. He smoothes my tousled hair from my cheek and kisses the top of my head as it rests on his chest. His fingers make patterns across my back, continuing to calm me.

I nuzzle into his caress as I rest my hand on his pecs. A glint catches my eye.

"Baz! When did you put this on me?" I ask, sitting up to stare at my right wrist.

He presses his lips to my side, and I shiver.

"While you dreamed of me, my Sleeping Beauty," he murmurs against my skin.

The Cartier Love bracelet diamond-paved in platinum is yet another gift from my husband. The timeless elegance of the piece is stunning. Its symbolism of a chastity belt that locks the loved one from any but the lover who has the key is powerful.

With a smirk, I reach into the nightstand to withdraw my red jewelry box.

"Your turn," I purr as place the box on his chest and brush my lips against his in thanks.

He returns my smirk and sits up. His Love bracelet is also platinum. But no diamonds as his is a quiet elegance.

I remove the screws and place the bracelet on his left wrist, right below his wedding band. So even if he removes his ring to spar with Borya or for some such reason, the bracelet remains as a symbol of me holding the key to his love. I kiss his palm and he cups my face for a kiss.

"I'm yours forever, baby, as you are mine. Thank you."

"You're so welcome, my lo—"

His mobile vibrates with a call on his nightstand.

Damn... Back to reality already. Our post-wedding brunch must start soon, and that's Sergeant Shelley to remind us. When Baz nods his head in confirmation, I laugh and climb out of bed to head to the shower.

Gotta love my mother-in-law. Impeccable timing!

SEBASTIAN

"*Y*ou appear well rested, Baz."

Harris' smirk taunts me.

But I laugh. My kid brother proved his level of maturity yesterday. He was correct in his assessment then and now. I clap him on the back as we end our bro hug.

"Marriage does a man good. You should try it soon," I tease him and he stutters, his face flushing red.

I know full well he's only twenty-nine and nowhere near ready for a wife. Hell, it took me until I was thirty-five for a relationship and thirty-six for marriage.

"Don't worry, bro," I assuage his fears. "You'll know when you're ready. In fact, she'll let you know like Lola did with me. One glance and one touch and I was hooked for life!"

I wave my left hand, showing him my wedding band.

He mumbles and scampers off in the opposite direction. My booming laughter follows him.

"You've scarred him for life, Sebastian."

I turn my gaze to Lydie, who I hadn't realized came to stand next to me. Her green eyes twinkle with mirth. I search her face for any signs of jealousy or trouble. I find none and release the breath I held, apprehensive she'd act up since Lola and I married. Thank fuck.

"Probably," I smile down at her. "At least until he 'meets The One' like Scott told me."

I put it out there to gauge her reaction. Not a flicker of emotion aside from her glee passes across her face. Good.

"How are you doing?" I ask, concerned genuinely.

We hadn't spoken except briefly regarding business since LEVELS London. Relief filled me since she hadn't gone postal and meant what she told Lola and me about seeing a therapist to work out her Daddy issues. Based on the normal conversations we had, I know her sessions have a positive impact on her. She seems more like her old self—confident, at ease, in control. I'm pleased for her. She'll find someone who deserves her love. Not someone her father wants to form alliances with for his gain.

"Great. I'm actually taking some time off. A much-deserved extended holiday, in fact," she beams.

"I'm happy for you, Lydie. I truly am," I respond.

"Hey lovebird! Where's your mate?"

Porter strides over to us. The debonair gent greets Lydie with a bow, then shakes my hand. I notice Lydie doesn't flinch at his reference to Lola. Progress, for sure.

We talk some more before we part to sit. I go in search of Lola, who I find chatting with Starr Knight. The ebullient beauty smiles at me as I approach. Her brown eyes glow with an inner warmth. Another new friend I'm thankful Lola has added to her circle.

"Good morning, Sebastian!" She stands as she hugs me. "Your aura is at peace, good!"

Not for a minute do I think she's quirky. Lola and I have taken some private virtual yoga and mediation sessions with her, and it works. I grin back at her.

"Good morning, Starr. I am at peace. Namaste," I clasp my palms together in front of my heart and bow to the light in her.

"Namaste," she bows in return.

As I straighten, I catch sight of Malcolm eyeing Starr from a distance. His stare is so focused he doesn't notice me observing him. He makes his way over. But a redheaded wedding guest waylaid him. A look of annoyance crosses his face when she steps before him.

Meanwhile, Starr excuses herself to head to the airport. She's off for another trip to an Indian ashram. Lola tells her we'll reschedule our sessions for after her return or ours. Then cocks an eyebrow at me, still piqued I haven't told her our honeymoon plans. Oh well. She'll learn soon enough.

"Where did she go?"

Lola and I turn to see an agitated Malcolm peering over our shoulders in the direction Starr walked away. We glance at each other and laugh. Not another one! My list grows.

* * *

Alone with Lola at last.

After brunch, Lola had some post-opening work to handle for a few hours with Luc. So I went to the office to meet with my father and siblings to discuss my transition to CEO and Chairman of the Board. I spoke privately with each of them to confirm their agreement with the change. As the eldest doesn't guarantee they really want me as their leader. I did not need for concern based on their enthusiastic responses. My father's speech last night proved his belief in me.

We decided the transition will start the week I return from my honeymoon and last for two months. He will make himself available as needed. But determined to have me fully on board within that timeframe. I assured him I'm up to his charge. Pleased, he clapped me on the back and left us to return to our mother with whom he had plans to take shopping. If people knew she had the Mighty Morgan wrapped around her finger, they'd laugh.

Just like Shelley and Morgan, Lola has me whipped. My goal is to keep her happy and surprised by what's coming at all times. She deserves nothing but joy for the rest of her life after being without a family since her parents passed away. Sure Leonie and Luc make up a part of her support system, but as my wife, we're bonded forever. Plus, my parents and siblings already love Lola. Soon we'll have our own family. Her happiness fuels mine.

Starting with our honeymoon. I wanted to make it an experience she'd never forget. Not the typical week at an all-inclusive Hawaiian beach resort or a big city trip to LA or New York or a Caribbean Sea cruise. No. Only something as unique and bold as Lola and me will do for our special time, starting our lives together as husband and wife.

I had Blair and Billie clear her schedule for two months. She'll be mine undisturbed and not distracted, fully focused on us. The best way to disconnect from the rest of the world and to remain in our universe is to go off the grid. No laptops, tablets, mobiles—aside from two emergency satellite phones. Lola, me, and the bits of clothing I'll sometimes let her wear. I can stare at her heavenly body all day and night.

We'll navigate the globe making stops in the Seychelles, Mauritius, the Maldives, Bali, Fiji, Bora Bora, and Tahiti. Private islands and beachfront bungalows await us. No neighbors, no guests, only the properties' staff. Bliss.

Lola was beyond excited when I surprised her with our itinerary. She jumped into my arms and covered my face with kisses. I had to put her down or we would miss our caravan.

I planned for the first night of our honeymoon to be just as remarkable as the island hopping. But opposite to the beach. Only an abundant amount of sand is similar.

Now she bounces next to me on the seat of the Range

Rover as we traverse the Arabia Deserta to kick off our honeymoon. Our destination is a tent next to an oasis outside of Dubai. Not just any tent. We're glamping in a luxury, temperature-controlled one. The floor covered in Persian rugs and oversized silk pillows; the walls lined with handwoven tapestries; a large, round bed strewn with sumptuous silk bedding takes up most of the interior space; a modern bathroom in a separate tent adjoins the main one.

As we hop out of the SUV, Lola's mouth drops at the romantic sight. Under a canopy sits two chairs, and a table covered with savory local dishes, wine, flowers, and flickering candles. The tent stands just behind the canopy with its flaps tied back to show the interior and netting covering the entry. A butler waits to assist us.

She squeals and throws her arms around my neck lifting onto her toes to kiss me passionately murmuring words of love. I return her kiss just as zealously.

After we eat dinner and each other, sated we lie on our backs stargazing through the night. The top of the tent is clear so the stars shine brightly above us.

I take Lola's left hand adorned with my rings and harness in mine and kiss her open palm. She turns her beautiful face towards me. Her hazel eyes shine as she smiles with a palpable intensity, mirroring my love for her.

Our future holds as many infinite possibilities as the uncountable stars above. They're so close, we can grab them and soar to heights unknown.

* * *

Sebastian & Lola's Story Continues: *Deepen My Desires*
Book 6

Turn the page for the Steele Family, Author's Note, and a Preview of
Ignite My Desires Roger and Leonie Part I **Book 3**

THE STEELE FAMILY

STEELE INTERNATIONAL, INC

Multigenerational, multibillion-dollar business luxury real estate development and management corporation

Headquarters & Family's Primary Residences:

The STEELE Tower, New York City

A modern, gray-tinted glass fifty-seven story mixed-use skyscraper on southwest corner of Fifty-Seventh Street and Fifth Avenue within Billionaires' Row

Global Offices:

- The United States of America (New York City, New Jersey, Chicago, California, Miami, Las Vegas)
- The Caribbean (St. Maarten, St. Barth's, St. Lucia)
- The French & Italian Rivieras (Nice, Cannes, Positano, Capri)
- Monaco (Monte Carlo)
- The United Arab Emirates (Abu Dhabi, Dubai)

STEELE FOUNDATION: A STRONG AND SUPPORTIVE HOUSE

Builds and manages attractive, affordable housing for urban, lower-income families

Available for download at **bit.ly/STEELEFamily**

Author's Note

Thank you for reading Part II of Sebastian and Lola's sexy, sizzling romance! I hope you enjoyed their Happy For Now story. If so, I'd love to hear your thoughts, please share a review at **bit.ly/CLBooksSI2Review** and tell your friends.

I couldn't stop telling their story! So later I added Part III —*Deepen My Desires*—after the start of Roger & Leonie's story. You can continue with Baz and Lola, but know the timing for Part III takes place after the conclusion of Roger and Leonie. So as always, the choice is yours!

The dynamism of Roger *The Responsible* and Leonie *The Lion*.
Click below or flip the page for a preview.

Ignite My Desires Roger & Leonie Part I

At **CharmaineLouise.com** take the *Four types of lovers. Which are you?* **Quiz** to match your Sexy Fantasy: sub, Voyeur, Dominatrix, or Dominatrix sub Switch.

Follow me on social media including my CLBooks Coterie Fan Club below or on your favorite channels below and subscribe to my newsletter at **bit.ly/ CLBooksNewsletter** for a **Free Book**.

Fulfill Your Desires.

xoxo

Charmaine Louise

STEELE International, Inc.
A Billionaires Romance Series Book 3

Ignite My Desires Roger & Leonie Part I

Click on the link below or visit books2read.com/u/
md6EZR to get your copy.
Keep reading for a sneak peek!

Ignite My Desires Roger & Leonie Part I

Books in the Series:

Discover My Desires Sebastian & Lola Prequel

(Available Exclusively to Subscribers)

Fulfill My Desires Sebastian & Lola Part I

Heighten My Desires Sebastian & Lola Part II

Ignite My Desires Roger & Leonie Part I

Stoke My Desires Roger & Leonie Part II

Justify My Desires Roger & Leonie Part III

Deepen My Desires Sebastian & Lola Part III

Capture My Desires Malcolm & Starr Part I

Embrace My Desires Malcolm & Starr Part II

Cherish My Desires Malcolm & Starr Part III

A Trilogy of Desires Sebastian & Lola Parts I-III

A Trilogy of Desires Roger & Leonie Parts I-III

A Trilogy of Desires Malcolm & Starr Parts I-III

Series Extras

Series Playlist

COMING NEXT: IGNITE MY
DESIRES ROGER & LEONIE PART I

PRESENT DAY— DUBAI, UNITED ARAB EMIRATES

ROGER

"*F*uck you, you slimy dick!"

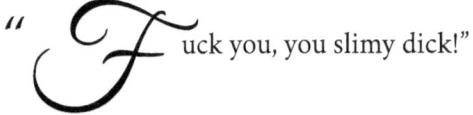

CRASH!

All I saw was red as that bastard Giovanni Mattei slid his hand up the dress of the blonde who'd been eyeing him for the past hour. We're at my future sister-in-law's opening night party for her luxury lingerie company, Lola's Coterie Dubai. The entire Steele clan is present to support her latest endeavor in her global expansion goal. Lola opened the flagship in Paris five years ago, followed by a location in London three years later.

Her initial goal to open boutiques in the United States started with New York and Las Vegas. But since meeting with STEELE Intentional, Inc. and my eldest brother Sebastian, the President of the Retail Properties Division, Lola's expansion now includes Abu Dhabi, Dubai, and Beverly Hills. Lola's Coterie Abu Dhabi opened last week, tonight is Dubai, and in a month another boutique will open in STEELE Galleria Rodeo Drive.

That fateful meeting a year ago between the two companies started a chain reaction. Sebastian and Lola dated within the week. Even moving in together. He surprised everyone since he was a notorious playboy.

Then, the spark hit me to fall for Leonie *The Lion* Beaulieu, the stunning supermodel, muse for Lola's Coterie, and Lola's best friend. Or as she calls it, *un coupe de foudre*—stroke of lightning, love at first sight. So we thought…

All I want to do right now is strike Mattei.

For the past year I've had to look at his smug face as he paraded around Monte Carlo, Las Vegas, Paris, the fucking globe with my woman on his arm.

Or at least she was for a brief two months.

The wildest two months of my life. I never knew what to expect with Leonie. One minute passionately wrapped in each other's arms, her long legs around my neck, my dick buried deep in her tight core. The next arguing about her not finishing reading assignments for her interior design degree from the Paris American Academy. The next, her feline amber eyes gazing lovingly at me to only narrow in anger when I reprimanded her lack of focus. My head aches as much as my dick just from thinking about Leonie.

What a fucking rollercoaster. We held on as long as we could before an argument went further than normal. Yeah, we had smaller disagreements. Bu nothing too major. The last one, though. No cuddles and coos of apology or incredible makeup sex could bridge the chasm we created. Words said, struck a chord and there was no going back. At least not at the time.

I let her get away from me once—well, I contributed hugely to her dumping me—and I won't let it happen again. First, I have to deal with the asshole she keeps going back to, fucking Mattei. He's always waiting in the wings to capture her with his charm. Only now she's distracted with the opening, as it's a work event for her representing Lola's Coterie. Mattei takes advantage of her lack of attention to *God's Gift* and shoves his hand up another woman's dress. Asshole.

Blondie wasn't the only one who couldn't keep her eyes or hands off the Italian playboy. Add the billionaire and nobleman status and he's irresistible to certain women. And any woman is irresistible to him... Without fail he flirted right back—a wink, a sly pinch on their rump, an unnecessary brush of his groin against their ass as he passed by them. Ridiculous.

Now observing Mattei and his shenanigans pisses me off. The self-proclaimed *God Has Shown Favor* shows only disrespect for Leonie. I would hate for his stupidity to upset her on such an important night. She deserves so much more. So I can't stop myself from telling him just that.

"You could at least have enough respect for the woman you're here with, then to feel up another woman within eyesight of her."

The sleaze turns his gaze towards me. His eyes take me in from head to toe as if assessing my seriousness.

Yeah, ass, I'm serious as fuck. If she's with him, he needs to act like a man and not a randy teenager who can't control himself. It's the middle child in me that demands balance and loyalty. I want Leonie for myself, but until she's fully mine again, he will respect her.

"What I do is of no concern of yours, Steele."

I'm surprised he knows who I am since we've never spoken. He must recognize my shock as his smirk widens.

"Oh, I know who you are, Steele," he starts. "You're the loser who can't keep Leonie satisfied. So she keeps coming back to me. You see..."

He leans closer for dramatically to pseudo-whisper. But loud enough so the blonde can hear his words.

"I know how to make her cum so hard on my big dick screaming my name, she forgets all about your sorry ass."

Fuck Roger *The Responsible* who knows better than to act crazy in public. This asshole just sent me over the edge with a vision of him pounding into my woman. No... Fucking... Way.

"Fuck you, you slimy dick!"

CRASH!

In a blind rage, my fist connects with Mattei's jaw and he falls back into mannequins. As they topple to the floor, he recovers and clips me with a punch to the chest. Damn, I didn't expect the pretty boy to know how to fight. We're even at six feet, three inches. I have ten pounds of muscle on him, though. Plus, I spar regularly. I use both size and skill to my advantage.

We exchange only a few blows before my brothers Malcolm and Harris grab Mattei. Luc Montaigne, Lola's mentor, and Sebastian grab me. Security stands by, ready to step in to take over.

Still pissed, I struggle against their hold as does Mattei, who tries to shrug my brothers off. Unmatched by their combined strength, Mattei and I can only glare at each other. Itching to square off again. I give two fucks as the crowd stares on in silence. I want to finish this shit once and for all.

Until the figure of my father Morgan, the Steele Patriarch and Alpha Dom, storms over with such a wrathful look that Mattei and I stand stock-still.

Fuck. My father is pissed.

"You will cease this outrageous, infantile behavior at once and apologize to Ms. Lewis and her guests. Then leave. Do… you… understand?" Morgan issues his edict.

All eyes turn to him, including that dickhead Mattei. Morgan's Dom stare knocks us down several notches. In fact, we're below ground by the time he finishes his chastisement of us. Everyone else stands in silent awe of his power.

Morgan's words reset my out-of-control brain. I shake my head to dispel the angry red haze. Sure, Mattei was disrespectful to Leonie and said some stupid ass shit. But I never should have allowed it to get to me. It sent me on a downward spiral of jealousy, driven by an intense need to flatten him for having what is mine.

No matter the circumstances, I should have maintained command of the situation. Particularly at a highly public event held by STEELE. Before Leonie, this would never have happened. It goes against every cell in my physiology.

I gain control before Mattei and turn to seek Lola out in the crowd gathered around. I hope she's not as upset as I imagine. I spot her standing between my mother and Leonie. My younger sister Haley and Lola's assistants Blair and Billie stand near them. All have shocked expressions on their faces. Damn.

I notice Mattei tries to walk to them. But Malcolm puts his hand on his chest to stop him since he recognizes that I headed their way already. Mattei has the sense to back down.

"Lola, I apologize for my poor behavior. Please forgive me," I beseech her.

With grace, she nods her head and accepts my outstretched hand. Her eyes meet mine before she searches for Sebastian, to whom she nods, too.

I turn my attention to the other women who stare at me, surprised by my unusual outburst.

"Mother, Leonie, I ask for your forgiveness, too," I say to both of them, but my eyes lock on Leonie whose amber gaze shies away.

My shoulders rise and fall on a disappointed sigh in response to her reaction. Not wishing to prolong the situation and knowing now is not the time to address Leonie's dismissal, I turn to the guests and apologize to them. Then excuse myself from the event.

As I pass Sebastian, he squeezes my shoulder to offer me support. I nod without breaking my stride. I don't even wait to hear Mattei's apology. I have to get out of here. Try to save some face from my lack of decorum.

Minutes after I exit the boutique, I feel my mobile vibrate in my trousers' pocket. I know who it is without even checking the name on the display. I answer on the first ring.

"Sorry. That was a shitshow Lola did not deserve. Does she really forgive me? Are you going to kick my ass?"

Of course it's Sebastian. I'm sure our father told him to call me or he would. I'd rather deal with my eldest brother than the elder Steele...

I must sound like a wreck since Sebastian doesn't go in on me, as would be his right. It's his woman's event for our family's company. He's the heir apparent to CEO and Chairman of the Board. So besides being the oldest who leads his siblings, he's the future leader of our multibillion-dollar business at which each of us leads divisions. I'm thankful when Sebastian doesn't add to my ill ease.

"Yes, and no. Dad gave the guests gift cards. What the fuck happened?" He asks.

I clue him in on the details. He tells me he understands. Baz is an Alpha male like me, although he's a Dom, too. So he understands protecting my woman's honor and my irrational possessive behavior. But he reminds me to keep my shit together in the future. Then teases me about not being responsible.

I grouse over the gibe. Then we hang up with a reminder about breakfast.

FUCK!

In my rage, I punch the wall. The plaster clatters to the floor, leaving a hole and splatters of blood. Too pissed to feel the pain, I stalk around the living room of my Rulers' Suite at STEELE Dubai I.

This shit is crazy. How can I allow myself to get so out of control that I make an ass of myself at a STEELE business function? So out of character for me—Roger *The Responsible*.

I roll my eyes in disgust at myself for letting Leonie upend my structured world. But I can't help myself. I call her mobile.

Leonie doesn't answer. What else is new...

I have no other choice than to leave a voicemail. How many will this one be? After twelve months, I've lost count. I just hope she'll listen to it and respond to me this time.

"How did we get here? Baby, I miss you. I'm so sorry. Tell me what to do. Please tell me, baby. Please…"

***

Click the Link Below or visit
books2read.com/u/md6EZR **for Your Copy**

Ignite My Desires Roger & Leonie Part I

I dedicate this novel to all the independent single ladies who find
pleasure in the arms of
powerful, possessive men.

Fulfill Your Desires.

xoxo
Charmaine Louise

WELCOME TO
CHARMAINELOUISE — THE
SENSUAL LIFESTYLE

GLITZY. GLAMOROUS. STEAMY.

CharmaineLouise New York, Inc. invites you to indulge in *The Sensual Lifestyle* through **CharmaineLouise Books** and **CharmaineLouise Intimates**. CLBrands immerse you in *Sexy Fantasies* with CLBooks contemporary romance novels and give you *Sexy Under Things & Loungewear* with CLIntimates.

Charmaine Louise Shelton the Founder, CEO & Author of CLNY loves all things classic, elegant, feminine, and of course with an erotic edge! Favorite outfit of choice is a cashmere cardigan, leather pencil skirt, and seamed silk stockings with stiletto heels. Sexy Fantasy Type: sub with a dash of Voyeur. When not writing and designing, Charmaine Louise travels and spends time with her Maltese buddies, ZIGGY and Jynger.

CharmaineLouise — *The Sensual Lifestyle*

~ Visit online at **CharmaineLouise.com**

~ Subscribe to **CharmaineLouise Newsletter**

~ Find us on Facebook **@CharmaineLouiseNewYork**

~ Instagram @**CharLouNY**

CharmaineLouise Books *Sexy Fantasies* launched summer 2020. Sizzling, contemporary romance with your soon-to-be favorite Alpha Doms, Powerful Billionaires, and the women they lust after and love for second chances, insta-love, enemies-to-lovers, and more.

Want to chat it up and share your thoughts with other CLBooks Lovers? Read our blog, join our Charmaine-Louise Books Coterie Fan Club and follow us on my author pages and social media to be in the know about the book release dates, exclusive content, giveaways, contests, and more!

~ **Purchase your eBook and paperback novels from my Author Page by clicking here!**

~ Read and subscribe to our blog *The World of Sex*

~ Connect on **Amazon Author Page**

~ **Goodreads Author Profile**

~ <u>**BookBub Author Profile**</u>

CharmaineLouise Intimates *Sexy Under Things &* *Loungewear* debuted in 2003. Inspired by the sensuous sirens and sylph swans of the past and present, the hand crochet cashmere and silk collections are for the sexy: hence, the line names Ginger — Bombshell; Diana — Showstopper; Jackie — Timeless; Lena — Classic. Also known as The Movie-Star from Gilligan's Island; Ms. Ross The Boss; Mrs. Kennedy Onassis; Ms. Horne.

Do you thrive on seduction and being sexy lounging at home? Read our blog and follow us on social media to receive the tips, the latest additions to the collections, private sales, and more!

~ Read and subscribe to our blog *The Art of Seduction*

~ Find us on Facebook **@CharmaineLousieIntimates**

~ Instagram **@CharmaineLouiseIntimates**

Fulfill Your Desires.